CROCODILE TEARS

"This is the eighth Alex Rider novel – and it seems amazing that it's been ten years since I sat down and wrote *Stormbreaker*. Alex has changed a lot since that first adventure. He's a little darker and more damaged which is hardly surprising after all the things that have happened to him, but he's also, I think, stronger. And that's just as well because, in many ways, *Crocodile Tears* is his toughest adventure. And in Desmond McCain he's surely up against his nastiest opponent yet." **AH**

Anthony Horowitz is one of the most popular contemporary children's writers. Both The Power of Five and Alex Rider are number one best-selling series enjoyed by millions of readers worldwide.

When Anthony launched the Alex Rider series in 2000 he created a phenomenon in children's books, spurring a new trend of junior spy books and inspiring thousands of previously reluctant readers. Hailed as a reading hero, Anthony has also won many major awards, including the Bookseller Association/Nielsen Author of the Year Award, the Children's Book of the Year Award at the British Book Awards, and the Red House Children's Book Award. The first Alex Rider adventure, *Stormbreaker*, was made into a blockbuster movie in 2006.

Anthony's other titles for Walker Books include the Diamond Brothers mysteries; *Groosham Grange* and its sequel, *Return to Groosham Grange*; *The Devil and His Boy*; *Granny*; and *The Switch*. His new collection of horror stories, *More Bloody Horowitz*, is coming in 2010. Anthony also writes extensively for TV, with programmes including *Foyle's War*, *Midsomer Murders*, *Poirot* and most recently *Collision*. He is married to television producer Jill Green and lives in London with his sons, Nicholas and Cassian, and their dog, Limpy.

You can find out more about Anthony and his books at:

www.anthonyhorowitz.com

www.alexrider.com

www.powerof5.co.uk

CROCODILE TEARS

ANTHONY HOROWITZ

WALKER BOOKS

AND SUBSIDIARIES

LONDON · BOSTON · SYDNEY · AUCKLAND

For LTD

First published 2009 by Walker Books Ltd
87 Vauxhall Walk, London SE11 5HJ

2 4 6 8 10 9 7 5 3 1

Text © 2009 Stormbreaker Productions Ltd
Cover design by Walker Books Ltd
Trademarks 2009 Alex Rider™,
Boy with Torch Logo™,
Stormbreaker Productions Ltd

This book has been typeset in Officina Sans

Printed and bound in Great Britain by Clays Ltd, St Ives plc

British Library Cataloguing in Publication Data:
a catalogue record for this book
is available from the British Library

ISBN 978-1-4063-2740-3

www.walker.co.uk

crocodile tears: fake or hypocritical tears. From the belief that crocodiles will pretend to cry in order to attract their victims ... and then cry for real as they devour them.

CONTENTS

FIRE STAR

Ravi Chandra was going to be a rich man.

It made his head spin to think about it. In the next few hours he would earn more than he had managed in the last twenty years: a fantastic sum, paid in cash, right into his hands. It was the start of a new life. He would be able to buy his wife the clothes she wanted, a car, a proper diamond ring to replace the flimsy band of gold she had worn since they were married. He would take his two young boys to Disneyland in Florida. And he would travel to London and see the Indian cricket team play at Lord's, something he had dreamt about all his life but had never thought possible.

Until now.

He sat hunched up beside the window of the bus that was taking him to work, as he had done every day for as long as he could remember. It was devilishly hot. The fans had broken down once again and of course the company was in no hurry to replace them. Worse still, this was the end of June, the time of year known in South India as *Agni Nakshatram* – or Fire Star. The sun was unforgiving. It was almost impossible to breathe. The damp heat clung to you from morning till night and the whole city stank.

When he had money, he would move. He would leave the cramped, two-room flat in Perambur, the busiest, most crowded part of the city, and go and live somewhere quieter and cooler with a little more space to stretch out. He would have a fridge full of beer and a big plasma TV. Really, it wasn't so much to ask.

The bus was slowing down. Ravi had done this journey so many times that he would have known where they were with his eyes closed. They had left the city behind them. In the distance, there were hills – steep and covered, every inch of them, with thick green vegetation. But the area he was in now was more like a wasteland, with just a few palm trees sprouting among the rubble, and electricity pylons closing in on all sides. His place of work was just ahead. In a moment, they would stop at the first security gate.

Ravi was an engineer. His identity badge with his photograph and full name – Ravindra Manpreet Chandra – described him as a plant operator. He worked at the Jowada nuclear power station just three miles north of Chennai, the fourth largest city in India, formerly known as Madras.

He glanced up and there was the power station

in front of him, a series of huge, multicoloured blocks securely locked inside miles and miles of wire. It sometimes occurred to him that wire defined Jowada. There was razor wire and barbed wire, wire fences and telephone lines. And the electricity that they manufactured was carried all over India by thousands more miles of wire. How strange to think that when someone turned on their TV in Pondicherry or their bedside light in Nellore, it had all begun here.

The bus stopped at the security point with its CCTV cameras and armed guards. Following the 9/11 attacks on New York and Washington, nuclear power plants all over the world had become recognized as potential terrorist targets. New barriers had been added; security forces had been enlarged. For a long time it had all been a damned nuisance, with people ready to jump on you if you so much as sneezed. But people had got lazy. Take old Suresh, for example, the guard at this outer checkpoint. He recognized everyone on the bus. He saw them at the same time every day: in at half past seven, out at half past five. Occasionally he'd bump into them, strolling past the shops on Rannganatha Street. He even knew their wives and girlfriends. It wouldn't have occurred to him to ask for ID or to check what they were carrying into Jowada. He waved the bus through.

Two minutes later, Ravi got out. He was a short, skinny man with bad skin and a moustache that sat uncomfortably on his upper lip. He was already wearing overalls and protective steel-capped shoes. He was carrying a heavy toolbox. Nobody asked him why he had taken it home. It was quite possible that he'd had to fix something in the flat where he lived. Maybe he'd been moonlighting, doing some jobs for the neighbours for a few extra rupees. Ravi was always carrying a toolkit. It was as much a part of him as an arm or a leg.

The bus had come to a final halt beside a brick wall with a door which, like every door at Jowada, was made of solid steel, designed to hold back smoke, fire or even a direct missile strike. Another guard and more television cameras watched as the passengers got out and went through. On the other side of the door, a blank, whitewashed corridor led to a locker room, one of the few places in the complex that wasn't air-conditioned. Ravi opened his locker (there was a pin-up of the Bollywood star Shilpa Shetty stuck inside the door) and took out a safety helmet, goggles, earplugs and a fluorescent jacket. He also removed a bunch of keys. Like most nuclear power stations, there were very few swipe cards or electronic locks on the doors at Jowada. This was another safety measure. Manual locks and keys would still operate in the event of a power failure.

Still clutching his toolbox, Ravi set off down another corridor. When he had first come to work here, he had been amazed how clean everything was – especially when he compared it with the street where he lived, which was full of rubbish, and potholes with muddy water, and droppings from the oxen which lumbered along pulling wooden carts between the cars and the motorized rickshaws. He turned a corner and there was the next checkpoint, the final barrier he would have to pass through before he was actually in.

For the first time, he was nervous. He knew what he was carrying. He remembered what he was about to do. What would happen if he were stopped? He would go to jail, perhaps for the rest of his life. He had heard stories about Chennai Central Prison, about inmates buried in tiny cells far underground and food so disgusting that some preferred to starve to death. But it was too late to back out now. If he hesitated or did anything suspicious, that was one sure way to get stopped.

He came to a massive turnstile with bars as thick as baseball bats. It only allowed one person in at a time and then you had to shuffle through as if you were being processed like some sort of factory machine. There were also an X-ray scanner, a metal detector and yet more guards.

"Hey – Ravi!"

"Ramesh, my friend. You see the cricket last night?"

"I saw it. What a match!"

"Two wickets down and we still came back. I thought we were finished!"

Cricket, football, tennis ... whatever. Sport was

their currency. Every day, the plant operators passed it between them and Ravi had deliberately watched the match the night before so that he could join in the conversation. Even in the cool of the corridor he was sweating. He could feel the perspiration beading on his forehead and he wiped it away with the back of his hand. Surely someone would stop him and ask him why he was still holding on to his toolbox. Everyone knew the correct procedure. It should be opened and searched, all the contents taken out.

But it didn't happen. A moment later, he was through. Nobody had so much as questioned him. It had gone just as he'd hoped it would. Nobody had lifted off the top tray of the toolbox and discovered the ten kilos of C4 plastic explosive concealed underneath.

Ravi walked away from the barrier and stopped in front of a row of shelves. He pulled out a small plastic device that looked like a pager. This was his EPD – or electronic personal dosimeter – which recorded his own radiation level and warned him if he came into contact with any radio-active material. It was set with his personal ID and security clearance. There were four levels of security at Jowada, each one allowing access to areas with different risks of contamination. Just for once, Ravi's EPD had been set to the highest level. Today he was going to enter the heart of the power station, the reactor chamber itself.

This was where the deadly flame of Jowada burned. Sixty thousand uranium fuel rods, each one 3.85 metres long, bound together inside the pressure vessel that was the reactor itself. Every minute of the day and night, twenty thousand tonnes of fresh water were sent rushing through pipes. The resulting steam – two tonnes of it every second – powered the turbines. The turbines produced electricity. That was how it worked. In many ways it was very simple.

A nuclear reactor is at once the safest and the most dangerous place on the planet. An accident might have such nightmarish consequences that there can be no accident. The reactor chamber at Jowada was made out of steel-reinforced concrete. The walls were one and a half metres thick. The great dome, stretching out over the whole expanse, was the height and breadth of a major cathedral. In the event of a malfunction the reactor could be turned off in seconds. And whatever happened in this chamber would be contained. Nothing could be allowed to leak through to the outside world.

A thousand safeguards had been built into the construction and the running of Jowada. One man with a dream of watching cricket in London was about to blow them apart.

The approach had come six weeks before at the street corner closest to his flat: two men, one a European, the other from Delhi. It turned out that the second man was a friend of Ravi's cousin

Jagdish, who worked in the kitchen of a five-star hotel. Once they had recognized each other, it seemed only natural to go for tea and samosas – particularly as the European was paying.

"How much do they pay you at Jowada? Only fifteen thousand rupees a month? A child couldn't live on that amount, and you have a wife and family. These people! They cheat the honest worker. Maybe it's time they were taught a lesson..."

Very quickly the conversation was steered the way the two men wanted it to go; and that first time, they left him with a gift, a fake Rolex watch. And why not? Jagdish had done them favours in the past, giving them free food which he stole from the kitchen. Now it was their turn to look after Ravi. The next time they met, a week later, it was an iPhone – the real thing. But the gifts were only a glimpse of all the riches that could be his if he would just agree to undertake a piece of business on their behalf. It was dangerous. A few people might be hurt. "But for you, my friend, it will mean a new life. Everything you ever wanted can be yours..."

Ravi Chandra entered the reactor chamber of the Jowada nuclear power station at exactly eight o'clock.

Five other engineers went in with him. They had to go in one at a time through an airlock – a white circular corridor with an automatic sliding door at each end. In many ways it looked like something out of a spaceship and its purpose was much the same. The exit wouldn't open until the entrance had closed. It was all part of the need for total containment. The five men were dressed identically, with safety helmets and goggles. All of them were carrying toolboxes. For the rest of the day they would carry out a series of tasks, some of them as ordinary as oiling a valve or changing a light bulb. Even the most advanced technology needs occasional maintenance.

As they emerged from the airlock into the reactor chamber they seemed almost to vanish, so tiny were they in these vast surroundings, dwarfed by the bright yellow gantries and walkways overhead, by electric hoists and cables, soaring banks of machinery, fuel rod transportation canisters and generators. Arc lamps shone down from the edges of the dome, and in the middle of it all, surrounded by ladders and platforms, what looked like an empty swimming pool plunged twelve metres down, with stainless steel plates on all four sides. This was the reactor. Underneath a one hundred and fifty tonne steel cap, millions of uranium atoms were splitting again and again, producing unimaginable heat. Four metal towers stood guard in the chamber. If they were shaped a little like rockets, they were rockets that would never fly. Each one was locked in its own steel cage and connected to the rest of the machinery by a network of massive pipes. These were the reactor coolant pumps, keeping the water rushing round on its vital journey. Inside each metal casing a fifty-tonne motor was spinning at the rate of fifteen hundred revs per minute.

The pumps were labelled north, south, east and west. The south pump was going to be Ravi's primary target.

But first of all he crossed to the other side of the reactor chamber to a door marked EMERGENCY EXIT ONLY. The two men had explained everything very carefully to him. There was no point attacking the reactor cap. Nothing could penetrate it. Nor was there any point in sabotaging the reactor chamber, not while it was locked down. Any blast, any radiation leak, would be contained. To achieve their aims an exit had to be found. The power of the nuclear reactor had to be set free.

And there it was on the blueprint they had shown him. The emergency airlock was the Achilles heel in the fortification of Jowada. It should never have been built. There was no need for it and it had never been used. The reason for a passageway between the reactor chamber and the back of the turbine hall, where it opened onto a patch of wasteland close to the perimeter fence, was to reassure the workers that there was a fast way out if it should ever be needed. But what it also provided was a single pathway from the reactor to the outside world. In one sense it was the barrel of a gun. All it needed was to be unblocked.

Nobody noticed Ravi as he strolled over to the

emergency door; and even if they had, they wouldn't have remarked on it. Everyone had their own worksheet. They would assume he was just following his. He opened the inner door – a solid metal plate – and let himself into the corridor. About halfway along, there was a control panel fixed high up in the wall. Standing on tiptoe, Ravi unscrewed it, using one of the few real tools he had brought with him. Inside, there was a complicated mass of circuitry but he knew exactly what to do. He cut two separate wires, then spliced them together. It was quite easy, really. The exit door slid open in front of him, revealing a patch of blue sky beyond a wire fence. He felt the sluggish air roll in. Somewhere, perhaps in the control room, someone would notice what had happened. Even now a light might be blinking on one of the consoles. But it would be a while before anyone came to investigate, and by then it would be too late.

Ravi went back into the reactor chamber and over to the nearest of the four reactor coolant pumps. This was the only way that wide-scale sabotage was possible. What he was aiming for was known in the nuclear industry as a LOCA – a loss of coolant accident. It was a LOCA that had caused the catastrophe at Chernobyl and had almost done the same at Three Mile Island in Pennsylvania, America. The pump was locked in its cage, but Ravi had the key. That was one of the reasons he had been chosen for this job. The right man in the right place.

He stopped in front of the cylindrical wall that rose more than twenty metres into the air. He could hear the machinery inside. The noise was constant and deafening. His mouth was dry now as he thought about what he was going to do. Was he mad? Suppose they traced this back to him. But at the same time, there was cricket, Ajala – his wife – Disneyland, a new life. His family were not in Chennai today. He had sent them to friends in Bangalore. They would be safe. He was doing this for them. He *had* to do this for them.

For a few brief seconds greed and fear hung in the balance, but then the scale tipped. He knelt down and placed the toolbox against the metal casing, opened it and removed the top shelf. The inside was almost filled with the bulk of the plastic explosive but there was just room for the timer: a digital display showing ten minutes, a tangle of wires and a switch.

Ten minutes. That would be more than enough time to leave the chamber before the bomb went off. He would exit the same way he had come in, and once he was on the other side of the airlock, he would be safe. If anyone questioned him, he would say he needed the toilet. After the blast, there would be panic, alarms, a well-rehearsed evacuation, radiation suits for everyone. He would simply join the crowds and make his way out. They would never be able to trace the bomb to him. There wouldn't be any evidence at all.

People might die. People he knew. Could he really do this?

The switch was right there in front of him. So small. All he had to do was flick it and the countdown would begin.

Ravi Chandra took a deep breath. He reached out with a single finger. He pressed the switch.

It was the last thing he did in his life. The men from the street corner had lied to him. There was no ten-minute delay. When he activated the bomb, it went off immediately, almost vaporizing him. Ravi was dead so quickly that he never even knew that he had been betrayed, that his wife was now a widow and that his children would never meet Mickey Mouse. Nor did he see the effect of what he had done.

Exactly as planned, the bomb had torn a hole in the side of the coolant pump, smashing the rotors. There was a hideous metallic grinding as the entire thing tore itself apart. One of the other plant operators – the same man who had been chatting about cricket just a few minutes ago – was killed instantly, thrown off his feet and into the reactor pit. The other engineers in the chamber froze, their eyes filled with horror as they saw what was happening, then scattered, diving for cover. They were too late. There was another explosion and suddenly the air was filled with shrapnel, spinning fragments of metal and machinery that had been turned into vicious missiles. The two closest men were cut to pieces. The others turned to run for the airlock.

None of them made it. Sirens were already sounding, lights flashing, as the machinery disintegrated. Everything in the chamber turned into a black and red hell. A cable whipped down, trailing sparks. There were three more explosions, pipes wrenching themselves free, fireballs spinning outwards, and then a roar as burning steam came rushing out like an express train. The worst had happened. Jagged knives of broken metal had smashed open the pipes, and although the reactor was already closing down, there were several tonnes of radioactive steam with nowhere to go. One man was caught in the full blast and disappeared with a single, hideous scream.

The steam thundered out, filling the entire chamber. Normally the walls and the dome would have contained it. But Ravi Chandra, in almost the last act of his life, had opened the emergency airlock. Like some alien stampede, the steam found it and burst through, out into the open air. All over the Jowada power station, systems were being shut down, corridors emptied, emergency safety measures put into place. But it was already too late.

The people of Chennai saw a huge plume of white smoke rise up into the air. They heard the alarms. Workers at Jowada were calling their relatives in the city, warning them to get out. The panic began at once. More than a million men, women and children dropped what they were doing and tried to find a way through traffic that had come to a complete standstill. Fights broke out. There were collisions and smash-ups at a dozen different junctions and traffic lights. But it had all happened too quickly and not a single person made it out of the city before the radioactive cloud, blown by a northerly wind, fell onto them.

The story appeared that night on television news all around the world.

It was estimated that at least a hundred people had died in the hour following the explosion. There had been casualties within the Jowada power station itself, but curiously far more were killed in the mad crush to get out of Chennai. By the following morning the newspaper headlines were calling it A NUCLEAR NIGHTMARE – in capital letters, of course. The Indian authorities were adamant that the steam cloud would have contained only low-level radiation and that there was no need for panic, but there were just as many experts who disagreed.

Twenty-four hours later, an appeal was made to help the people of Chennai. Further casualties were being reported. Homes and shops had been looted. There were still riots in the streets and the army had been called in to restore order. The hospitals were full of desperate people. One British charity – it called itself First Aid – came forward with a comprehensive plan to distribute food, blankets and, most important of all, potassium iodate tablets for every one of the eight million people of Chennai to counter possible radiation sickness.

As always, the British people were unfailing in their generosity, and by the end of the week they had raised one and a quarter million pounds.

Of course, if the disaster had been any greater, they would have raised much, much more.

REFLECTIONS IN A MIRROR

Alex Rider took one last glance in the mirror, then stopped and looked a second time. It was strange, but he wondered if he recognized the boy who was looking back. There were the thin lips, the slightly chiselled nose and chin, the fair hair hanging in two strands over the dark brown eyes. He raised a hand and, obediently, his reflection did the same. But there was something different about this other Alex Rider. It just wasn't quite him.

Of course, the clothes he was wearing didn't help. In a few minutes he would be leaving for a New Year's Eve party being held at a castle on the banks of Loch Arkaig in the Highlands of Scotland – and the invitation had been clear. Dress: black tie. Reluctantly Alex had gone out and rented the entire outfit: dinner jacket, black trousers and a white shirt with a stick-up collar that was too tight and dug into his neck. The one thing he had refused to put on was the pair of polished leather shoes that the shop assistant had insisted would make the outfit complete. Black trainers would have to do. What did it all make him look like, he wondered, as he straightened the bow tie for the tenth time. A young James Bond. He hated the comparison but he couldn't avoid it.

It wasn't just the clothes. As Alex continued his examination, he had to admit that so much had happened in the last year, he'd almost lost track of who – and what – he was. Standing in front of the mirror, it was as if he had just stepped down off the merry-go-round that his life had become. He might be still but the world around him was spinning.

Just two months ago he had been in Australia – not on holiday, not visiting relatives, but, incredibly, working for the Australian Secret Intelligence Service, disguised as an Afghan refugee. He had been sent to infiltrate the people-smuggling gang known as the snakehead, but his mission had taken him much further than that, setting him against Major Winston Yu and the potential devastation of a huge bomb buried deep inside a fault line in the earth's crust. It had also brought him face to face with his godfather, the man he had known only as Ash. Thinking about him now, Alex saw something spark in his eyes. Was it anger? Grief? Alex had never known his parents and he'd thought Ash would somehow be able to explain where he'd come from, to make sense of his past. But his godfather had done nothing of the sort and their meeting had led instead to betrayal and death.

And that was really it, wasn't it? That was what the boy in the mirror was trying to tell him. He was still only fourteen years old but this last year – a year whose end they were about to celebrate – had almost destroyed him. If he closed his eyes, he could still feel Major Yu's walking stick smashing into the side of his head, the crushing weight of the water under the Bora Falls, the punishment he had taken in the Thai boxing ring in Bangkok. And those were just the most recent in a string of injuries. How many times had he been punched, kicked, beaten, knocked out? And shot. His wounds might have healed but he would still be reminded of them every time he undressed. The scar left by the .22 bullet fired into his chest by a sniper on a rooftop in Liverpool Street would always be with him. And the memory of pain. They say that never leaves you either.

Had it changed him? Of course it had. Nobody could survive all this and stay the same. And yet...

"Alex! Stop admiring yourself in the mirror and get downstairs!"

It was Sabina. Alex turned and saw her standing in the doorway, wearing a silver dress with lots of glitter around the neckline. Her dark hair – she had grown it long – was tied back. Unusually for her, she was wearing make-up: pale blue eyeshadow and glossy pink lipstick.

"Dad's waiting. We're about to leave."

"I'll be one minute."

Alex twisted the bow tie again, wondering what he had to do to stop the damn thing going crooked. He looked ridiculous. Nobody under the age of fifty should have to dress like this. But at least he'd been able to resist Sabina's suggestion that he should go to the party dressed in a kilt. She'd been teasing him about it since Christmas.

Despite everything, the last six weeks had been fantastic for Alex Rider. First of all, Sabina and her parents had unexpectedly arrived in England. Edward Pleasure was a journalist. He had almost been killed once, investigating a pop star called Damian Cray. Alex had blamed himself for that, and when, at the end of it all, Sabina had left for America, he had been certain he would never see her again. But now she was back in his life and although she was a year older than he was, the two had never been closer. It helped perhaps that she was one of the few people who knew about his involvement with MI6.

Better still, the Pleasures had invited Alex to join them for New Year at the house they had rented in the West Highlands of Scotland. Hawk's Lodge was a Victorian pile that had been named after an obscure poet rather than the bird. It stood three storeys high on the edge of woodland with Ben Nevis in the background. It was the sort of house that needed roaring log fires, hot chocolate, old-fashioned board games and too much to eat. Liz Pleasure, Sabina's mother, had supplied all of this and more from the moment they had arrived. In the past few days the four of them had gone hillwalking and fishing. They had visited ruined castles and isolated villages and strolled along the famous white sands of Morar. Sabina had hoped it might snow – there was good skiing over at Cairn Gorm and she had brought her gear with her – but although it was freezing outside, so far the weather had only managed a few flurries. There was no television in the house and Edward had banned Sabina from bringing her Nintendo, so they had spent the evenings playing Scrabble or Perudo – the Peruvian game of liar dice which Alex nearly always won. If there was one thing he had learnt in his life, it was how to lie.

Meanwhile, Jack Starbright, Alex's housekeeper and in many ways his closest friend, was in Washington. She had been invited up to Scotland too but had decided to go home for New Year to see her parents. As he followed her out of the house, it had crossed Alex's mind that one day she would go back to America for good. Her parents and the rest of her family were there. He wondered what would happen to him when she did. She had looked after him since his uncle had died, and as far as he knew there was nobody to take her place. As if reading his thoughts, she had given him a hug while the taxi driver loaded her cases.

"Don't worry, Alex. I'll see you in a week. Just try and have a good time in Scotland. See if you can make it past New Year without getting into trouble. Don't forget, school starts on the sixth."

And that was another reason to be cheerful. Alex had managed to complete almost half a term at Brookland without getting kidnapped, shot at or recruited by one of the world's security agencies. He had begun to feel like an ordinary schoolboy again, being told off for talking in class, sweating over his homework, listening out for the bell that meant the end of day.

He took one last look in the mirror. Jack was right. Forget James Bond. He'd had enough of all that. He was leaving it behind.

He went down two flights of stairs to the wood-panelled hall with its rather gloomy paintings of Scottish wildlife. Edward Pleasure was waiting with Sabina. It seemed to Alex that the journalist had got quite a lot older since they had last met. There were definitely more lines in his face. He now wore glasses all the time. And he had lost a lot of weight. He also limped, supporting himself with a heavy walking stick, metal-tipped and with a brass handle shaped like a duck's head. His wife had bought it for him in an antique shop in London. She had joked that if any of the people he wrote about ever tried to attack him again, at least he'd have something he could use to defend himself.

That was what Alex liked most about this family. They stuck together and, no matter what happened, they always seemed to be cheerful. He had found it easy spending time with them, slipping into their routine. And Alex liked to imagine that in many ways his parents would have been just like Edward and Liz.

The journalist had also put on black tie for the evening but Alex saw at once that there was a problem.

"What is it?" he asked.

"Mum's not coming," Sabina replied. She was looking frustrated. Alex knew she had spent hours getting ready for the party. Now, at the last minute, something had gone wrong.

"She says she's not feeling up to it," Edward explained. "It's nothing serious. Just a touch of flu."

"Then I think we should all stay," Sabina said.

"That's nonsense, Sabina. The three of you go and enjoy yourselves." Liz Pleasure had appeared at one of the doorways. She was a pleasant, easy-going woman with long, straggly hair. She didn't care how she looked and she liked to run a house without rules. Right now she was wearing a baggy jersey and jeans, holding a box of tissues. "I don't much like parties anyway and I'm certainly not going out in this weather."

"But you don't want to be here for New Year on your own."

"I'm going to have a hot bath with some of that expensive oil your dad bought me for Christmas.

Then I'm going to bed. I'll be asleep long before midnight." She went over to Sabina and put her arm round her. "Honestly, Sab, it doesn't bother me. We can celebrate New Year tomorrow and you can tell me what I've missed."

"But, Mum, we won't enjoy it without you."

"Of course you will. You love parties. And you look terrific – both of you." Liz Pleasure had made up her mind. "You have to go. Your dad's got the tickets and they're worth a fortune." She beamed at Alex. "You look after her, Alex. And remember. This is a party in a real Scottish castle – Hogmanay and all the rest of it. I'm sure you're going to have a fantastic time."

There was no point in any further argument, and twenty minutes later, Alex found himself being driven along the twisting roads that led north to Loch Arkaig. The weather had got worse. The snow that Sabina had been hoping for was falling more heavily, swirling in front of the headlights as they cut through the night. Edward Pleasure was driving a Nissan X-Trail which he had rented at Inverness Airport. Alex was glad he had chosen a four-by-four. The snow was already settling. Any thicker and they would need the extra traction.

Sabina was stretched out in the back, untangling her iPod. Alex was in the front. It was the first time he had been alone with Edward Pleasure since the South of France and he felt a little uncomfortable. The journalist must have known about his involvement with MI6; Sabina would have told him everything that had happened. But the two of them had never discussed it, as if it was somehow impolite.

"It's good to have you with us, Alex," Edward muttered. He was deliberately keeping his voice down so that Sabina, plugged into Coldplay, wouldn't hear. "I know Sab was really glad you could tag along."

"I've had a great time," Alex said. He thought for a moment, then added, "I'm sorry about tonight, though."

Edward smiled. "We don't have to stay too long if you don't want to. But what Liz said was right. Nobody celebrates New Year like the Scottish. And Kilmore Castle is quite a place. Dates back to the thirteenth century. It was torn down in the first Jacobite rising and stayed more or less in ruins until it was bought by Desmond McCain."

"Isn't he the man you're writing about?"

"That's right. He's the main reason we're going. The Reverend Desmond McCain." Edward reached down and flicked a switch, blowing hot air over the windscreen. The wipers were doing their best but snow was still sticking to the glass surface. It was warm and cosy inside the car, in marked contrast with the world outside. "He's an interesting man, Alex. Do you know anything about him?"

"Not really."

"I thought you might have read about him in

the papers. He was brought up in an orphanage in east London. No parents. No family. Nothing. He'd been abandoned in a supermarket trolley, wrapped in a plastic bag – McCain Oven Chips. That's how he got his name. He was fostered by a couple in Hackney, and from that moment things started going better for him. He did well at school ... at least in sport. By the time he was eighteen, he had become a famous boxer. He won the WBO middle-weight title twice and everyone thought he'd make it a hat-trick, except he got knocked out in the first round by Buddy Sangster in Madison Square Garden in 1983."

"Didn't something happen to Sangster?" Alex asked. He'd heard the name somewhere before.

"That's right. He died a year later. He fell under a train in the New York subway. They showed his funeral on TV. One of his fans even sent him a hundred black tulips. I remember hearing that..." Edward shook his head. "Anyway, Desmond McCain wasn't boxing any more. His jaw had been smashed up pretty badly. He went to some plastic surgeon in Las Vegas but it was a botch job and it never healed properly. To this day he can only eat soft food. He can't chew. But it wasn't the end of him. He went into business – property development – and he was very good at it. There were a dozen families in Rotherhithe, down on the River Thames, and somehow he persuaded them to sell cheaply to him and then he knocked down their houses and put up a bunch of skyscrapers and made a fortune.

"That was about the time that he became interested in politics. He'd donated thousands of pounds to the Conservative Party and suddenly he announced he wanted to be an MP. Of course, they welcomed him with open arms. He was rich, he was successful – and he was black. That was part of it too. And the next thing you know, he managed to get himself elected in a corner of London which hadn't voted Conservative since the nineteenth century, and even then it was only by mistake. People liked him. It was the typical rags to riches story – you could say plastic bag to riches in his case. He got a big majority, and a year later he was a minister in the department for sport. There was even talk that he could one day become our first black PM."

"So what went wrong?"

Edward sighed. "Everything! It turned out that his business hadn't been doing as well as people thought. One or two of his developments had fallen behind schedule and he had huge financial problems. The bank was closing in and it looked as if he might go bankrupt – and of course you're not allowed to be a member of Parliament if that happens. God knows what he was thinking, but he decided to set fire to one of his properties and claim on the insurance. That was his way out of the mess. Well, the property in question was a twenty-four-storey office block overlooking

St Paul's, and one night it simply burned to the ground. The next day, McCain put in a claim for fifty million pounds. Problem solved."

They came to a sharp bend in the road and Edward Pleasure slowed down. By now the whole road was snow-covered, with dark pine trees looming up on both sides.

"At least, that's what he thought," he went on. "Unfortunately the insurance company smelled a rat. They started asking questions. Like, for example, why had the alarms been switched off? Why had the security staff been allowed to leave early? There was a lot of gossip in the press – and then, suddenly, a witness appeared. It turned out there'd been a homeless person sleeping in the underground car park. He'd been there when McCain drove in with six gallons of petrol and a cigarette lighter. He was lucky to get away alive. Anyway, McCain was arrested. There was a fairly sensational trial, and he was sent to prison for nine years."

Alex had listened to all this in silence. "You called him the Reverend McCain," he said.

"Well, that's the strange thing. In a way, McCain's whole life had been bizarre – but while he was in jail, he converted to Christianity. He did a correspondence course and became a priest in some Church no one's ever heard of. And when he got out – that was five years ago – he didn't go back into business or politics. He said he'd spent his whole life being selfish and he wanted to put all that behind him. Instead he set up a charity. First Aid. That's what it's called. It provides a rapid response to emergencies all over the world."

"How much further?" Sabina's voice came from the back seat. She was still plugged into her iPod.

Edward Pleasure held up a hand and opened it twice, signalling ten minutes.

"You interviewed him?" Alex said.

"Yes. I've done a big piece for *GQ*. They'll be publishing it next month."

"And...?"

"You'll meet him tonight, Alex, and you can see for yourself. He has an enormous amount of energy and he's channelled it into helping people less fortunate than himself. He's raised millions for famine relief in Africa, bush fires in Australia, floods in Malaysia – even that accident in South India. Jowada."

Alex nodded. He'd read about it when he'd been working as a ball boy at Wimbledon. It had made the front pages. "The nuclear reactor," he said.

Edward nodded. "For a time it looked as if the whole city of Chennai could have been affected. Fortunately it wasn't as bad as that, but a lot of people were killed in the panic. First Aid were up and running the very next day, getting anti-radiation stuff to the women and kids, helping with supplies, that sort of thing. Nobody was quite sure how they got off the mark so quickly but that's how they work. Instant response. Their aim is to be the first charity in."

"And you really think this man, McCain, is genuine?"

"You mean ... do I think he's another Damian Cray?" Edward smiled briefly. It had been his article exposing Cray as a maniac that had almost got him killed. "Well, I did have my doubts when I first met him. I mean, even if he wasn't a crook, he was a Tory politician, which didn't exactly recommend him. But you don't need to worry, Alex. I did a lot of research into his charity. I interviewed him and I met people who knew him. I spoke to the police and I opened their old files. The truth is, I couldn't find anything bad to write about him. He really does seem to be a rich man who made a bad mistake and who's trying to make up for it."

"How come he owns a castle? If he went bankrupt..."

"That's a good question. After he went to prison, he lost all his money, everything. But he had powerful friends – both in the City and in the Tory Party – and they did what they could to help him out. Thanks to them, he managed to hang on to Kilmore Castle. He also has a London flat and he's the part-owner of a business somewhere in Kenya."

A car suddenly appeared in the road beside them, overtaking. Edward slowed down to let it pass. He watched as it was swallowed up by the whirling snow. "I'll be interested to hear what you think of McCain," he muttered.

"Did he invite you?"

"Yes. When I met him, I mentioned I was planning to be in Scotland for New Year and he gave me four tickets. And it's just as well. They actually cost three hundred pounds each."

Alex let out a low whistle.

"Well, it's all for charity. All the profits will go to First Aid. There'll be a lot of rich people there tonight. They'll raise tens of thousands."

There was another brief silence. The road had begun to climb steeply uphill and Edward changed down a gear.

"We never really talked about Damian Cray," Edward said.

Alex twisted in his seat. "There's nothing to say."

"My book about him sold a million copies. But I never mentioned you, or your part in what happened."

"I prefer it that way."

"You saved Sabina's life."

"She saved mine."

"Can I give you some advice, Alex?" Edward Pleasure had to keep his eyes on the road but just for a moment he turned them on Alex. "Stay away from all that. MI6, intelligence, all the rest of it. I've a good idea what's been going on over the past year. Sabina's told me some of it but I have contacts in the CIA and I hear things. I don't want to know what you've been through but, believe me, you're better off out of it."

"Don't worry. I don't think MI6 are interested in me any more. They didn't even send me a Christmas card. That part of my life is over. And I'm glad."

The road was even steeper now and the trees had fallen away on one side to reveal an expanse of black water, Loch Arkaig, stretching out below. It was still snowing but the flakes didn't seem to be making contact with the half-frozen surface, as if the two were somehow cancelling each other out. The loch was said to have its own monster – a giant water horse – and, looking down, Alex could well believe it. Loch Arkaig had been left behind by the glaciers. Twelve miles long and in places a hundred metres deep, who could say what secrets it had managed to keep to itself for the past million years?

And there was Kilmore Castle looming up above him, almost invisible behind the sweeping snow. It had been built on a rocky outcrop above the loch, completely dominating the surrounding land-scape, a massive pile of grey stone with towers and battlements, narrow slit-like windows, soar-ing archways and solid, unwelcoming doors. There was nothing about the place that had been built for comfort. It existed only to rule and to keep those inside it in power. It was hard to imagine how it had ever fallen or, for that matter, how it had been built. Even the Nissan X-Trail with its 2.2

litre four-cylinder turbo diesel engine seemed to be struggling as it negotiated the tight hairpin bends that were the only way up. Had soldiers once come here on horseback? How could they possibly have penetrated those massive walls?

They were in a queue of traffic now, with other partygoers just visible behind the frosted windows of their cars. The last bend brought them to a wide open space which had been converted into a car park with attendants in Day-Glo jackets frantically signalling where to go. Two fiery torches had been placed on either side of the main entrance, the flames fighting the snow. Men and women in heavy coats, their faces lost behind scarves, were hurrying across the gravel and bundling themselves in. There was something almost nightmarish about the scene. It didn't look like a party. These people could have been refugees, running for their lives from some freak act of nature.

Edward Pleasure parked the car and Sabina took off her iPod.

"We don't have to stay until midnight," her father told her. "If you want to leave earlier, just let me know."

"I wish Mum had come," Sabina muttered.

"Me too. But you know she wouldn't want us to worry about her. Let's just have fun."

They got out of the car, and after the warmth of the interior Alex was immediately hit by the deep chill of the night, the snow dancing in front of his eyes, the wind rushing through his hair. He had no coat and broke into a run, hugging himself, using his shoulders to battle through the elements. It was as if the very worst of the winter had somehow been concentrated on this rocky platform, high above the loch. The flames of the beacons writhed and twisted. Somebody shouted something but the words were snatched away.

And then they had reached the archway and passed through into an inner courtyard where at least the wind couldn't penetrate. Alex found himself in an irregularly shaped space with high walls, cannons and a huge bonfire. About a dozen guests were crowded round it, feeling the warmth and laughing as they brushed snow off their sleeves. A second archway stood ahead of him, this one with carved eagles and an inscription in Gaelic, the letters glowing red and shimmering in the light of the fire.

CHA DÈANAR SGRIOS AIR NÀIMHDEAN
GUS AM BITHEAR FIOS AIR CÒ IAD

"What's that?" Sabina asked.

Edward shrugged, but next to him one of the other guests had overheard. "It's the motto of the Kilmore clan," he explained. "This was their ancestral home. They were here for three hundred years."

"Do you know what it means?"

"Yes. 'You cannot defeat your enemies until you know who they are.'" The guest pushed forward and disappeared into the castle.

Alex stared at the inscription. He wondered if in some way it wasn't speaking to him. Then he dismissed the thought. A new year was about to begin and with it a new set of rules. There were no more enemies. That was what he had decided.

"Come on, Alex..."

Sabina grabbed his arm and together they went in.

CARDS BEFORE MIDNIGHT

Alex had never been to a party like it.

The banqueting hall at Kilmore Castle was huge, but even so it was jammed with people: five or six hundred of them had been invited and this wasn't an invitation anyone was going to turn down, even if it came with a three hundred pound price tag. Within minutes Alex had spotted half a dozen TV celebrities and soap stars, a clutch of politicians, two celebrity chefs and a pop star. The men were in black tie or kilts. The women had fought to outdo one another with yards of silk and velvet, plunging necklines and a dazzling assortment of diamonds and jewels.

A whole army of waiters in full Highland dress were pushing their way through the crowd carrying trays of vintage champagne, while a trio of bagpipe players performed on a gallery above. There were no electric lights. Over a hundred candles flickered in two massive chandeliers. Torches blazed from iron braziers mounted in the walls. The far wall was dominated by a massive stone fireplace with flames leaping up the chimney and throwing red shadows across the flagstone floor.

The Kilmores hadn't lived at the castle for centuries but they were certainly present tonight. Life-size portraits hung on the walls – grim-looking men with swords and shields; proud-eyed women in tartan and bonnets. Suits of armour had been mounted in many of the alcoves and crossed swords stood guard over every archway and door. The animals they had killed – stags, foxes, wild boar – looked down on the scene with their disembodied heads and glass eyes. Coats of arms dotted the walls, the fireplace, even the windows.

Desmond McCain must have spent a fortune on the party, ensuring that at the very least his guests would get value for money. A buffet table reached from one end of the hall to the other, piled high with salads and great slabs of beef and venison, whole salmon, and – on a giant silver platter – a roast suckling pig complete with angry eyes and an apple in its mouth. There were dozens of different wines and spirits, punchbowls and as many as fifty brands of malt whisky in bottles of various shapes. One archway led to a dance floor, another to a billiard room with a tournament already under way. Somehow McCain had managed to park a brand-new Mini Cooper Convertible in the hallway. It was the first prize in a raffle that also included a Kawasaki Ultra 260X Jet Ski and a two-week Caribbean cruise – all of them given free to First Aid by wealthy sponsors.

Outside, the snow was still falling. The wind was cutting through the night like a scalpel. But all that was forgotten as, inside, the guests enjoyed the warmth of each other's company and the spirit of the celebration as the minutes ticked down to New Year.

And yet, despite all this, Alex and Sabina felt a little out of place. Not many other teenagers had been invited and the ones they met all lived locally, seemed to be at least six feet tall, and clearly regarded them as outsiders. They ate together, had a couple of drinks, and made their way to the dance floor, but even here they didn't feel comfortable, surrounded by adults twisting and swaying to music that had been written before Alex was born.

"I've had enough of this," Sabina announced as the band lurched into an Abba classic.

Alex knew what she meant. The centre of the dance floor was dominated by three bald men in kilts jabbing their fingers into the air to the tune of "Money, Money, Money". He glanced at his watch. It was only ten past eleven. "I don't think we can leave yet, Sabina," he said.

"Did you see where Dad went?"

"He was talking to one of the politicians."

"Probably hoping to get a story. He never stops."

"Come on, Sabina. Cheer up. This place is hundreds of years old. Let's go and explore."

They pushed their way off the dance floor and headed down the nearest corridor. It twisted round and the music and the noise of the party were cut off almost at once. Another corridor led off it, this one decorated with tapestries and heavy gilt mirrors with glass blackened by age. At the end they came to a staircase which led to one of the towers and suddenly they found themselves outside, surrounded by stone parapets, looking out into the white-spotted blackness that the night had become.

"That's better," Sabina said. "I was suffocating in there."

"Are you cold?" Alex could see the snow falling gently onto her bare neck and shoulders.

"I'll be all right for a minute."

"Here." He took off his jacket and handed it to her.

"Thanks." She slipped it on. There was a pause. "I wish I didn't have to go back to America," she said.

Her words jolted Alex. He had forgotten that she would be returning in a few days' time. She'd enrolled at a school in San Francisco, where the family was living, and it would be a while before they saw each other again. He'd be sorry when she'd gone. He'd got used to having her around.

"Maybe I could come over in the Easter holidays," he said.

"Have you been to San Francisco?"

"Once. My uncle took me on a business trip. At least, that's what he told me. He was probably working with the CIA, spying on someone or some-thing."

"Do you ever think about Damian Cray?"

"No." Alex shook his head. The question seemed to have come out of nowhere. He glanced at Sabina and was surprised to see that she was looking at him with something close to anger in her eyes.

"I do. All the time. It was horrible. He was mad. And the way he died! I'll remember that for the rest of my life."

Well, that made sense. Sabina had been there at the very end. In fact, she had been at least partly responsible for his sensational death.

"I thought you said you were going to stop all that," she went on. "Playing at being a spy..."

"It was never my choice," Alex replied. "And anyway, I've already told your dad. I've stopped. It's not going to happen again."

Sabina sighed. "San Francisco's great," she said. "Great shops. Great food. Great weather. But I miss England." She paused. "I miss you."

"I'll come out. I promise."

"You'd better..."

They had only been outside for a couple of minutes but in this weather it was more than enough. Alex could see the flakes of snow in Sabina's hair. "Let's go downstairs," he suggested.

"Yeah. Let's find Dad and get out of here. I want to get back to Mum. I'll go to the main hall. You look in the other rooms. If you ask me, this party sucks. All these men in kilts and not one of them with decent legs..."

She handed him his jacket and the two of them made their way back down the twisting staircase, then split up, searching for Edward Pleasure. Alex watched Sabina hurry down the corridor, then went the other way, past more unsmiling portraits of long-dead ancestors. He wondered why anyone would want to live in a place like this. Maybe Desmond McCain needed somewhere to hide from the world. When he wasn't trying to help it.

He heard the murmur of voices, the clink of a glass and a woman laughing. He had come to a set of double doors, opening into what had to be the castle's library. There were shelves of leather-bound books that looked hundreds of years old and were surely never read. He saw at once that the library had been converted into a casino, with card tables, a spinning roulette wheel and croupiers in white shirts, waistcoats and bow ties. As he walked in, the roulette ball tumbled into its slot with a loud clunk, the audience laughed and applauded and the croupier called out "Eighteen, red, even..." and began to sort out the chips. There were almost a hundred people playing the different games, most of them holding drinks and one or two of them puffing on cigars. This was the only room in the castle where smoking was allowed and a film of smoke hung in the air.

Alex didn't mean to go in. He looked briefly at

the cards sliding across the green baize, the fresh chips stacking up in front of the roulette wheel, the men and women, some standing, some sitting, leaning forward, their faces flushed with excitement. The main focus of attention seemed to be at the far end of the room. There was a game in progress with six players, but one of them had just lost. Alex saw him throw his cards down with disgust and get up, leaving an empty chair. At the same time, the winning player laughed, a deep, rich sound that warmed the room.

Desmond McCain. It had to be him. Alex would have known it even if he hadn't been the only black man there. McCain was lolling back in his chair in front of a great window which had the effect of framing him, putting him in the centre of the picture. Almost despite himself, Alex moved forward to get a closer look. He had been thinking about McCain only a few minutes ago. It couldn't hurt to see what the laird of Kilmore Castle was really like.

McCain was gathering up his cards, which almost disappeared in his oversized hands. He was a huge man with an extraordinary presence that somehow drew Alex to him. He was completely bald, with a round, polished head that had surely never seen a single hair. His eyes were a strange shade of grey – they were dark but they were still electric – and his smile was quite simply dazzling. Like everyone else, he was dressed in black tie; but unlike so many others, he looked completely comfortable, as if he always dressed this way.

He picked up a tumbler of whisky, which he drank as if it were a cocktail, using a straw at the side of his mouth, and Alex remembered what Edward Pleasure had told him about the boxing injury. It was true. The man he was looking at had received a blow that had permanently dislocated his jaw. Worse than that, it had been put back together in such a way that it no longer fitted properly. It was as if someone had taken a photograph of his head, cut it horizontally in half and then fixed the two pieces a few millimetres apart. His eyes and nose were no longer exactly over his mouth.

McCain said something, turned his head and laughed a second time. That was when Alex saw it. He was wearing a silver crucifix, not around his neck but in his ear. It was one centimetre long, pinned into the lobe. The jewellery was very striking, set against the intense dark skin. This was a man who wore his faith openly, who dared you to argue against it.

Alex drew closer. The six of them had been playing a version of poker – Texas hold 'em – in which five cards turned face up are used by everyone at the table. And the stakes couldn't have been higher. Alex saw that at once from the number of different-coloured chips spilling across the table, marked £50, £100 – even £500. Each one had been bought at its face value. The casino was using real money, with a percentage of the winnings going to First Aid.

Alex could feel the tension in the air. A scattering of cards, a few minutes' playing time and thousands of pounds could be changing hands. At the moment, McCain was clearly in the lead. There was a whole mountain of chips stacked up in front of him and only one of the players – a man with a shock of silver hair and a thick, fleshy face – came anywhere close.

McCain looked up and noticed Alex. At once the smile was there, drawing him in, making him feel that the two of them had known each other for years.

"Good evening," he boomed. "Welcome to the Kilmore Casino. You're frankly a little young to be gambling, I'd have said. What's your name?"

"Alex Rider."

"And I'm Desmond McCain. We're just about to play the last hand. Why don't you join us? It's all in a good cause so I think we can turn a blind eye to the age limit." He gestured at the seat that had just been vacated. Alex could already hear that his broken jaw made it difficult for him to speak. Words beginning with *f* or *r* came out slightly distorted. "The cards have been quite interesting this evening. Let's see if they have anything more to say before midnight."

Alex knew he was making a mistake. He was meant to be looking for Edward Pleasure. He had agreed with Sabina. They were going to leave. But it was almost as if McCain had challenged him. If he walked away now, he would look like some little kid who was out of his depth.

McCain had won the last hand and was neatly stacking up all the chips, including those of the man who had just left. Alex sat down in the empty chair.

"Good!" McCain beamed at him. "Do you know the rules of Texas hold 'em?"

Alex nodded.

"We're taking this very seriously. It costs two hundred pounds to join the table – that goes straight to First Aid – and minimum bets are fifty pounds. Have you brought your pocket money with you?"

A couple of the other players laughed. Alex ignored them. "I didn't bring any money at all," he said.

"Then we'll let you off the entrance fee and I'll stake you. This is the last hand of the evening, so five hundred ought to be plenty." He slid the chips over. "It makes it more fun with more people. And you never know. You could win enough to buy yourself a new PlayStation!"

With Alex making up the numbers, there were six players at the table: three men, two women and him. McCain was at one end with a dark-haired woman – Alex vaguely recognized her as a television presenter – at his side. Then came an elderly man who could have been a retired soldier, sitting rigidly with a straight back and a face fixed in concentration. The silver-haired man was beside him. He reminded Alex of an accountant or a banker. After Alex, the circle was completed by a Scottish woman with ginger hair, sipping champagne even though it was clear she'd already had more than enough.

The croupier shuffled the deck and each player was dealt two cards, face down. These were known as the hole cards. Alex had learnt the basics of the game, playing with his uncle, Ian Rider, and Jack Starbright at an age when other children were probably reading Postman Pat. Texas hold 'em is largely a game of bluff. You try to make pairs, three of a kind, a full house and so on. But everything depends on your hidden cards. They may be great; they may be terrible. The secret is to make sure no one guesses either way.

Alex watched as McCain raised the corners of his cards with a thumb and smiled, not even attempting to conceal his pleasure. Of course, it was possible that he was bluffing but Alex sensed that this wasn't a man who was too clever when it came to hiding his emotions. He had to have something good under there – high cards or a pair. Alex examined his own cards. There was nothing to get excited about but he kept his own face blank.

"Come on, then," McCain said.

Now the betting began.

Alex looked at all the money he had been given,

thinking that there had to be better ways to spend five hundred pounds. McCain started the bidding with a hundred and the TV presenter folded at once.

"There's no point playing against you, Desmond," she said. She had a thick Scottish accent. "You always win."

"'We are all running in the race,'" McCain said. "'But only one receives the prize.'" He laughed briefly. "That's Corinthians, Chapter 9, Verse 24." He turned to the soldier. "Are you in, Hamilton?"

Hamilton also folded. The accountant, Alex and the ginger-haired woman all slid their hundred-pound chips in front of them.

The croupier was a pale, unsmiling man in his late twenties. He looked uncomfortable having a teenager in the game but dealt three more cards – the flop – face up on the table, waiting while each player made another bet.

By the time the last card had been dealt, this was what Alex was looking at, spread out on the green baize surface:

J♦ 7♥ A♣ 9♥ J♥

He had spent three hundred pounds to get here, betting against McCain.

There were just three players remaining. The other woman had folded, leaving Alex, the accountant and McCain to fight it out. The fact that the ace of clubs had now been joined by a pair of jacks made this an even more extraordinary game. McCain had asked if the cards had anything to say and it seemed that they were screaming. If this had been a real casino, with more people at the table, the betting might have climbed to hundreds of thousands of pounds. Even so, it was going to be expensive. Alex had just two hundred pounds left but the accountant had almost as much as McCain. And, even with such high sums, it was obvious that there was more to this than money. McCain was still relaxed, still smiling – but he really wanted to win the game. It was his party, his castle, his evening. It was a matter of personal pride.

And the other people in the room had sensed it too. Alex realized that the roulette wheel had stopped spinning. Everyone had gathered round the table to watch this strange contest – two men, a boy and five white rectangles which, combined with the turned-down cards, could mean so much or so little.

"Interesting cards," McCain muttered. "If either of you has another ace, you'll have two pairs. You could win the entire pot..."

Why had he said that, Alex wondered. The odds of two pairs at poker are not huge. Why even mention it? Was he perhaps challenging them? Or could it be that he was trying to divert their attention? Suppose he had three of a kind...

"I'll tell you what," McCain went on. "It's the

last game of the evening, so why don't we have a bit of fun?"

McCain lifted his hands theatrically, touched the two thumb tips together, then laid his palms flat on the table. There was a stir from the audience as he used the wedge to slide all his chips forward, the piles collapsing on top of one another as at least fifteen thousand pounds was spread across the table. One or two people clapped. Everyone knew what was happening here. It was all or nothing. This was one of those games that any serious gambler would remember for the rest of his life.

"I'm going to make it easy for you," McCain said. He ran a hand across his jaw as if he were trying to smooth it back into place. "I know the two of you don't have enough money to match my bet but I'm feeling charitable." He smiled at his own joke. "Put all your money in and we'll call it quits."

The accountant drummed his fingers on the table. "Are you trying to pretend you've got the third jack, Desmond?" he asked. He had a clipped, nasal way of speaking. His eyes were small and almost colourless and Alex watched them dart from McCain to the cards on the table and somehow knew that he was about to make a mistake. "I think you're bluffing," he went on. "You're just trying to scare us away. Well, it's not going to work." He slid his own pile into the centre, the plastic chips mingling with McCain's. He'd added about ten thousand pounds of his own.

Twenty-five thousand pounds in total. Any thought of charity had suddenly disappeared. It was a fantastic sum of money to be determined by the turn of a few cards.

Alex glanced at his own pile. It looked pathetic in comparison with the others but he assumed McCain's invitation extended to him. "I'm in," he said.

"All right, Leo!" McCain nodded at the accountant. "Let's see what you've got."

The accountant flicked over his two cards. There was a mutter of approval from the spectators. He did indeed have another ace – the ace of diamonds – plus a two of spades. Adding them to the face-up cards gave him two pairs – aces and jacks – a very good hand. McCain really would need three of a kind to do better.

It should have been Alex's turn to show his cards next but McCain ignored him. "Too bad, Leo!" he crowed. "God has delivered you into my hand – as it says in the Book of Samuel, Chapter 23." The silver crucifix glimmered briefly as he leant forward and picked up his cards. He paused for a moment, then turned them over, one at a time.

The first card was the jack of clubs. Three of a kind. It beat Leo easily. But then came the real triumph. He turned over the second card to reveal the other black jack – the jack of spades. The audience exploded. The odds of getting four of a kind in Texas hold 'em are four thousand one hundred and sixty-four to one. It was incredible luck. It was almost miraculous.

Now Alex understood why McCain had talked about three of a kind. He had actually been under-selling himself to draw the other players in. And the tactic, at least in part, had worked.

"I have the knaves and that makes it my evening," McCain roared. His eyes were bright with pleasure. He began to sweep all the chips towards him.

"What about my cards?" Alex said quietly.

"Your cards?" McCain blinked. He had forgotten Alex was even there. He glanced down at the table as if to reassure himself. Nothing could beat four jacks ... could it? He relaxed. "Do forgive me, Alex," he said. "I should have let you show your cards first. But we would all love to see them. What have you got?"

Alex waited. He was aware that everyone was looking at him. But for some reason he wanted McCain to remember this. Maybe it was just that he didn't like being taken for granted.

He turned over the eight of hearts. And then the ten of hearts.

There was a long silence as the truth sank in. Then the audience gasped. The seven, nine and jack of hearts were already on the table, face up. Put them together with Alex's cards and he had a straight flush: seven, eight, nine, ten, jack. And in the rules of poker a straight flush beats four of a kind.

Alex had won.

McCain froze with his hands still cradling the chips, and in that moment Alex stared at the huge mound spread out in front of him. They were all his! He had just won more money than he had owned in his whole life. But even so, he regretted what he had done. McCain was his host. This was meant to be his big night. But he had just lost around twenty-five thousand pounds betting against someone who had been using *his* money in the first place. Worse than that. He had been shown up in front of a large crowd of his friends by an unknown fourteen-year-old. How would he take it?

Alex glanced up. McCain was staring across the table with raw anger in his eyes.

"I'm sorry..." Alex began.

McCain slammed his hands together as if to break the mood. At the same time, he leant back and roared with laughter. "Well, there's a lesson in pride," he exclaimed loudly, for everyone to hear. "I jumped in too quickly. I was too sure of myself and it seems I've been undone by a child I don't even remember inviting. Never mind! Alex, you've beaten me fair and square." He used his huge hands to push the chips away, as if trying to distance himself from them. "You can cash in the money with the croupier. I bet you must be the richest thirteen-year-old in Scotland right now."

"Actually, I'm fourteen," Alex said. "And I don't want the money. You can give it all to First Aid."

That drew a round of applause from the audience. McCain stood up. "That's very generous of you," he exclaimed. "Donating my own money to my own charity!" He was joking but there was an edge to his voice. "I can promise you it will be well spent."

He moved away from the table, a few people patting him on the back as he left. Alex glanced down one last time at McCain's cards: the knaves, as he had called them. They were strangely ugly – almost like freaks, joined at the chest with flowing hair and strange multicoloured tunics.

Scowling knaves versus his own brave hearts. But of course, it didn't mean anything. They were only cards; and even as he watched, they were swept away and shuffled back into the deck.

OFF-ROAD VEHICLE

Twenty-five thousand pounds!

Even as he made his way back into the main body of the castle, Alex thought about what he had just done. It had been an awful lot of money to give away without thinking. He could have kept a bit of it, bought something for Jack or Sabina. He shook his head, annoyed with himself. Charity was what this evening was all about. The money wasn't his and never had been. He remembered the look of anger in Desmond McCain's eyes as he had revealed his straight flush. McCain might be a born-again Christian but he hadn't liked being beaten, and somehow Alex doubted that he was going to be invited back.

Sabina had disappeared but Alex stumbled across Edward Pleasure in yet another of the castle's many passageways, leaning on his walking stick while he talked on his BlackBerry. There was a spiral staircase just behind him, leading up to the next floor.

He closed up the phone as Alex approached.

"That was Liz," he said. "She's not feeling any better and I'm beginning to think maybe we ought to get back after all."

"That's fine by me," Alex said. "In fact, Sabina wants to leave too."

It was half past eleven. In just thirty minutes there would be the countdown to midnight, balloons, more champagne and a chorus of "Auld Lang Syne" before what had been billed as the biggest fireworks display in Scotland. Guests were already streaming past, making their way into the banqueting hall. But Alex didn't mind missing it. There was something about Kilmore Castle that he found unsettling. Maybe it was the fact that it was so ancient and remote, perched high up above the loch as if it didn't want to belong to the twenty-first century. He would be glad to see in the new year somewhere else.

"Where is Sabina?" Edward asked.

"She was looking for you."

"Well, let's wait for her here. She's bound to turn up sooner or later."

Alex could hear music coming from the dance floor – now they'd shifted into Michael Jackson. A few more guests hurried past. One of them recognized him from the casino and smiled at him. Once again the two of them were alone.

"So, are you looking forward to school?" Edward asked, as much to fill the silence as anything else.

"Yes, I am." If the question had taken Alex by

surprise, so did the answer. He really was looking forward to the start of the spring term. He felt safe at school. He felt normal.

"What was that essay you were working on?"

Alex had brought homework with him to Scotland. After having so much time off, he was trying as best he could to catch up. "I'm doing a project about GM crops," he said.

"GM?"

"You know, genetically modified. It's something we've been looking at in geography. How scientists can muck around with crops and make them do different things." Alex dredged his mind, trying to remember what he'd been learning the term before. "It's something Prince Charles is always going on about," he said. "He's afraid they'll accidentally destroy the world."

"The real problem with GM crops could be the corporations who end up controlling them," Edward said. "Have you heard of the terminator gene?"

Alex shook his head.

"It's something they've built into plants that effectively turns them off. It stops them reproducing. So if you want more wheat or barley seeds or whatever, you have to go back to the same company and pay them. You see what I mean? Whoever controls the genes could end up controlling the planet. It might be a good subject for me to write about myself. The real danger of genetically modified food..."

There was the sound of footsteps on the spiral

staircase and suddenly Desmond McCain was there, coming down towards them. Sitting at the card table, Alex hadn't realized how tall the man was. He was almost seven foot, built like an American football player with oversized shoulders and arms. Given his life story, he must have been at least fifty but he looked much younger. He obviously still kept himself in shape.

And he was alarmed.

He was trying to hide it, but it was there in his face. His eyes were clouded and the zigzag that was his mouth was stretched tight. He had clearly overheard Alex and Edward talking and something had disturbed him. But what? They had only been discussing Alex's homework.

Edward Pleasure turned round. "Reverend McCain!" he exclaimed.

"Mr Pleasure..." McCain came to a halt. Alex saw the rapid calculations being made as he took stock of the situation. He was forcing himself to calm down. He walked down the last of the stairs. "I'm very glad you could make it to my little affair," he said. He gestured at Alex. "Are the two of you together by any chance?"

"Yes. Have you met?"

"Alex and I were playing cards just a few minutes ago." McCain's smile had returned but it seemed a little strained and artificial. "If I'd known he was your guest, perhaps I wouldn't have been so rash with my betting. He cleaned me out." They were now all standing on the same level but McCain still loomed over them. "How is the article?" he asked.

"It's finished."

"I hope it won't contain any unpleasant surprises."

"You won't have long to wait. It'll be out next month."

"Have you delivered it?"

"Not yet."

"I'm looking forward to reading it." McCain examined the journalist as if it were his mind that he was trying to read. For a moment, neither of them spoke. Then McCain blinked, suddenly losing interest. "But now you must forgive me," he said. "I have a speech to make. Thank you so much for coming to Kilmore Castle. It was very good to see you again. And a pleasure to meet you, Alex."

He swept past them in the direction of the banqueting hall.

Edward Pleasure was looking puzzled. "What was all that about?" he asked.

Alex shrugged. "I don't know." He hesitated. "I thought he looked upset about something."

"I thought so too."

"Maybe he's worried about what you're going to write."

"He shouldn't be. I've already told you. I had nothing bad to say. Actually, I think he's quite a remarkable man. Take tonight, for example. All these people have come here because of him.

66

And it's all for charity. He never rests—"

He stopped as Sabina appeared, hurrying down the corridor towards them.

"Dad!" she said. "I've been looking for you every-where."

Edward Pleasure put an arm round her. "We're leaving," he said. "Mum's still awake. We can toast the new year when we get in."

They had left their coats by the main door so they had no choice but to leave through the banqueting hall. By now all the guests had assembled and were standing together, champagne glasses in hand, facing the gallery where the pipers had been performing and where McCain was about to make his speech. At least nobody would notice the three of them leaving early. Alex and Sabina followed Edward Pleasure and they made their way down the side of the buffet table – which had been partly cleared – on their way out.

There was a sudden fanfare, a single trumpeter standing at the back of the hall, his instrument glowing golden in the candlelight. The notes echoed across the chamber and the guests stopped talking and looked up expectantly. McCain appeared on the gallery. Two of the Highland pipers flanked him, a guard of honour. Alex couldn't help wonder-ing if they were about to burst into tune. But they stood back as McCain reached the front and looked down on the crowd.

"I want to thank you all for coming," he began,

his voice booming out. "I'll be brief. It's midnight in exactly twenty minutes and that's when the party really gets going. For those of you who stay the course, we'll be serving haggis, neeps and tatties and then a good Scottish breakfast to see you off. And the champagne will be flowing all night."

A few people cheered. The invitation had made it clear that everyone was welcome until sunrise.

"We're here to enjoy ourselves," he went on. "But at the same time, we can't forget the many terrible things that are happening around the world and the many millions of people who need our help. I want you to know that tickets sold for tonight's party, along with the raffle, our silent auction and private donations, have raised a fantastic four hundred and seventy-five thousand pounds for First Aid."

There was another burst of applause. Hearing it, Alex felt ashamed of himself. Whatever mistakes he had made in the past, McCain had more than redeemed himself. The whole evening was about helping other people, and in his own small way Alex had inadvertently spoilt it.

McCain held up a hand. "I have no idea how that money will be spent, but thank God it's there." He stressed the word "God" as if the two of them were personal friends. "This past year we've had those terrible floods in Malaysia, the volcano eruption in Guatemala and, most recently, the incident at the Jowada nuclear power station in India, which could have been much, much worse. We were there first and the money went straight to the people who needed it. Charity is the bond of perfectness, as it says in the Book of Colossians. And the next time disaster strikes, wherever in the world it happens, we will be ready..."

Edward Pleasure had got the coats. Sabina had already slipped hers on. One of the waiters had opened the door to reveal a maelstrom of snow against an unforgiving night. It was time to go. Alex took one last look back, and it seemed to him that at that moment, standing on his own at the front of the gallery, Desmond McCain stared straight at him, locking him into a final eye contact that ignored the six hundred people between them.

"Alex?" Sabina called out to him.

And then they were gone, out of the warmth of the castle, hurrying towards the car, which Edward Pleasure was already unlocking, using the remote control on his key fob. The rear lights blinked a welcome orange in the darkness. It had been snowing all evening. There was a thick carpet on the ground and on top of all the cars. If it continued much longer, Sabina might get her skiing break after all.

They threw themselves into the Nissan X-Trail, slamming the doors behind them. Once again Alex was glad that they had an off-road vehicle. They would need it tonight.

"What a night!" Edward Pleasure muttered,

echoing Alex's thoughts. He turned the key in the ignition and the engine began to throb reassuringly. He found the heating and turned it up as far as it would go. Alex was next to him. Sabina was once again in the back. "I'm afraid we're actually going to have New Year on the road," he said. "It'll take us at least an hour to get home."

"I don't mind." Sabina was already untangling the wires of her iPod. "That place gave me the creeps."

"I thought you liked parties."

"Yes, Dad. But not when I'm the youngest person there by about two hundred years."

They set off, the tyres crunching on the new snow. The weather had briefly cleared – which was just as well. Edward Pleasure would need all the visibility he could get to negotiate his way down the series of hairpin bends that led to the main road beside the loch. Alex took one last look at the great bulk of Kilmore Castle. He could see the firelight glowing behind the windows of the banqueting hall and could imagine McCain's speech ending, the balloons cascading, the kissing and the singing, and then more drinking and dancing into the new year. He was glad they'd left early. He'd been having a great time in Scotland but, like Sabina, he'd felt slightly uncomfortable at the party. He loosened his bow tie, then pulled it off. He'd have preferred to spend the evening at home.

The accident was so sudden, so unexpected, that none of them even realized what was happening until it was almost over. For Alex, it was as if the journey down the hillside had been broken into a series of still pictures. There was Edward Pleasure changing gear as the car picked up speed. How fast were they going? No more than twenty-five miles per hour. The headlights were shooting out, two separate columns, distinct from each other. Sabina said something and Alex half turned round to answer her.

And then there was a cracking sound. It seemed to come from a long way away but that wasn't possible. It had to be something in the engine. The car shuddered and lurched crazily to one side. Sabina cried out.

There was nothing anyone could do. It was as if a giant hand had seized the back of the car and swung it round like a toy. Alex felt the tyres slide helplessly across the road. Edward wrenched the steering wheel the other way but it was useless. They were spinning round, out of control, the night sky rushing towards them. And then came the moment when the tyres left the icy surface, and with a surge of terror Alex knew that they had come off the edge of the road, that they were in the air with the black, frozen waters of Loch Arkaig far below.

For half a second the car hung there.

Then it pitched forward and plunged down.

DEATH AND CHAMPAGNE

They couldn't stop. There was nothing they could do. The last thing Alex saw was Edward Pleasure clutching the steering wheel as if he had been electrocuted, his arms rigid, his eyes staring. Outside, the world had turned upside down. The headlights were bouncing off the surface of the loch, which was rushing towards them, covering the front window.

They hit the water. The actual impact was brutal, whipping them forwards and backwards at the same time. Alex realized that there must be a thin coating of ice stretching across the loch – he heard it and felt it splinter. It was like smashing through a mirror into another dimension. The car didn't float, even for a second. Carried on by its own momentum, it plunged into the darkness, huge tentacles of water reaching out and drawing it in. The real world of Scotland and castles and New Year was wiped out as if it had never existed, to be replaced by ... nothing. All the lights in the car had gone out. It was as though steel shutters had fallen on the other side of the windows. Alex would never have believed that darkness could be so total.

Something was pressing against him, smothering him. He panicked, punching out with his fists, trying to get whatever it was off him. He couldn't breathe. What was this huge thing, pushing him back into his seat? Where had it come from? He forced himself to think straight, to fight against the sense of blind terror. It was the airbag. That was all. It must have been activated at the moment of impact.

Air. He was going to need it. They were still sinking, getting deeper and deeper. He couldn't see anything but he could feel the pressure in his ears. There was no let-up. It was getting worse and worse. How deep was the loch? Some of these Scottish lakes continued down for hundreds of metres. They would keep going until they reached the bottom and that was where they would die. What had seconds before been a twenty thousand pound luxury car had become their steel coffin.

There was a soft thud and a shudder as the tyres came into contact with mud. Alex was aware of a ton of blackness weighing down on him. They weren't moving any more. That was something to be grateful for. But how far down had they gone? More to the point, how long did they have? The car wouldn't be able to keep the water out for more than a few minutes. It was already splashing down onto his feet, presumably coming through the air vents. The water was freezing cold, numbing the flesh at first touch. Already it was over his ankles. It was as if his legs were being taken away from him, one inch at a time.

"Alex?" It was Sabina's voice, coming from the back seat. She sounded a mile away.

"Are you OK, Sabina?"

"Yes. I think so. What about Dad?"

Edward Pleasure hadn't spoken since they had left the road. Alex reached out and found him. The journalist was resting against his own airbag ... unconscious, injured, perhaps even dead. It was impossible to say. Alex couldn't see anything. He drew his hand back and held it in front of his face, so close that it was brushing against his nose. He couldn't see it. It was impossible to breathe normally. His heart was racing, trapped inside him just as he was trapped in this car. He couldn't deny it. He was terrified.

He swallowed hard and somehow managed to speak. "Your dad's unconscious," he said.

"What happened?" He could hear the tears in Sabina's voice. Like him, she was struggling for control.

"I don't know."

"What do we do?"

It should have been silent here at the bottom of Loch Arkaig but Alex was aware of noise all around him. The engine was ticking and clanking as it cooled. There were strange ghostlike echoes coming from the lake itself. The Nissan was groaning as it fought against the pressure outside. And – most terrible of all – a steady stream of water continued to seep into the car.

It was still climbing. Alex felt it rise over his knees, a blanket of ice. He was sure that the water had only been at ankle level a few moments ago, but time didn't exist down here. Minutes were hours and a whole life could be over in seconds.

There was the sound of fumbling in the back, then Sabina spoke again. "Alex ... the door's locked."

"Don't even try to open it!"

Different thoughts were spinning uselessly through his mind. The Nissan might have a self-locking system. If the doors had locked themselves electronically, it would be impossible to get out. But there was no point in getting out anyway. Inside or outside, they would die.

"What are we going to do?"

Alex was still blind. He reached up, hitting his hand on the ceiling. Where was the light switch over the mirror? He found it and turned it on. Nothing. Of course, the car's electrical circuits would have flooded. But then he remembered. Edward Pleasure had consulted a map just after they'd left Hawk's Lodge – and he'd used a torch. Where had he put it?

He pushed the airbag out of the way – he was still cradling it in his lap – and felt for the glove compartment. Somehow he managed to get it open and more water poured out. God! They couldn't have more than a few minutes left. The water had risen over the edge of his seat, rushing between his legs. It was unbelievably cold. The whole lower part of his body no longer belonged to him. The water was already climbing up his stomach. Soon it would cover his head.

But he had found what he was looking for. A heavy rubber cylinder. Edward's torch. He flicked it on and to his utter relief it worked. The beam leapt out of his hand.

Alex had experienced more than enough in the past year but he would never forget what he saw right then in the uncertain light of the torch. It was the perfect nightmare. There seemed to be no way out.

The car was already half filled with water, which looked as black and as thick as oil. It was now pouring out of the ventilation ducts in two steady streams. Outside the windows, there was nothing. The glass didn't even look like glass. They could have been buried alive rather than deep under the surface of Loch Arkaig – it would have made no difference. The two airbags took up most of the space in the front of the car. Edward Pleasure was slumped against his, a great gash on the side of his head where he had somehow knocked himself out. Alex undid his seat belt and twisted round. Sabina was looking more frightened than he had ever seen

her. She had drawn her legs up as if she was cow-
ering away from the water, but it had reached her
anyway. It completely covered the back seat. The
bottom of her silver dress was soaked. She was
shivering with cold and fear.

They were in a tomb. And they were alone.
Nobody would have seen them leave the road. Nobody would ever find them. It would simply seem
that they had vanished into thin air.

"Alex..." Sabina was staring at the torch as if
it could somehow save her life. "What happened?"
she asked again.

"I don't know. The car lost control."

"Is Dad...?"

"He's OK. He's still breathing." The torch flickered
and for a brief second total darkness fell on them. It
couldn't go out now! Alex tightened his grip as if he
could somehow will the batteries to keep working.
"We're going to have to open the window, Sabina."

"Why?"

"To make the pressure inside the car the same as
the pressure outside. Then the doors will open."

"Yeah. And then we'll drown."

"No." Alex shook his head. "We didn't sink that
far. I don't think we can be more than twenty
metres down."

"Twenty metres is a long way, Alex."

Alex drew a breath. He knew that there couldn't
be too many more breaths in this cramped compartment available to him. The water was rising

fast, the air space beneath the ceiling becoming narrower and narrower. But once the water reached the level of the vents, it would stop. They would be sitting in a bubble of air which would quickly diminish as they breathed out carbon dioxide. Sabina was wrong. They wouldn't drown. They would suffocate.

"We have to get out of the car and swim for the surface," he said. "There's not much time."

"What about Dad?"

"Don't worry about him. I'll look after him."

"But how do we open the window?"

All the windows in the Nissan were electric and even if the car battery still had power, it wouldn't be enough to move them. The pressure outside was too great. They had to break the glass. Alex thought about leaning back and kicking out, using the heel of his shoe. But he knew it wouldn't work. He couldn't get the right angle; and anyway, the glass was toughened. He'd never have the strength.

He needed a hammer or an axe. Something metal. A fire extinguisher? There wasn't one. Golf clubs? Edward Pleasure had brought golf clubs with him but they weren't in the car. He'd left them back at Hawk's Lodge.

Then Alex remembered.

"Sabina, where's your dad's walking stick?"

"It's here."

"Pass it to me." He couldn't keep the panic out of his voice. He could feel the seconds ticking away.

Sabina handed it across and Alex quickly examined it in the light of the torch. The handle was metal and shaped like a duck's beak. He could use it like a hammer, except the stick was too long. He didn't have enough room to swing it. It would have to be shorter. How?

"Take this." He handed the torch to Sabina. "Shine it on me."

"What are you doing?"

He didn't answer her. He fed the walking stick through the steering wheel, slanting it diagonally across the dashboard so that the tip was in the far corner. The bulk of the walking stick was now in front of him. Using all his strength and his own body weight, he slammed forward, pushing against the stick. There was a creak of straining wood but the stick held. The water was rising over his chest. He could feel its grip, as cold as death. He tried again and this time he was successful. The walking stick snapped in half.

There was no time to lose. He dropped the bottom half and took the splintered end in his hand. He now had something like a hammer, about half a metre long.

"I'm going to break the window," he shouted. "Take a deep breath. As soon as the water's over your head, you'll be able to open the door."

Sabina nodded. She was either too cold or too frightened to speak.

Alex clutched the walking stick. Then, at the last

minute, he remembered something he had learnt from his days scuba-diving with his uncle. "Don't hold your breath!" he exclaimed. It was one of the most common reasons for diving accidents. If he and Sabina held their breath as they rose through the different pressure levels, they would end up puncturing their lungs. "Swim as fast as you can," he said. "But remember to hum as you go."

"What do you want me to hum, Alex – 'Auld Lang Syne'?"

Alex almost smiled. Only Sabina could still make jokes at a time like this. "Hum anything, Sabina," he said. "As long as you're humming, your lungs will be open."

He unfastened Edward's seat belt and checked that the driver's door was unlocked. The car was filling more slowly now but there couldn't be much more oxygen left. He tightened his grip on the broken walking stick, then swung it with all his strength, aiming for his own passenger window, as high up as possible. The duck's beak handle slammed into the glass. Sabina had pointed the torch towards him and he saw a series of spidery cracks. Water oozed in, but the window held. Was it his imagination or was it already getting more difficult to breathe? He had seconds left. He swung the makeshift hammer again, then once more.

On the third strike the window shattered and Alex was almost torn from his seat by the torrent of water that came rushing in, filling up the available space. The torch died and the blackness returned so suddenly that he wondered if the force of the water had knocked him out. But he was still conscious. Still thinking. Had Sabina managed to open her door? There was nothing more he could do. He had to get himself out – and Edward Pleasure.

Fumbling, blind, Alex searched for the door handle. He had underestimated just how powerful the rush of water would be. There were iron bands around his chest, crushing him, trying to empty his lungs. He squeezed the handle and felt the door open. At once he lurched sideways, fighting his way out of the car.

But he didn't dare go too far. Everything was black. If he lost contact with the car, he would never find it again and Edward Pleasure would drown. With the icy water swirling around his face, he hooked a hand underneath the door frame and felt his way over the roof and down the other side. Where was the door handle? He was already beginning to strain for air. He should have opened it from the inside. That might have saved a few precious seconds.

His hand smashed into the wing mirror but it didn't matter because he couldn't feel anything. Somehow he managed to curl his fingers round the handle and pull. The door opened. Alex's natural buoyancy was dragging him up but he kicked out, forcing himself to stay down. He reached inside and put his arms around Edward Pleasure but he couldn't get him out. He seemed to be stuck, jammed against the steering wheel.

With his own air running out and the surface at least twenty metres away, Alex thought the unthinkable. It was like some devil voice whispering in his ear. Leave him. Look after yourself. You can always tell Sabina you were unable to free him. If you stay down here any longer, both of you will die.

It was the airbag, pinning him in place, that was the problem. Alex still had the walking stick. At the last moment, without really knowing why, he had slipped it through his belt, taking it with him. Now he drew it out and, holding it this time by the handle, jabbed the splintered end into the nylon skin. He felt it puncture and there was a rush of bubbles against his fist. He was briefly tempted to breathe them in, but somehow he remembered that there would be nitrogen rather than air inside the bag and it wouldn't do him any good. The bag crumpled. Alex pulled again. Edward Pleasure came free.

They were out of the car – but which way was up? Alex couldn't even see the bubbles escaping from his lips. Nor could he feel them. The intensity of the cold had punched right through him and his entire body was numb. He was still gripping Edward Pleasure and he kicked out with his legs, hoping that gravity, buoyancy, whatever would tell him which was the right direction. The journalist was dragging him down. He was a deadweight in

Alex's arms and once again that voice was in his ear. Let him go. Forget him. Save yourself. But he just gripped all the tighter, kicked and kicked again.

Alex was following his own advice and humming – not a tune, more a soft moan of despair. Suppose he was wrong? The Nissan could have plunged thirty metres or even fifty. He looked up but saw no light, no sign of the surface. He kicked. It didn't feel as if he was making any progress. And what about Edward? How could Alex be sure he was still alive?

His chest was beginning to ache. His lungs were screaming for air and Alex knew that he wouldn't be able to resist them much longer. It could only have taken him thirty seconds to clamber across the car. Another thirty to get Edward out. Perhaps a minute since then. Surely he could hold his breath longer than that!

But not in this cold. The icy chill of Loch Arkaig had weakened him. It was all over. His humming faltered and stopped. There was no more air to come out. With a sob of pure despair Alex opened his mouth...

...and breathed air. He didn't even know how or when he had reached the surface. He hadn't felt his shoulders break through the ice. Somehow he was just there. As his vision cleared, he saw the blurred outline of the moon, lost behind clouds, and a scatter of still-falling snow. He had to struggle to keep Edward Pleasure's head above water and he wondered, with a sense of dread, if the rescue had all been in vain. He wasn't sure that Sabina's father was still breathing. He looked horribly like a corpse.

And where was Sabina? Alex tried to call her name but he was too frozen ... his chest, his vocal cords. He jerked round in the water. There was Kilmore Castle, floodlit, high above him. The shore was about twenty metres away. He was alone. She hadn't made it.

"Aaah..."

No. He was wrong. There was a splashing sound as the black surface of the lake parted, and suddenly Sabina was beside him, light rippling around her. Her face was white. Her long hair had come loose and was trailing in the water. She had tried to call his name but it was too much for her. The two of them stared at each other, saying more with their eyes than they could ever have managed with words. Then Sabina reached out and took hold of her father, sharing the weight. The two of them began an awkward, stumbling swim to dry land.

And even as they went, Alex knew that their ordeal wasn't over yet. They hadn't drowned but they could still die of cold. Their body temperature had to be dangerously low. Once they were on the shore, they would have to find help – and quickly, before their entire system shut down. But how? Kilmore Castle was too high up, too far away. None of the guests would be leaving yet. And Edward Pleasure needed immediate attention – unless it was already too late.

There was a loud bang, and for a horrible moment Alex thought that someone was shooting at them, but a second later the sky exploded with a blaze of white and silver and he realized McCain had just launched his first fireworks. So this was New Year – and what a way to begin it, with this hideous midnight swim. All around him the water shimmered with a brilliant array of colours as the display continued overhead. He could imagine the guests sipping their champagne, wrapped up in their coats and scarves as they watched from the battlements with the usual oohs and aahs as each five hundred pound missile was outdone by the next. What would they think if they could see what was happening below? Death and champagne. It seemed incredible that the two could be so close, existing side by side.

It took them five minutes to reach the water's edge, and climbing out onto the shore was a horrible, brutal experience. It was covered in shingle, slate grey and jagged. No feeling had yet returned to Alex's arms and legs. He was filthy, coated in some sort of oily film. Water was still streaming down his face. It was in his eyes and mouth. He must look barely human.

But his only thoughts were for Edward Pleasure. Helped by Sabina, he turned the journalist onto his back, then knelt beside him. The time he had spent in the Brecon Beacons being trained by the SAS hadn't included life saving. Fortunately he'd learnt that at school. There was a hiss and a scream from a rocket and for a second the sky blazed red, illuminating Edward's face. His eyes were still closed. Alex checked that his mouth wasn't blocked. He found his heart, placed both fists on top of it and pushed hard. He did it again, then continuously.

Sabina was shaking violently. She might have been sobbing but she made no sound. She had no strength left. She could only watch in growing despair as Alex kept up the massage. Edward Pleasure lay flat out, still. But suddenly, on the tenth or eleventh attempt, he coughed and water gushed out of his mouth. Sabina grabbed hold of his arm and he opened his eyes. Alex let out a deep breath. He'd been about to try mouth-to-mouth resuscitation and was relieved that it wasn't going to be needed.

Silver sparks crackled and exploded, hundreds of them, spread out across the darkness, then rained slowly down onto the loch.

"We have to get help." Alex tried to speak but he was so cold he couldn't make himself understood and the words came out as no more than single letters. "W-w-w v-v-v g-g-g..." His whole body was out of control. His teeth were chattering. The muscles in his neck and shoulders seemed to be locked rigid. He could see the snow settling on Sabina's hair. He had never been so cold. A few more minutes out here and the three of them would freeze solid.

But the greatest miracle of the night was still to come. Alex heard the sound of footsteps on the shingle and turned round. There was a man hurrying towards them, carrying a blanket. He had appeared as if by magic. In fact, it seemed so unlikely that he was there at all that Alex wondered if he was hallucinating. It was impossible to make out the man's features in the shifting colours of the night, but vaguely Alex registered that he wasn't dressed in black tie. He wasn't a guest from the party.

The man reached them. "I saw what happened!" he exclaimed. "I thought you must be dead. Are you all right? Can you move?"

"Our car..." Alex pointed out at the loch. For a moment, the water blazed emerald green. A great circle of fire hung in the sky then blinked out.

"I know. I saw. We have to get you, quickly, into the warm." The man draped the blanket over Sabina and as he leant forward another firework exploded, the glare revealing the side of his face. Alex saw that he was a young man in his early twenties, either Indian or Pakistani. As Sabina clutched the blanket and drew it round her shoulders, the man peeled off his coat and gave it to Alex. "Put this on," he instructed. "Do you think you can walk? My van is just up on the road. It's only five minutes from here. Once you're inside, you'll be OK."

Edward Pleasure was recovering his strength. He dragged himself up onto one elbow and broke into another fit of coughing. "What happened?" he demanded. His voice was little more than a whisper.

"Not now, sir. Not now. We have to go..."

The fireworks display had come to an end. Alex heard clapping and the blare of those plastic horns like the ones given away in crackers. Slowly they staggered to their feet. Sabina and Alex had to support Edward Pleasure and all three of them needed the help of the man who had come out of nowhere. Somehow he managed to guide them across the beach, the snow whirling around them as if unwilling to let them go. There was a track leading down from the main road, and a white van with its headlights on and side lights blinking. The sight of it lent them new strength. They stumbled off the shingle and threw themselves into the back.

"Don't worry!" Without his jacket the man was also shivering. He paused beside the doors. "I'll take you to hospital. You'll be all right." He closed the doors, locking them in.

They were lying on bare metal, a puddle of water all around them. Sabina was almost hidden in her blanket. Edward Pleasure was barely conscious. Alex heard the driver get into the front, and a few seconds later they moved off. At the same time, he realized that his senses were returning. The man had turned the heating up to full and Alex could actually feel the warm breeze against his skin.

It took them an hour to reach the hospital in Inverness and Liz Pleasure arrived two hours after that. By then all three of them had been treated for hypothermia and shock and were tucked up in bed with hot-water bottles and soup, being looked after by nurses who had agreed to work through New Year's Eve and who, Alex decided, really were true angels. The man who had rescued them had left without giving his name. He had told them he was a supplier on his way to Kilmore Castle. But what had he been supplying so late at night? Alex hadn't liked to ask him but it struck him now that something didn't quite add up. After all, the back of the van had been empty.

They were released the next morning, Edward Pleasure blaming himself for the car accident, all of them too shaken to discuss it. Between them they had decided to cut the holiday short. The Highlands and lochs of Scotland held no attraction after what had happened. They needed the reassurance of the city.

Waiting for the plane that would take them back to London, Alex wondered if he should tell them what he knew, what he had seen a split second before the car swerved and left the road. But in the end he decided against it. He still wasn't one hundred per cent sure. He wanted to believe that he was wrong.

Just before the car had lost control, he had heard a distant cracking sound. And at the same moment, out of the corner of his eye, he thought he'd seen a tiny flash of light in the darkness, behind them and high up above. He hadn't imagined it. It had been there. And he understood exactly what it meant.

A marksman positioned on the battlements of Kilmore Castle.

Edward Pleasure hadn't skidded on the ice. One of the tyres had been blown out and it had been done quite deliberately by someone who wanted to force them off the road. Anyone else would have thought they were imagining it but Alex knew better. He had been a target too many times before. Someone had just tried to kill them.

But who?

Desmond McCain? Because he had lost at cards? No – that was insane. There had to be someone else. An old enemy perhaps. Alex had plenty of them. Or maybe it had nothing to do with him. Edward Pleasure could have been the target. Journalists too had a long list of people who wanted to settle scores.

He said nothing. The last time he had been with the Pleasure family, in the South of France, they had been attacked. How could he possibly tell them that it had happened a second time? Sabina would never want to see him again. It was much better to persuade himself that he was wrong, that he was tired, that he had an overactive imagination. Anyway, in a few minutes they would be in the air, flying south, leaving it all behind them.

And yet secretly he knew that he was lying to himself. As their flight was called and he picked up his hand luggage, Alex gritted his teeth. Trouble never seemed to leave him alone. Well, let it follow him to London. He'd just have to be ready for it when it showed up again.

NINE FRAMES PER SECOND

Alex was glad to be home.

Jack was there, waiting for him, surrounded by presents that she'd bought in the American sales. Alex sometimes wondered what people made of the two of them, living together the way they did. With her baggy clothes, her wild red hair and her constant smile, Jack was more like a big sister than a housekeeper. And although she was actually his legal guardian, she never nagged him or told him off. They were really just friends and Alex knew that he couldn't have got through the last year without her. She knew what he was doing. She had tried to talk him out of it. But she had never stood in his way.

She'd bought him new jeans, two shirts, a Barack Obama baseball cap and a pair of fake Police sunglasses. And over their first dinner together he told her what had happened at Loch Arkaig – but with no mention of any sniper. He had decided not to worry her.

"I just don't believe it, Alex!" Jack exclaimed. "You go off for a nice New Year's Eve party and you end up twenty metres under a frozen loch. Only you could manage that!"

"It wasn't my fault," Alex protested. "I wasn't driving."

"You know what I mean! How's Edward? How's Sabina?"

"They're OK. They were shaken up. We all were."

"I'm not surprised. Do you know how it happened?"

Alex hesitated. The one thing he wasn't going to do was lie to Jack. "Nobody's quite sure. They haven't got the car out yet. It's possible they never will. But Edward thinks one of the tyres blew out. He felt something just before he lost control."

"And what about the man who helped you?"

"He didn't hang around. He didn't even wait to be thanked."

Alex wouldn't have mentioned the accident at all but he knew it would come out at the weekend when he and Jack went to Heathrow Airport to say goodbye to Sabina and her parents. It was an uneasy last meeting, the five of them standing together, hemmed in by the crowds and suitcases and bright lights of Terminal Three.

"We'll see you again in the spring," Edward Pleasure said, reaching out and shaking Alex's hand. "We've got a spare room and we can head down the coast. I'm sure you'd enjoy trekking in

Yosemite or we could stay on Big Sur."

Sabina's mother gave him a hug. "I know what you did," she said quietly. "Sabina told me. Edward would still be in that car if it hadn't been for you." Alex said nothing. For some reason, it always embarrassed him, being thanked. "I hope you'll come and see us. And you too, Jack. Maybe you should come over together."

And then it was Sabina's turn. She and Alex moved a little to one side.

"Bye, Alex."

"Bye, Sabina."

"I thought you were brilliant in the car. When I started to swim up to the surface, I was sure I was going to die. But I knew my dad would be all right because you'd promised you'd look after him."

"It seems that every time I'm with your family, something bad happens," Alex said. It was true. In Cornwall, the South of France and now in Scotland, sudden violence had never been far away.

"Will you come to San Francisco?"

"There'll probably be an earthquake or something."

"I don't mind. I still want to see you."

Sabina glanced at her parents. They were standing with their backs to her, talking to Jack. She quickly leant forward and kissed Alex on the cheek. Then, suddenly, the three of them were picking up their hand luggage and making their way through to passport control and the security checks. Sabina looked round one last time and waved. Then they were gone.

The next day, Alex went back to school and the Christmas holidays were forgotten in a whirl of timetables, textbooks, new teachers and old friends. Brookland was a sprawling mixed comprehensive half a mile north of Chelsea. It had only been built about ten years ago and it prided itself on its modern architecture with double-height windows and bright primary colours. At the same time, though, it still had an old-fashioned, friendly feel. Everyone wore uniforms, sober shades of blue and grey. The school had a motto and it was even in Latin: *Pergo et perago*, which sounded like the story of two Italian cannibals but which actually meant "I try and I achieve".

"No running in the corridor, Alex."

Miss Bedfordshire, the school secretary, greeted Alex with one of her favourite phrases, even though Alex had only been walking quickly. She had stepped out of a classroom, blocking his path.

"Hi, Miss Bedfordshire."

"It's good to see you. Did you have a nice Christmas?"

"Yes, thanks."

"And do you plan to stay with us for the whole term? It would certainly make a change."

Alex had recently been away almost as much as he'd been at school and Miss Bedfordshire had always had her doubts about the series of strange illnesses that had been listed on his doctor's notes.

"I hope so," he said.

"Maybe you should eat more fruit. You know. An apple a day..."

"I'll give it a try." Alex hurried on his way, aware that the secretary was watching him as he went. Sometimes he wondered how much she really knew.

And then there were twenty minutes catching up with the usual crowd. Tom Harris was late as always and looked incredibly scruffy in a new uniform that was one size too big for him. His parents had recently got divorced and he had spent the Christmas holidays with his elder brother in Naples. Alex had got to know them both when he'd come up against Scorpia for the first time – and Tom was the only one in the school who was aware of his involvement with MI6. There were a couple of girls with him and together they all piled into the sports hall for year group assembly.

This began, as usual, with a hymn, which the head teacher, Mr Bray, insisted on – even though every other school in the area had jacked it in. There were three hundred of them packed into the hall and they were horribly out of tune. The last chords faded away and everyone sat down to listen to an uplifting speech which, as usual, went on too long. This term it was all about respect. "Respect for others; respect for yourself; above all, respect for the community." Alex noticed that

Tom was listening intently with one hand resting against the side of his head. Only he could see the white wires of an iPod trailing back down the other boy's sleeve, and hear the faint *tish-ta-ta-tish* coming from his ear.

Then it was on to school business. Mr Bray introduced a new class tutor and mentioned a couple of teachers who were leaving.

"One last thing," he announced. "I'm very happy to tell you that the science block is finally open again after the mysterious fire which did so much damage last year." Alex shifted uncomfortably. He had been at the very centre of the fire and knew exactly what had caused it. He was glad that Tom wasn't listening. Watching Alex squirm, and knowing as much about him as he did, his friend might have put two and two together. "I hope you'll enjoy the new facilities. I wish you all a hard-working and successful term..."

The assembly finished and lessons began. For Alex that meant history followed by maths and then citizenship studies, a cheerful assortment for the morning of the first day of term. After lunch the first lesson of the afternoon was geography, with Mike Gilbert, a young teacher who had only arrived the term before. He was curly-haired with glasses, and specialized in brightly-coloured ties. He hadn't been teaching long enough to lose his enthusiasm and it had been he who had set the class the project on genetic engineering that Alex had described in Scotland. It was part of the year's work on resources and food.

"I hope you've all thought a little about this very serious subject," he began. "I'm going to want to see your written work completed by half-term. And I've got some good news." He picked up a letter and showed it to the class. "At the end of last term I wrote to the Greenfields Bio Centre in Wiltshire. I'm sure you know who they are; they're always in the news. Greenfields is a private organization, one of the world leaders in plant science and microbiology. They've been doing more than anyone else to develop new techniques in genetic engineering and they've got a huge facility on the edge of Salisbury Plain. I asked if we could visit, look at their work, and maybe talk to some of their professors – and rather to my surprise they've agreed. To be honest with you, I didn't think they'd allow school visits, because so much of their work is secret. But we'll be heading down there next week. You'll need permission from your parents and I'll hand out forms at the end of the lesson. Don't forget to get them signed!"

He put the letter down and went over to the board.

"Now, I want to find out how you're getting on with your projects. But first of all, I asked you to come up with some of the pros and cons of GM crops. Can anyone give me an example of how this science has helped society?"

GM crops.

Alex couldn't help himself. He remembered the moment he had told Edward Pleasure about his homework, just as Desmond McCain had come down the stairs, and suddenly he was back at Kilmore Castle, half an hour before New Year. McCain had been alarmed about something. But what was it and could it really have led to the gunshot and their near death in Loch Arkaig?

There had been no gunshot. Alex put the idea out of his head. The car had blown a tyre, that was all. And yet he still remembered McCain, the gleaming bald head, the silver cross, the strange line where the two halves of his face failed to meet.

No. This was crazy. McCain ran a charity. He had made a mistake in his life but he had paid for it. He wasn't a killer.

"Rider?"

Alex heard his name, realized it had been called out twice and forced himself to focus back on the class. Just as he had feared, Mr Gilbert had asked him something but he hadn't even heard the question. He'd been miles away.

"I'm sorry, sir?" he said.

Mr Gilbert sighed. "You don't turn up to school very often, Rider. But it would be nice if you actually listened when you did. Hale?"

James Hale was another of Alex's friends, a neat-looking boy with brown hair and blue eyes, sitting at the next desk. He glanced apologetically at Alex and then answered. "GM science can make crops grow extra vitamins," he said. "And there was a special sort of rice that was changed so that it could grow underwater for a few weeks without dying."

"That's right. Obviously it was very useful in countries with too much rainfall. Anyone else...?"

Alex made sure he concentrated until the end of the lesson. The first day of term was far too early to get into trouble. Somehow he made it to three forty-five without further incident and then he was part of the crowd, pouring out of the school gates, his backpack over his shoulder. For once, he hadn't brought his bike with him. Alex owned a Condor Junior Roadracer which had been built for him as a twelfth birthday present. But he'd noticed recently that it wasn't giving him a comfortable ride. The truth was that he was growing out of it and the saddle wouldn't adjust any more. He would be sorry to see it go. It belonged to his old life, before his uncle had died, and there was precious little of that left.

Perhaps it was thinking of his uncle that drove Alex to take a short cut across Brompton Cemetery. This was where Ian Rider had been buried after the so-called car accident that had killed him. It was at the funeral that Alex had first begun to learn the truth about his uncle: that he had never worked in a bank, that actually he had lived and died as a spy. Alex often walked through the cemetery but today, acting on impulse, he left the main path and went over to the gravestone. He looked at the name, carved in a square slab of grey marble, with the dates below it and a single line:

A GOOD MAN TAKEN BEFORE HIS TIME

Well, that was one way of putting it. Somebody had left flowers, quite recently. Roses. The petals were dead and withered but there was still a little colour in the leaves. Who had been here? Jack? And if it was her, why hadn't she mentioned it to him?

Alex bent down and brushed the plants to one side. He thought about the man who had looked after him all his life but who had been gone now for almost a year. He could still see Ian Rider – halfway up a mountain, on a dive boat in full scuba gear or racing on jet skis around the Bahamas. He had taken Alex all over the world, always challenging him, pushing him to the limit. Adventure holidays, he had called them. And how could Alex have known that all the time, he was being trained, being prepared to follow in his uncle's footsteps?

Footsteps that had brought him here.

"Alex Rider?"

They must have crept up behind him while he was crouching beside the grave, and even without looking up Alex knew he was in trouble. There was something about the voice – soft and threatening, with a slight foreign inflection.

Slowly Alex turned and looked up. Sure enough, there were three men standing at the foot of the grave, all of them Chinese, dressed in jeans and loose-fitting jackets. They were completely relaxed, as if they had strolled into the cemetery and come upon him by chance. But Alex knew that wasn't the case. They might have followed him from school. They might have known that he sometimes took this short cut, and waited for him. But there was nothing chance about this meeting. They were here for one single purpose.

"I'm sorry," Alex said. "My name is James Hale. You've got the wrong person."

Even as he spoke, he was glancing left and right. It was close to sunset. There was nobody else around. No passing vicar, no other kids from Brookland on their way home. Apart from his back-pack Alex had nothing with him. He knew he wasn't going to find a weapon in a cemetery but there was always a chance that a gravedigger had been careless enough to leave behind a spade.

He was out of luck. There was an open grave, waiting for its occupant, about six headstones away, but no sign of any tools. What else? A small stone angel stood next to him, a monument to "a great dad, a much-missed granddad and a wonderful husband". Why did no one ever have anything bad to say about people who had died?

The nearest man smiled unpleasantly, revealing nicotine-stained teeth. "You are Alex Rider," he insisted. "This is the grave of your uncle."

"You're wrong. He used to live next door."

Just for a moment, the three men hesitated, wondering if, after all, they had made a mistake. But then the leader made up his mind. "You will come with us," he said.

"Why? Where do you want to take me?"

"No more questions. Just come!"

Alex remained where he was, crouching beside the gravestone. He wondered what would happen next. He quickly found out. The man who had spoken gave a signal and suddenly all three of them were armed. The knives had appeared in their hands like an unpleasant magic trick. Alex examined the silver blades, one in front of him, one on either side. They were notched, designed to inflict the most vicious wounds. The men had got into position, surrounding Alex, without his seeing them. They were standing in combat stance, their weight spread evenly over their feet, each knife exactly the same distance from the ground. These were professional killers. They had done this many times before.

"What do you want?" Alex demanded, trying to keep his voice neutral. "I don't have any money."

"We don't want money." One of the other men spat on the grass. He had furious eyes, lips twisted into a permanent sneer.

"Major Yu sent us to see you," the leader said.

Winston Yu! So that was what this was about. Somehow the head of the snakehead gang that Alex had helped break up in Thailand had reached out from whatever hell he had been sent to. He had left instructions for revenge.

"Major Yu is dead," Alex said.

"You killed him."

"No. The last time I saw him he was running away. If he's dead, that's the best thing that ever happened to him. But it had nothing to do with me."

"You're lying."

"What difference does it make? He's finished. The whole thing's over. Coming after me isn't going to bring him back."

"You must pay for what you did. That's why we're here."

They were about to make their move. Alex could almost see the knives jabbing forward, striking at his stomach and chest. They would leave him in the cemetery, bleeding to death, and the next funeral that took place here would be his. But he wasn't going to let that happen.

Alex acted first. He was still holding the dead roses that he had been clearing from his uncle's grave. He could feel the sharp thorns digging into the palm of his hand. Swinging his arm up, Alex threw them, scattering them across the first man's face. For just a second, the man was blinded, in pain, the thorns cutting into him. A single dead rose was hanging under one eye. Alex sprang up, then followed through with a powerful back kick, the ball of his foot ramming into the man's stomach. The man's eyes widened in shock and he crumpled, gasping for breath. That just left two.

They were already lunging towards him. Alex had to get out of their range and there was only one way. His hand came down on Ian Rider's gravestone and he cartwheeled over it, landing on the ground just behind. He needed a weapon and he snatched up the only one he could see – the stone angel from the grave next to his uncle's. He hoped the much-missed granddad wouldn't mind. The angel was heavy. Alex swung it round and hurled it at the second man, the one who hadn't spoken. It hit him in the face, breaking his nose. Blood poured over the man's lips and he reeled away, howling.

The last of the three men swore in Chinese and launched himself towards Alex, the knife sweeping in great arcs, cutting at the air. Alex fled. With his attacker getting closer all the time, he ran across six of the graves, then leapt over the open trench. But the moment he landed, he stopped and turned round. The man, who had also jumped, was taken completely by surprise. He had expected Alex to keep running. Instead Alex had both feet firmly planted on the ground, while *he* was in mid-air. There was nothing he could do as Alex lashed out with a front jab – the *kizami-zuki* he had been taught in karate, leaning with all his weight forward for maximum reach.

Alex's fist caught the man in the throat. The man's eyes went white and he plunged down like a stone, disappearing into the grave. He hit the mud at the bottom and lay still. The first man was on his knees, wheezing, barely able to breathe. The second was still bleeding. Alex alone was unhurt. So what should he do? Call the police on his mobile. No. The last thing he needed right now was a load of tricky questions.

He went back to Ian Rider's grave, snatched up his backpack and walked away. But even as he left, there were some questions of his own nagging at his mind. If Major Yu had given orders for him to be killed, why hadn't they just gone ahead and done it? They could have tiptoed up behind him and stabbed him. Why had they felt the need to announce themselves? And for that matter, why had none of them been carrying a gun? Wouldn't that have made the whole thing easier?

As Alex left the cemetery, he didn't see the fourth man, fifty metres away, hiding behind one of the Victorian mausoleums. This was a European or perhaps an American, with fair hair down to his neck, smiling to himself as he watched Alex through the 135mm telephoto lens that was attached to the Nikon D3 digital SLR camera he was holding. He had taken more than a hundred shots of the encounter, clicking away at a rate of nine frames per second, but he took a few more, just for good measure. *Click*. Alex dusting himself down. *Click*. Alex turning away. *Click*. Alex heading for the main gate.

He had it all recorded. It was perfect. The man had been chewing gum but now he took it out of his mouth, rolled it into a ball and pressed it against one of the gravestones.

Click. One final shot of Alex leaving the cemetery and the whole thing was in the bag.

BAD NEWS

Alex was having dinner with Jack when the doorbell rang.

"Are you expecting anyone?" she asked.

"No."

The doorbell sounded again, longer and more
insistent. Jack put down her knife and fork and
frowned. "I'll get it," she said. "But why would
anyone call at this time of night?"

It was half past seven in the evening. Alex had
got in, changed, done his homework and had a
bath. He was sitting at the kitchen table of the
Chelsea home that had once belonged to Ian Rider
but which he and Jack now shared. He was wearing jeans and a sweatshirt. His hair was still damp
and his feet were bare. Jack liked to call herself a
ten-minute cook because that was the maximum
amount of time she spent preparing a meal. But
tonight she had served a home-made fish pie and
Alex suspected she had cheated on the time.

He was feeling guilty. He hadn't told her yet

about the fight at the cemetery, partly because he was waiting for the right moment, partly because he knew what she would say. There was no way he could keep something like that from her but nor did he want to ruin the evening. He had been about to bring it up when the doorbell rang.

He heard voices out in the hall – a man speaking, polite but insistent. Jack arguing. There was a pause, then Jack returned on her own. Alex could see at once that she was concerned.

"There's someone here who wants to see you," she said.

"Who is it?"

"He says his name is Harry Bulman."

Alex shook his head. "I've never heard of him."

"Then let me introduce myself."

A man had appeared at the kitchen door behind Jack, strolling into the room, looking around him at the same time. He was in his thirties, with long beach-blonde hair falling in a tangle, broad shoulders and a thick neck. He was handsome – but not quite as handsome as he thought. There was an arrogance about him that was apparent in every move he made, even the way he had followed Jack in. He was dressed smartly in grey slacks, a blazer and a white shirt open at the collar. He had a gold chain around his neck and a gold signet ring with the letters HB on his third finger. To Alex it was as if he had stepped out of an advertisement for clothes – or perhaps toothpaste. This was a man who enjoyed being himself and wanted to sell his talents to the world.

Jack spun round. "I don't remember inviting you in."

"Please. Don't ask me to wait outside. If you want the truth, I've been waiting for this moment for quite a long time." He looked past Jack. "It's a great pleasure to meet you, Alex."

Alex slid his food aside. "Who are you?" he demanded.

"Do you mind if I sit down?"

"You don't need to sit down," Jack growled. "You're not staying long."

"You might change your mind when you hear what I've got to say." The man sat down at the head of the table, opposite Alex. "My name is Harry Bulman," he said. "I'm sorry I've come round so late but I know you're at school, Alex – at Brookland – and I wanted to catch you while you were both in."

"What do you want?" Alex asked.

"Well, right now I could murder a beer if there's one going." Nobody moved. "OK. I'll get to the point. I've come here to speak to you, Alex. As a matter of fact, although you won't believe it, I want to help you. I hope the two of us are going to be seeing quite a bit of each other. I think we're going to become friends."

"I don't need any help," Alex said.

Bulman smiled. His teeth were as white as his

shirt. "You haven't heard what I've got to say."

"Then why don't you get on with it?" Jack cut in. "Because we were having supper and we didn't want to be disturbed."

"Smells good." Bulman drew a business card out of his wallet and slid it across the table. Jack came over and sat next to Alex. They both read it. There was the name – Harry Bulman – and beneath it his job description. Freelance journalist. There was also an address in north London and a telephone number.

"You work for the press," Jack said.

Bulman nodded. "The *Mirror*, the *Express*, the *Star*... If you ask around, you'll find I'm well known."

"What are you doing here?" Alex asked. "You said you could help me. I don't need a journalist."

"As a matter of fact, you do." Bulman took out a packet of chewing gum. "Do you mind? I've given up smoking and I find this helps." He unwrapped a piece and curled it into his mouth. "This is a nice place you've got here."

"Please get on with it, Mr Bulman."

Alex could hear that Jack was running out of patience. But the journalist had already wrong-footed them twice. He had simply walked in here and for the moment neither of them was asking him to leave.

"All right. Let's cut to the chase." Bulman rested his elbows on the table and leant forward.

"Most journalists have a specialist area. It might be food, football, politics ... whatever. My speciality is intelligence. I spent six years in the military – I was in the commandos – and I hung on to my old contacts when I left. I always figured they might come in handy. I was actually thinking about writing a book but that didn't work out, so I started touting myself around Fleet Street. MI5, MI6, CIA ... any bits of gossip I managed to pick up, I'd string together as a story. It wasn't going to make me rich. But I did OK."

Alex and Jack were listening to this in silence. Neither of them liked the way it was going.

"And then, a couple of months ago, I began to hear these strange rumours. They started with an event that took place at the Science Museum last April, when Herod Sayle was about to launch his Stormbreaker computer system. What happened to the Stormbreakers, by the way? There was going to be one in every school in the country, but suddenly they were recalled and that was that. They were never seen again.

"Anyway, back to the Science Museum. It seems that someone, an agent of MI6 Special Operations, parachuted through the roof and took a shot at Sayle. No names, no pack drill. Nothing unusual about that. But then I was talking to a mate in the pub and he told me that the bloke on the end of the parachute wasn't a man at all. It was a boy. He swore to me that Special Operations had gone out and recruited a fourteen-year-old and that this was their latest secret weapon.

"Of course, I didn't believe it at first. But I decided to have a nose around and so I started asking questions. And do you know what? It all turned out to be true. MI6 had taken some poor bloody kid, trained him up with the SAS in the Lake District and sent him out on active service no fewer than three times. It took me a while longer to find out the name of this boy wonder. In the SAS he was known as Cub. But I persisted – I'm not so bad at this job – and in the end I got what I wanted. Alex Rider. That's you."

"I don't know what you're talking about," Alex said.

"You're making a mistake, Mr Bulman," Jack added. "Your story is ridiculous. Alex is still at school."

"Alex *is* still at Brookland," Bulman agreed. "But according to the school secretary, a very nice lady called Miss Bedfordshire, he's been away an awful lot recently. Don't blame her, by the way. She didn't know I was a journalist. I pretended I was calling from the local council. But let me see..."

Bulman took out a notebook.

"You were away for the first time last March. You were also away in November, at exactly the same time that a teenage boy dropped in on an oil rig in the Timor Sea, fighting alongside the Australian SAS. And who was that kid at Heathrow Airport when Damian Cray had a nasty accident in a jumbo jet? Now there's a funny thing, isn't it? An international pop star and multi-millionaire. One minute he's in perfect health; the next we're being told he's had a heart attack. Well, I suppose I'd have a heart attack if someone pushed me into the turbine of a plane." Bulman snapped the notebook shut. "Nobody's been allowed to write anything about any of this. National security and all the rest of it. But I've spoken to people who were at the Science Museum, at Heathrow and in Australia." He fixed his eyes on Alex. "And they've all described you."

There was a long silence. Jack's fish pie had gone cold. Alex was stunned. He had always supposed MI6 would protect him from publicity. He had never expected a journalist to turn up at his home.

Jack was the first to speak. "You've got it all wrong," she said. "Alex took a bit of time off last year because he was sick. You can't possibly think—"

"Please don't treat me like an idiot, Jack," Bulman cut in, and suddenly there was steel in his voice. "I've done my homework. I know everything. So why don't you stop wasting my time and face up to the facts?"

He reached into his jacket pocket and took out a bundle of photographs. Alex winced. He knew what was coming even before the journalist spread them on the table.

And he was right. The pictures had been taken just a few hours earlier in Brompton Cemetery. They showed Alex in action against the three men who had attacked him, kicking out in one frame, spinning over the gravestone in another.

"When were these taken?" Jack asked. She was obviously shaken.

"This afternoon," Alex replied. "They followed me from school and came up to me in the cemetery." He looked accusingly at Bulman. "You set it all up."

The journalist nodded. "Believe me, Alex. They weren't going to hurt you. But I had to be one hundred per cent certain. I wanted to see you in action for myself. And I have to say, you more than lived up to your reputation. In fact, I'm going to have to pay the guys double what I promised them. You put two of them in hospital! Oh, and there's something you should listen to."

Bulman produced a miniature digital voice recorder and pressed a button. At once Alex heard his own voice, a little tinny and distant, but definitely him.

Major Yu is dead.

You killed him.

No. The last time I saw him he was running away...

"All three of them were wired for sound." Bulman flicked the machine off. "You knew all about the snakehead so don't play innocent with me. By the way, I never found out how Major Yu died. I'd be interested to know how it happened."

Alex glanced at Jack. They both knew there was no point denying it any more. "What exactly do you want?" he demanded.

"Well, we could start with that beer I was talking about."

Jack stiffened. Then she stood up, went to the fridge and took out a can of beer. She gave it to the journalist without a glass but he didn't seem to mind. He cracked it open and drank.

"Thank you, Jack," he said. "Look, I can tell you're both a bit thrown by this and I can understand that, but you've got to remember what I said when I first came in. I'm on your side. In fact, I want to help you."

"Help me ... how?"

"By telling your story." Bulman held a hand up before Alex could interrupt. "Wait a minute. Just hear me out." He had obviously rehearsed what he was about to say. "First of all, I think what's happened to you is an outrage. It's more than that. It's a national scandal. In case you hadn't noticed, the law says that you can't join the army until you're sixteen. So the idea that MI6 can just stroll along and use a kid like you quite frankly beggars belief. Did you volunteer?"

Alex said nothing.

"It doesn't matter. We can come to all that later. But here's the point. When this gets out, heads are going to roll. The way I see it, you're the victim in all this, Alex. Don't get me wrong – you're also a hero. If even half what I've heard about you is true, then what you've done is absolutely amazing. But it should never have been allowed to happen and I think people are going to be horrified when the story breaks."

"The story will never break," Jack muttered. "They won't let you write it."

"I'm sure they'll try to stop me. But this is the twenty-first century, Jack, and it's not so easy any more. You think the Americans wanted anyone to know about the torture practices carried out in the Abu Ghraib prison in Iraq? Or what about all the British MPs who were trying to hide their crooked expenses? There are no secrets any more. If they stop me going to the newspapers, I can put it on the Internet; and once the story's broken, the press will come running. You'll see. And if we keep it exclusive – if we go to the *Sunday Times* or the *Telegraph* – we'll clean up.

"But it's not just about the newspapers. The way I see it, there's a book in this. It shouldn't take more than three months to write and it'll sell all over the world. Tony Blair was offered six million pounds for his memoirs, which nobody even wants to read, and I reckon we could make ten times that amount. Then there'll be syndication in the world press, exclusive interviews – Oprah Winfrey alone will pay a million – and almost certainly a bidding war for the rights to make a major Hollywood film. You're going to be the most famous person in the world, Alex. Everyone is going to want a piece of you."

"And who gets the money?" Jack asked. She already knew the answer.

"We'll come to an agreement, Jack. Whatever you may think of me, I'm not greedy and there's going to be more than enough to go around. Fifty-fifty! Alex will tell me the full story and I'll write it down. I've got all the contacts: publishers, lawyers, that sort of thing. I'll be like Alex's manager, and I promise you I'll look after him. Like I said, I'm a fan. And after what he's been through, he deserves to rake it in. From what I hear, MI6 haven't even paid him a salary. Now that's what I call exploitation."

"Suppose I'm not interested," Alex said. "Suppose I don't want the story to be told."

Bulman drank more of his beer. The chewing gum was still in his mouth. "It's too late for that now, Alex," he explained. "It's going to happen anyway. The story's out there and someone will write it, even if I don't. If you sit back and refuse to cooperate, it'll only make it worse. You'll have to live with what people say about you and you won't get a chance to tell your side.

"But in a way, if you don't mind my saying so, you're lucky that you've got me in the driving seat. You think anyone else would offer you equal partnership? In fact, most hacks would have just gone ahead and broken the news without even coming here. I can imagine you're probably a bit confused right now and I'm sorry I pulled that stunt on you in the cemetery. But believe me, once you get to know me better, we're going to be friends. I'm a professional. I know what I'm doing."

Bulman finished his beer and crumpled the can. Alex didn't know what to say. Too many thoughts were going through his head. Fortunately Jack took over.

"Thank you for being so frank with us," she said. "But if you don't mind, we'd like some time to think about what you've said."

"Of course. I can understand that. You have my number. I can give you to the end of the week." Bulman stood up. "I reckon it'll be quite fun, Alex. I'll come here every evening and we'll talk for a couple of hours. Then I'll write it up the next day while you're at school. You can read it at week-ends." He gestured at the photographs. "You can hang on to those. I've got copies."

He went over to the door, then turned round one last time.

"I meant what I said. You're a real hero, Alex. I hope I made that clear from the start. There aren't many boys your age who actually believe in their country. You're a patriot and I respect that. I'm really privileged to have met you." He waved a hand. "Don't get up. I'll show myself out." And then he was gone.

Neither Jack nor Alex said anything until they heard the front door close. Then Jack went out to make sure the journalist really had left. Alex stayed where he was. He was in shock. He was trying to think what it would all mean. He would become world famous. There was no doubt of that. His photograph would be in all the newspapers and magazines and he would never be able to walk down the street again, not without being pointed out as some sort of curiosity ... a freak. He would have to leave Brookland, of course. He might even have to leave the UK. He could say goodbye to his home, to his friends, to any chance of a normal life.

He felt a black anger welling up inside him. How could he have allowed this to happen?

Jack came back into the room. "He's gone," she said. She sat down at the table. The photographs were still spread out in front of her. "Why didn't you tell me about the cemetery?" she asked.

There was no accusation in her voice but Alex knew she was upset. "I was going to," he said. "But it happened so soon after Scotland that I thought you'd be worried."

"I'd be more worried if I thought you weren't telling me when you were in trouble."

"I'm sorry, Jack."

"It doesn't matter." Jack gathered the photographs into a pile and placed them face down. "He wasn't quite as clever as he thought," she said.

"He didn't know everything about you. He'd only found out about three of your missions. And he said you trained in the Lake District. He got that wrong too."

"He knew enough," Alex said.

"So what are we going to do?"

"We can't let him write this story." Alex felt a hollow in his chest. "He doesn't care about me. He just wants to use me. He's going to ruin everything."

Jack reached out and touched his hand. "Don't worry, Alex. We'll stop him."

"How?" Alex thought for a moment, then answered his own question. "We're going to have to go and see Mr Blunt."

It was the only course of action. They both knew it. There were no other options.

"I don't like you going back there. Every time you set foot in that place, something bad comes out of it." Jack was only saying what Alex was thinking. "I was beginning to think they'd forgotten all about you. This will just remind them."

"I know. But who else is going to stop him, Jack? We need their help."

"They've never helped you before, Alex."

"This time it's in their interest. They're not going to want Harry Bulman writing about them." Alex pushed his plate away. He had barely eaten but he no longer had any appetite. "I'll go after school tomorrow."

"I'll come with you."

"Thanks."

He was going back. The decision had been made. But as Alex got up and helped clear the table, he wondered if in truth he had ever really left.

THE LION'S DEN

The evening seemed to have drawn in early at Liverpool Street. It was only half past four as Jack and Alex came out of the station but already the street lamps were on and the first commuters were on their way home, snatching their free newspapers without even breaking pace. There must have been a slight mist in the air because it seemed to Alex that the offices were glowing unnaturally, the light behind the windows not quite making it to the world outside.

Punched in the chest.

Unable to breathe.

The pavement, cold and hard, rushing towards him.

This was where Alex had been shot and he would never be able to return without experiencing it again. The flower seller that he saw now, standing on the other side of the café, the old woman coming out of the shop – had they been there that day? It had been five o'clock, almost the same time as now, but at the end of summer. There was the roof where the sniper must have lain concealed, waiting for Alex to come out. He had sworn that he would never come back, but somehow he had been trapped. It was like one of those dreams when you keep on running but always end up in the same place.

"Are you OK?" Jack asked. She could guess what was going on in his head and she was alarmed.

Alex pulled himself together. "It feels strange, being back."

"Are you sure you want to go through with this?"

"Yes. Let's get it over with."

They stopped in front of a tall, classical building that would have been just as much at home in New York, but for the Union Jack that hung limply from a pole jutting out from the fifteenth floor. A black-painted door invited them in and on the wall to one side a brass plaque read ROYAL & GENERAL BANK PLC. LONDON.

Strangely, the bank was fully operational with counters, cash machines, cashiers and clients, and Alex wondered how many people had accounts here without knowing what the real purpose of the building was. The entire place belonged to the Special Operations division of MI6. The bank was nothing more than a cover. And for that matter, how many men and women had come out of that door and never returned? Alex's uncle had been one of them, dying for queen and country or whatever else motivated them. What difference did it make when you were dead?

"Alex?" Jack was watching him anxiously and he realized that despite what he had just said, he hadn't moved. "The lion's den," she muttered.

"That's what it feels like."

"Come on..."

They went in.

The door took them from the cold reality of the city into the warmth and deception of a world where nothing was ever what it seemed. They were in a reception area with a row of lifts, a marble floor, half a dozen clocks – each one showing the time in a different country – and the inevitable potted plants. But there would be hidden cameras too. Their images would already be on the way to a central computer equipped with face recognition software. And the two receptionists, both female and pretty, would know exactly who they were before they said a word.

One of them looked up as they approached. "Can I help you?"

"We have an appointment with Mrs Jones."

"Of course. Please take a seat."

It was all so normal. Alex and Jack took their places on a leather sofa. A scattering of financial magazines lay on the table in front of them. Alex had come straight from school so he was still in his uniform. He wondered what he must look like to passers-by. A rich kid, perhaps, opening his first account.

A few minutes later, one of the lifts opened

and a dark-haired woman in a black suit stepped out. As usual she was wearing very little jewellery, just a simple silver chain around her neck. This, of course, was Mrs Jones, the deputy head of Special Operations and the second most important person in the building. Despite the impact that she'd had on his life, Alex knew very little about her. She lived in a flat in Clerkenwell, near the old meat market. She had been married once. She had two children but something had happened to them and they were no longer around. And that was it. If she'd ever had a private life, she'd left it behind her when she became a spy – and the spy was all that was left.

"Good afternoon, Alex." She didn't seem particularly pleased to see him. Her face was completely neutral. "How are you?"

"I'm fine, thank you, Mrs Jones."

"We're ready to see you." She turned to Jack. "I'll bring Alex back down in about half an hour."

"Wait a minute." Jack stood up. "I'm coming too."

"I'm afraid not. Mr Blunt wants to see Alex on his own."

"Then we're leaving."

Mrs Jones shrugged. "That's your choice. But you said on the phone that you needed our help..."

"It's all right, Jack." Alex could see the way this was going and he had quickly made his decision. It was possible that Alan Blunt would agree to help him – but it would only ever be on his own terms. Any argument and Alex would be thrown out in the street. It had happened before. "I don't mind seeing them on my own if that's what they want."

"Are you sure?"

"Yes."

Jack nodded. "All right. I'll wait for you here." She glanced at the magazines. "I can catch up with the latest banking news."

Alex and Mrs Jones walked over to the lifts and Mrs Jones pressed the button for the sixteenth floor. She knew that the button would read her fingerprint and that if she wasn't authorized to travel up, two armed guards would be waiting when she arrived. She was also aware of the thermal intensifier concealed behind the mirror, as well as the early warning chemical detector which had been added recently. Even the floor was examining the soles of Alex's shoes. The dust and residue under his feet might, in certain circumstances, provide valuable information about where he had been.

Mrs Jones seemed more relaxed now that the two of them were on their own. "So how is school going?" she asked.

"OK," Alex said. Mrs Jones sounded friendly enough but he had learnt to treat even the most casual question with suspicion.

"And how was Scotland?"

How did she know he had gone to Scotland for

New Year? Did she know what had happened there? Alex decided to put her to the test. "I had a great time," he said. "I really liked Loch Arkaig. In fact, I made quite an in-depth visit."

Mrs Jones didn't even blink. "I haven't been there myself."

They arrived at the sixteenth floor and left the lift, walking down a heavily carpeted corridor with doors that had numbers but no names. They stopped outside 1605. Mrs Jones knocked, and without waiting for an answer they went in.

Alan Blunt was sitting behind his desk as if he had been there for ever, as if he never left. It was the same grey man in the same grey suit with the same files open in front of him. Sometimes Alex tried to imagine the head of Special Operations with a wife and children, going to a film or playing sport. But he couldn't do it. Like Mrs Jones, Blunt had no life outside these four walls. Was this what he had dreamt about when he was young, being locked into a job that would never let him go? Had he actually ever *been* young?

"Sit down, Alex." Blunt waved Alex to a chair without looking up from his paperwork. He wrote something down and underlined it. Alex wondered what he had just done. He could have been ordering extra office stationery; he could have just sentenced someone to death. The trouble with Blunt was that, either way, he would have shown the same emotion.

He glanced briefly at Alex. "You're getting taller." He sounded disapproving – but that made sense. The younger and more innocent Alex looked, the more useful he was to MI6.

There was a long silence. Alex took the seat he had been offered. Mrs Jones sat down beside the desk. Blunt made a few last notes, the nib of his pen scratching against the page. At last he finished what he was doing.

"I understand you have a problem," he said.

Jack hadn't said very much on the telephone. She'd had enough dealings with MI6 to know that nobody says anything important on an unsecured line. So Alex quickly explained what had happened: the fight in the cemetery, Harry Bulman's visit, the newspaper story he was intending to write.

He finished talking. Blunt reached out and wiped a speck of dust off the surface of the desk.

"That's very interesting, Alex," he said. "But I'm not sure there's very much we can do."

"What?" Alex was astonished. "Why not?"

"Well, as you've often reminded us, you don't actually work for us. You're not part of MI6."

"That's never stopped you from using me."

"Perhaps not. But it's not our business to interfere with the freedom of the press. If this man, Bulman, has found out about your activities over the past year, we can't really stop him. Are you asking us to arrange an accident...?"

"No!" Alex was horrified. He wondered if Blunt was even being serious.

"Then what exactly do you have in mind?"

Alex drew a breath. Maybe Blunt was trying to confuse him deliberately. He wasn't sure how to respond. "Do you really want him to go ahead and write this story?" he asked.

"I don't see that it matters one way or another. We can always deny it."

"What about me?"

"You can deny it too."

He could. But it would make no difference. When Bulman's story came out, his life would still be in pieces. In fact, if MI6 denied the story, it would only make it worse. Once again he felt a rising sense of anger. It was Blunt who had put him in this situation in the first place. Was he really going to sit back and wash his hands of the whole affair?

But then Mrs Jones came to his rescue. "Maybe we could have a word with this journalist," she suggested. "It might be possible to make him see things from our point of view."

"Talking to him would only compromise us," Blunt insisted.

"I absolutely agree. But in view of what Alex has done for us in the past..." She hesitated. "And what he might do for us in the future..."

Blunt looked up, his eyes, behind the square, gun-metal spectacles, locking into Alex's for the first time. "Would you ever consider coming back?" he asked.

It was as if the thought had only just occurred to him but suddenly Alex understood. Everything in this room had been rehearsed. Mrs Jones had known he had been to Scotland. They knew what was going on at Brookland. They probably even got copies of his homework. And they had steered this conversation exactly where they wanted. These two never left anything to chance.

"There's something you want," Alex said. His voice was heavy.

"Not at all." Blunt drummed his fingers. Then he seemed to remember something. He opened a drawer in his desk and took out a file which he laid in front of him. "Well, since you mention it, there is one thing. But it's a very simple matter, Alex. Hardly worthy of your talents."

Alex leant forward. The file that Blunt had selected was stamped with the usual red letters: TOP SECRET. But there was another word written underneath it in black ink. Alex read it upside down. GREENFIELDS. It meant something. Where had he heard it before? Then he remembered and he reeled back. He almost wanted to laugh. How did they do it?

Greenfields was the name of the research centre that he was about to visit with the rest of his class. His geography teacher, Mr Gilbert, had been talking about it only the day before.

"What do you know about genetic engineering?" Blunt demanded.

"I've been doing a project on it," Alex said. But of course, Blunt knew that already. He was sure of it.

"It's an interesting subject," Blunt continued, in a tone of voice that suggested it was anything but. "Genetic science can do incredible things. Grow tomatoes in the desert or oranges the size of melons. There's no question that companies like Greenfields could change the way we live. Of course" – he clenched his fingers beneath his chin – "there are also certain dangers."

"Whoever controls the food chain controls the world." Alex remembered what Edward Pleasure had said when they were in Scotland.

"Exactly. Anything that puts too much power into the hands of one individual is of interest to us. And there is one individual working at Greenfields who is causing us particular concern."

"His name is Leonard Straik," Mrs Jones said.

"Straik is the director and chief science officer. Aged fifty-eight. Unmarried. He was a brilliant student, reading biology at Cambridge back in the seventies. He invented something called the biolistic particle delivery system – also known as the gene gun. It uses helium pressure to fire new DNA into existing plant organisms ... something like that, anyway. The long and the short of it is that, thanks to Straik, it's become much easier to mass-produce GM seeds.

"For twenty years Straik ran his own company, Leonard Straik Diagnostics – or LSD, as it was called. It all went well for a time but, like many scientists, he was less brilliant when it came to business and the whole thing collapsed. Straik lost all his money and went freelance. Six years ago he was hired as the director of Greenfields and he's been there ever since."

"Why are you interested in him?"

"Because of something that happened a couple of months ago." Blunt opened the file. "Last November the police got a call from a whistle-blower inside the company, a biotechnician by the name of Philip Masters. He said he knew something about Straik and wanted to talk. Given the security implications, the police passed the information to us and we arranged a meeting – but one day before it could take place, there was an accident and Masters was killed. Apparently he came into contact with some sort of toxic material and it poisoned his entire nervous system. By the time he turned up in the local morgue, he was unrecognizable."

"An accident..."

"Exactly. It seemed a bit of a coincidence."

"We don't like coincidences," Mrs Jones said.

"Since then we've been taking a close look at Greenfields," Blunt went on. "It's a major operation. As well as research and development, it's also one of the largest suppliers of genetically modified seeds in the world, using the gene gun that Straik pioneered. There are whole countries in Africa and South America that are dependent on it. We cannot risk having a loose cannon at the centre of an operation like that. Masters knew something about Straik. We need to know what it was."

Alex nodded. He was beginning to see where this was going.

"We've managed to put a tap on Straik's landline and we intercept all the calls he makes on his mobile. But we need more than that."

"We want to get into his computer," Mrs Jones said.

Blunt nodded. "There may be nothing in this. After all, people die all the time. Accidents do happen and there are plenty of toxic plants on the site. I understand Straik keeps a whole greenhouse full of them. He's been doing research into natural cures – antivenoms. But we have to get someone into Greenfields – and it can't be a security guard or a maintenance engineer. That's exactly what he'd be expecting. We have to take a different approach."

Alex had heard it all before. People with something to hide would always suspect an adult, particularly if they knew they were under surveillance. But nobody would think twice about a schoolboy on a class trip. Alex remembered what Mr Gilbert had said. *I didn't think they'd allow school visits, because so much of their work is secret.*

Somehow they had been persuaded to make an exception for Brookland. Had MI6 been working quietly behind the scenes?

"It would be easy for you to slip away from the group during your visit," Mrs Jones continued. "And it'd take you no time to download everything from Straik's computer."

"Won't it have a password?" Alex asked. "And how would I even get into his office?"

"We can have a word with Smithers about all that," Blunt replied. "But it's up to you, Alex. It seems fairly straightforward to me. We can't even be sure that Straik is up to no good. It may all be a fuss about nothing. However, it seems that we can do each other a favour. You agree to help us and we'll have a word with this man – Harry Bulman – and see if we can persuade him to leave you alone."

Blunt smiled but Alex wasn't fooled. He knew what was going on. If he refused to help, he would be left out in the cold and his life would be torn apart. Blunt was pretending to offer him a choice, knowing exactly what Alex would do. The decision had already been made.

He should have expected it. He had agreed to walk into the lion's den – so he could hardly complain when he got scratched.

"It's a pleasure to see you as always, Alex," Smithers said. "I rather fancy you've grown a bit.

Unless, of course, Mr Blunt has supplied you with a pair of my new trainers. I'm rather pleased with them, I must say."

"Do they fire missiles?" Alex asked.

"Oh no. Nothing like that. They're for agents who need to change their appearance rapidly in the field. There's a hydraulic system built into the heel and they can add three inches to your height."

"Do you have a name for them?"

Smithers folded his arms across his ample stomach. "Pumps!"

The two of them were sitting in Smithers' office on the eleventh floor. The room looked ordinary enough but Alex knew that everything in sight actually disguised something else – from the X-ray anglepoise lamp to the incinerator out tray. Even the filing cabinet concealed a lift to the ground floor.

Smithers was exactly as Alex remembered him. He was dressed in an old-fashioned three-piece suit that must have been specially tailored to fit his bulk, with a striped tie that was surely of the old school variety. As usual, there was a broad smile across his face and above his various chins. Smithers was the one person in MI6 that Alex was always pleased to see. He was also the only agent Alex trusted.

"So I understand you're going to look into Greenfields for us," Smithers continued. "Very good of you, Alex. I'm always amazed how helpful you are."

"Well, Mr Blunt is very persuasive."

"That's certainly true. At least it shouldn't be too dangerous this time ... although do look out. That chap Masters was a bit of a mess. He'd definitely trodden in something that he shouldn't – so just make sure you look where you're going." Smithers coughed, realizing that he'd said too much, and added hastily, "I'm sure no one will even notice you."

"How do I get into Straik's office?" Alex asked.

"I've got a few things for you right here." Smithers opened a drawer in his desk and took out an old-fashioned pencil case. It was made of tin, slightly battered, decorated with a picture of the Simpsons – the sort of thing Alex might have been given for Christmas three or four years ago. "It's unlikely that you'll be searched," Smithers said. "But we know Greenfields has a very efficient security system so better safe than sorry."

He pushed the case towards Alex. "The tin is rather clever," he explained. "I actually developed it for international air travel. It has a lead lining so it won't show any of the hidden circuitry if it passes through an X-ray machine. But at the same time, there are silhouettes of pens and rulers fused inside the lid so if the tin is scanned they'll show up as ghost images. You could carry anything you wanted inside and nobody would notice."

He opened the tin. Alex was surprised that it actually did contain pens and rulers – along with other pieces of school equipment. "Since this is a school trip, I've concealed all the gadgets inside things you might reasonably be expected to have with you," Smithers said. With a pudgy finger and thumb he picked out a rather large eraser. "The Memory Stick that you'll need for Straik's computer is inside this. Just tear open the rubber and plug it in. You won't need passwords or anything like that. It's completely automatic. In around thirty seconds everything that's on the computer will be on the Memory Stick."

He took out a library card. It was already stamped with Alex's name and had a magnetic strip on the back. "Straik's office will almost certainly be locked. This will get you in. It looks like a library card but actually it's an all-purpose swipe card." He lifted the tin and for the first time, Alex noticed a narrow slot near the bottom. "You take the library card and you swipe any door that you want to open. Then you feed it into the tin. There's a miniaturized flux reversal system hidden in the bottom. It will work out the code you need and reprogramme the card. These are now standard equipment for all MI6 agents, although this is the first time I've hidden one in a Simpsons pencil case!"

"How do I find Straik's office?"

"I'm working on that, Alex. Greenfields is a big place and I doubt there'll be signs. But I've got a rather neat idea and I'll send it to you in a couple of days."

Alex picked up a pencil sharpener. "What does this do?"

"It sharpens pencils." Smithers reached out for it. "But it also converts into a knife. It's tiny, of course, but the blade is diamond-edged and will cut through almost anything." He lifted what looked like a small pocket calculator out of the tin. "No need to worry about CCTV cameras. Just press the plus button three times and it will send out a square wave frequency signal which should jam any transmissions within fifty metres. On the subject of jam, it's almost time for tea. Would you like some?"

"No thanks." Alex took the calculator. "Does it do anything else?"

"As a matter of fact, it's also an extremely sophisticated communications device. Press the nine button three times and you can talk directly to us. It'll work anywhere in the world."

"999," Alex muttered. "In case of emergencies..."

Smithers smiled. "And finally, I know you like your explosions, Alex, so you'll enjoy this." He took the last two items out of the tin.

"They look like pens," Alex said.

"Yes, they do. They're gel ink pens ... but the gel in this instance is short for gelignite." Smithers held them in front of him. "There are two colours here. The red one is much more powerful than the black one. Remember that. It's the difference between blowing a door off its hinges and blowing the lock off the door. They both have time fuses concealed in the cap. Twist once for fifteen seconds then pull the plunger upwards to activate. You have a delay of up to two minutes. They're also magnetic. And, of course, they write."

He put everything back into the tin and closed the lid.

"There you are, old chap. Everything you need, nice and neat. I'm sure this mission is going to be a piece of cake – which reminds me once again that it really is time for tea. Are you sure you won't join me?"

"No thanks, Mr Smithers." Alex took the pencil case and got to his feet. "I'll see you."

"I'm sure you will, Alex. I don't know what it is about you, but you just don't seem able to stay away. Take care – and do come and see me again soon."

Back on the sixteenth floor Alan Blunt was still behind his desk, listening as Mrs Jones read from a report. It had been printed and handed to her a few minutes before. There were just two pages: a black and white photograph followed by about fifty lines of text.

"Harry Bulman," she was saying. "Educated at Eton. Expelled when he was sixteen. Drugs. He went into the Marines – and it's true what he told Alex. He actually made it into the commandos, but they threw him out. Dishonourable discharge for cowardice. His unit came under attack in Afghanistan and he was found buried in a sand dune. He was hiding. After that he managed to get odd jobs in journalism. Writing about defence issues some of the time but mainly it was just smut. Three-in-a-bed headlines and that sort of thing. Married and divorced. No children. Lives in north London. Thirty-seven years old."

There was a brief silence as Blunt took this in. Nothing showed behind his eyes but Mrs Jones knew that he would be considering every possibility and that within seconds he would have come up with a plan of attack. This was his great strength. It was the reason why he had headed up Special Operations for so long.

"Invisible Man," he said. He had made his decision. "We'll give it to Crawley. He hasn't been out in the field for a while. He'll enjoy it."

"Right." There was a shredder beside the desk. Mrs Jones fed the report into it and the blades began to rotate. Harry Bulman was looking out from the photograph. There was a half-smile on his face, as if he was pleased with himself. Slowly he disappeared into the machine, sliced into ribbons and dropping into the bin below.

INVISIBLE MAN

There were at least ten thousand guests in the auditorium and they were all applauding. Harry Bulman made his way through the crowd, occasionally pausing to shake hands and receive congratulations from people he didn't even know. Ahead of him the stage beckoned. A dozen golden statuettes stood in a line and one of them had his name on it: journalist of the year. It was glimmering in the spotlight, twice the size of any of the others; and as he walked towards it, it seemed to grow even bigger. At the same time, a bell began to ring and...

He woke up. It was seven thirty in the morning and his alarm had just gone off.

It had been a dream, of course, but a very pleasant one – and Bulman had no doubt that very soon it would become a reality.

He was going to be famous. Newspaper editors who were usually too busy to give him the time of day would be queuing up to employ him. There would be television chat shows, celebrity parties and piles of awards. It occurred to him that maybe he had been a little too generous offering Alex fifty per cent of his earnings. After all, he was the one doing all the work. It was *his* story. Maybe forty or even thirty per cent would be closer to the mark. In fact, at the end of the day, the journalist didn't need to pay him anything at all. It wasn't as if Alex could do anything about it.

It was incredible really that the two of them had finally met. Bulman remembered the first time he had heard the story of a teenage spy. It had been in a pub, the Crown in Fleet Street, a late night drinking session with an old friend in the army who had been at the Science Museum when the parachutist came through the roof. He hadn't believed it then, but something had told him to stick with it and very soon he had found himself on what had become nothing less than a quest. He had spent weeks doggedly following leads that had gone nowhere, meeting contacts who had clammed up at the last moment, calling in favours and, when necessary, making threats. But piece by piece he had put the story together. And in the end it had led him to Alex.

Bulman slept in a circular bed with black silk sheets on the top floor of a modern block of flats in Chalk Farm. His bedroom had views of the railway lines leading into Euston Station. The place had only been built twenty years ago but already there were cracks appearing, maybe because of the vibrations from the trains. One was passing now. When he'd first moved in here, the grinding wheels had woken him up, but he had soon got used to it. In fact he quite liked it. He wouldn't have been able to afford the flat if it had been anywhere more expensive.

It was the end of the week. Four days since he had been in Alex's Chelsea house. He had decided to give the boy time to work things out and to realize he had no alternative. He and that housekeeper of his would have talked things over and they probably blamed each other for what had happened. Now that he thought about it, maybe that was another interesting angle. The girl – Jack – was quite pretty. What was she doing living with a fourteen-year-old boy? The *News of the World* would like that! Well, this afternoon Bulman would go back. He would be there waiting with a digital recorder when Alex finished school.

He threw back the covers and went into the kitchen, where the plates from dinner last night – and the night before – were still stacked up in the sink. Bulman liked good food but he couldn't be bothered to cook for himself, and the packages from ready meals, mainly Marks & Spencer, were spilling out of the bin. He found a clean mug and made himself a coffee, glancing at the newspaper articles that were pinned to a cork board above the sink.

SECRETS OF ARMY'S BASRA BREAKFAST

INTELLIGENCE CHIEF'S FACEBOOK DISGRACE

SAS COMMANDER MISSES FLIGHT

He wasn't proud of his work. Nobody took much notice of what he wrote and the stories were always nearer the back of the paper than the front. What did it matter anyway? They were read and then forgotten ... if they were read at all.

Bulman opened the fridge. He took out the milk and sniffed it. It was sour. He poured it into the sink and drank his coffee black. What was he going to do until four o'clock? It was a beautiful day, a cold January sun glinting off the railway tracks. He watched a second train rumble past on its way into the city, packed with commuters heading for their boring jobs. He could almost imagine them, squashed into the newspapers they were trying to read. A month from now, those newspapers would belong to him.

A late breakfast. Shopping. A couple of beers at the Groucho Club in Soho. He mapped out his day as he got dressed in his usual open-necked shirt, blazer and slacks. He never wore jeans. He liked to keep himself smart. He fastened the shirtsleeves with brightly polished silver cufflinks, each one decorated with a miniature engraving of the Fairbairn-Sykes dagger, used by the commandos since the Second

World War. Finally he scooped up the briefcase that he always carried with him, grabbed his wallet from the bedside table, finished his coffee and went out.

There was a news-stand opposite his building with a display showing the morning headlines. JOURNALIST KILLED. He couldn't help smiling as he read the words. He wondered if it was anybody he knew; probably someone taking a bullet in Afghanistan or somewhere. He had often tried to get himself sent abroad ("...our man Harry Bulman, embedded with the allied forces in Iraq...") but none of the editors had been interested. Well, serve them right, whoever they were. Probably some stupid amateur who didn't know when to duck.

He was about to cross the road and buy the paper, when he remembered that he had used the last of his change in the pub the night before. He'd been drinking with a couple of freelance journalists and somehow they'd all ended up round the fruit machine, shovelling coins into the slot. At one stage he'd won over fifteen pounds, but of course he'd put it all back in again. That was his problem. He never knew when to stop. He took out his wallet and opened it. All he had was a few credit cards. He had no cash at all.

The nearest cash machine was by the traffic lights, the other side of Camden Market. Bulman thought about walking but, as luck would have it, a bus appeared at that exact moment, rumbling towards him down the hill. At least he had his

Oyster card; it was valid for any Tube or bus in London. He hurried over to the bus stop, arriving just as the driver pulled in and the doors hissed open. A couple of people got on ahead of him but then it was his turn. He pressed his card against the scanner. The machine made a discouraging sound.

"I'm sorry, mate," the driver said, glancing at the screen which displayed how much money had been taken. "You've got nothing on your card."

"That's not possible," Bulman replied. "I took the Tube yesterday and I had about thirty quid."

"Well, it's showing zero now." The driver pointed at the screen.

"Your machine must be broken."

"It worked for everyone else."

Bulman held his card against the screen for a second time – but with the same result. It was definitely showing £00.00. The four noughts seemed to mock him. He glanced round. The bus was crowded with people waiting to move off. They were all watching him impatiently. "All right." He scowled. "I'll walk."

Bulman had decided it wasn't worth the argument. The bank was near by and the sun was shining. He stepped back onto the pavement and the bus moved off. He was still holding his Oyster card. He glared at it. When he had a spare minute, he would send a letter to Transport for London to complain. Maybe he would even write an article about his experience. Idiots. Why couldn't they get their technology to work?

By the time he had walked down to the bank it was almost eight thirty. All around him the shops were opening. People were hurrying out of the coffee bars, clutching their styrofoam cups, then disappearing into their offices – another busy London day. Propping his briefcase under his arm, Bulman selected a credit card and fed it into the cash machine. He needed money for breakfast, to pick up a few groceries – and later on he might treat himself to a taxi over to Chelsea. He punched in his PIN, touched the button for £50 and waited.

The screen went black. Then a message came up:

> **CARD REJECTED. PLEASE CALL**
> **PROVIDER FOR FURTHER ADVICE.**

Bulman stared at the screen, then punched CANCEL to get his card back. Nothing happened. Not only was the machine refusing to give him any money, it had decided to keep his card! There was nothing wrong with his account. The last time he'd looked, he'd had over two hundred pounds. Someone must have vandalized the cash dispenser, some Camden Town lout who'd had too much to drink.

The bank wouldn't be open for another half-hour but there was a building society just a few minutes further down the high street. This time there was a queue. Bulman stood behind an elderly woman who seemed to take an age to withdraw her money. Well, at least it proved that this machine worked. Bulman selected a second credit card and fed it into the slot. All his cards used the same PIN – his date of birth backwards. Angry, but taking care not to make a mistake, he keyed it in.

The same thing happened again. A blank screen. A stark white message. His card was swallowed up.

He swore. A couple of people had queued to use the same machine and they were looking at him with a sort of pity, as if they imagined that he was broke, that there was nothing in his account. What was he to do now? He was hungry – he needed breakfast. He had no money and his Oyster card wasn't working.

Then he remembered. His car, a second-hand Volkswagen Golf, was parked round the corner from his flat. He didn't often use it during the day – even with the congestion charge, there was still too much traffic in London – but he often drove it at night and he kept spare cash in the glove compartment, usually about ten pounds. That wouldn't buy him much but it was better than nothing, and he could use it for breakfast while he waited for the bank and the building society to open. He'd feel better with a bit of food inside him. He'd go in and shout at the silly fat girl behind the cash desk (in his experience, cashiers were always silly and fat). And once it was sorted, he would get on with his day.

He found the side street and strolled down to where the car was parked.

The car wasn't there.

Bulman stood on the pavement, blinking. He had the beginnings of a headache. He had definitely parked the car on this spot. He might have had a few too many drinks the evening before – and yes, he was probably well over the limit – but he was certain this was where he had left it. Now there was a blue Volvo in his space. He looked up and down the road. There was no sign of his Volkswagen. He forced himself to think. Dinner, pub, fruit machine, one last drink, then home around midnight. The car had to be here. The car wasn't here. So what had happened?

It had been stolen! Cars were always being taken in this part of town. A lot of the residents had those clumsy-looking locks that fitted over the steering wheel, but he had never bought one. He shook his head. What a day this was turning into. He'd be in a bad mood when he caught up with Alex Rider later this afternoon. It would be their first session together – but even so he was going to give the boy a hard time.

First things first. Bulman took out his mobile to call the police. He wondered what number to use. This wasn't really an emergency but he decided to call 999 anyway. He thumbed the button three times and held the phone to his ear.

Nothing.

It wasn't ringing. There wasn't even a dialling tone. Bulman brought the phone down – it was a brand-new BlackBerry – and examined it.

No signal.

It was ridiculous. He was in the middle of Chalk Farm. There was always a signal here. He walked a few paces along the pavement, held the phone up, tried it at a different angle. The screen remained the same. He was squeezing the phone so tightly that he was almost crushing it. He forced himself to calm down. There was an old-fashioned phone box at the end of the road. He didn't need coins to make a 999 call. He would contact the police from there.

He retraced his steps and entered the phone booth, which was plastered with advertisements for models and smelled of cigarette smoke and urine. At least the phone itself seemed to be working. He balanced his briefcase against the glass and made the call.

"Which service do you require?" the operator asked him.

"My car has been stolen," Bulman said. He was almost relieved to hear another human voice. "I need to speak to the police."

There was a pause and he was put through.

"I'd like to report a stolen car," he said. "I parked it in Chilton Street last night and now it's gone."

"Can I have the registration number?" It was a

woman's voice. She didn't sound very concerned. She also spoke with a foreign accent, making him wonder if he'd been re-routed to a call centre abroad.

Forcing himself not to lose his temper, he gave the registration number. "KL06 NZG."

"KL06 NZG?"

"Yes."

"Is that a green Mercedes SLR Coupé?"

"No!" Bulman shut his eyes. His headache was getting worse. "It's a silver Volkswagen Golf."

"Can you give me the registration number again?"

Bulman repeated it, leaving a space between each letter and digit. Whoever was at the other end of the line obviously didn't have much skill with computers.

"I'm sorry, sir." The woman was adamant. "That number is registered to a Mercedes. Can I take your name?"

"It's Bulman. Harold Edward Bulman."

"And your address?"

He told her.

"Could you hold on a moment?" There was another silence, longer this time. Bulman was about to hang up, when the woman came back on the line.

"Mr Bulman, how long have you had this car?"

"I bought it two years ago."

"I'm afraid we have no record of that name or that address."

Finally Bulman lost his temper. "Are you telling me that I don't know where I live and that I've forgotten the make and the colour of my own car?" he demanded. "I'm telling you, my car has been stolen. I left it here yesterday and it's gone."

"I'm sorry, sir. The registration number you've given us doesn't match up with the information I have here."

"Well, your information is wrong."

Bulman slammed the phone down. His head was throbbing.

He needed money. He felt naked without cash and he wanted to eat. He looked at his watch. At least that was still working. Five past nine. The banks would have opened by now. Bulman had ID on him and he'd feel better once he had a full wallet. He could deal with the car later.

He turned and walked back the way he had come. Twenty minutes later, he found himself in the local branch of his bank, talking to one of the personal managers who had a desk in the main hall. The manager was a young Asian man dressed in a suit, with a neat beard. He was clearly alarmed as this new customer came striding up to him, and Bulman realized that what with all the tramping back and forth trying to deal with the events that seemed to have ganged up on him in the past hour, he must look half crazy. He no longer cared.

"I need to withdraw some money," he said. "And your machine doesn't seem to be working."

The manager frowned. "We haven't had any complaints."

"It doesn't matter. I don't need to use the machine. I want to withdraw some money from you."

"Do you have a card, sir?"

Bulman handed over his last remaining credit card and watched as the manager brought up his details on the computer. He gazed at the screen, perplexed.

"I'm very sorry, sir, I can't find—"

"Are you saying I don't have an account with you?" Bulman's voice quavered.

"No, sir. You *used* to have an account. But you closed it down a year ago. You can see for yourself." The manager swivelled the computer round and there it was again: a row of zeros at the bottom of his account. Every last penny had been removed exactly twelve months before.

"I never closed my account," Bulman said.

"Would you like me to talk to head office?"

But Bulman had already gone, spinning out of the chair and making his way through the main door, out into the fresh air. What the hell was going on? The Oyster card, then the bank cards, his mobile phone, his car, now his accounts – it was as if his identity was being taken from him one piece at a time. He leant against the corner of the building, steadying himself, and as he stood there a commuter hurried past, throwing a newspaper into a bin right in front of him, almost as if he wanted him to see what was on the front page.

It was a photograph of himself.

Bulman gazed at it in horror, remembering the headline that he had seen as he came out of his flat. JOURNALIST KILLED. He was looking at the same headline now. He felt the pavement lurch beneath him as he stepped forward and plucked out the newspaper. The story was very short.

> Harold Bulman, a freelance journalist who specialized in stories relating to the army and intelligence services, was yesterday morning found dead in his north London flat. Mr Bulman, thirty-seven, had been stabbed.
>
> Police have appealed for any witnesses who might have seen or heard anything between ten o'clock and midnight to come forward. Detective Chief Superintendent Stephen Leather, who is heading the investigation, said: "Mr Bulman may well have made enemies in his line of work and at this stage we are not ruling anything out."
>
> Harold Bulman was divorced and had no close family or friends.

It was him. They were saying he was dead! How could they have made a mistake like that? Was this the reason why his phone wasn't working, why there was no money in his account? Suddenly it all made sense. Somehow he'd been confused with somebody else. And as a result, a whole series of switches had been pulled as, automatically, his life was turned off.

He had to get to a telephone. He had to talk to his editors, to the people who employed him. He had no money. But there was a phone in his flat. That was the answer. Bulman didn't want to be on the street any more. He had become a non-person, an invisible man. For some reason, he felt exposed. How could he be sure that there wasn't someone out there who really did want to stab him? He had to get inside.

He was sweating by the time he got back to his apartment block and his hand shook as he tried to force the key into the lock. It didn't seem to want to go in. In the end, after three attempts, he realized that the key didn't fit. And that was impossible too. He used it every day. He had used it last night. But someone, in the last nine hours, had changed the lock.

"Let me in!" he shouted. There was nobody to listen to him. He was shouting at the glass door and the brickwork. "Let me in!" He kicked the door, using the sole of his foot. But the glass was reinforced, shatterproof, and held in place by powerful magnetic plates. He kicked out a second time. He was screaming now. Anyone passing would think he was mad.

"Are you all right, sir? Can I help you?"

He hadn't heard the police car draw up behind

him, but when he turned round, there were two policemen standing on the pavement. Bulman was glad to see them. After all, he'd been trying to call them just a few minutes ago.

"I'm locked out," he said.

"Do you live here, sir?"

"Well, obviously I live here. If I didn't live here, I wouldn't be trying to get in." Bulman realized he was being rude. He tried to force a smile to his face. "I have a flat on the top floor," he explained. "This has never happened before."

"Can I try for you?"

Bulman noticed that the policeman had dropped the "sir". He handed the keys over and watched as the policeman tried them in the lock – also without success. The policeman examined the keys, then the lock. He straightened up. "You're not going to open this door with these," he said. "The lock is Banham. These are Yale."

"But that's not possible..."

"What's your name?" the second policeman asked.

"Harry Bulman. I'm a journalist."

"And you say you live here?"

"I don't just say I live here. I do live here. But I'm locked out."

"Just one moment, sir..."

The first policeman was talking on his radio. Bulman passed his briefcase from one hand to the other. It was suddenly feeling very heavy. Considering it was only January, the weather was

157

far too hot. The second policeman was looking at him suspiciously. He was only about nineteen years old with light brown hair and sticking-out ears. He still had a schoolboy face.

"Are you sure this is where you live?" the first policeman asked. He had finished his radio conversation.

"Yes. Flat 37. On the top floor."

"There was a Harold Bulman, a journalist, registered to this address, but he was killed two nights ago."

"No. That was in the papers. I just read it. But it's a mistake. I'm Harry Bulman."

"Would you have any identification on you?"

"Of course I have." Bulman took out his wallet. But two of his cards had been swallowed by the cash machines and he had left the third in the bank. His driving licence was in the flat. His fingers were shaking as he fumbled through the leather sleeves. He had a press card but that seemed to have disappeared. "I can give you ID once I get into my flat," he said.

The two policemen looked at each other. The younger one seemed to notice Bulman's briefcase for the first time. "What are you carrying?" he asked.

The question took Bulman by surprise. "Why do you want to know?" he snapped.

Before he could stop him, the first policeman had picked up the briefcase. "Do you mind if we look inside?"

"Yes. As a matter of fact, I do—"

It was already too late. The policeman had opened the briefcase and was looking at the contents, his face full of horror. With a sense that his whole life was draining away from him, Bulman leant forward. He knew what was inside: a notepad, a couple of magazines, pens and pencils. He was wrong. The policeman was holding the case open and Bulman could clearly see a kitchen knife, about fifteen inches long, the blade covered in dried blood.

"Wait—" he began.

The two policemen acted incredibly quickly. Without even knowing quite what had happened, Bulman found himself face down on the pavement with his arms gripped behind his back. He felt the metal edges of the handcuffs bite into his flesh as they clicked shut. The first policeman was back on his radio, talking rapidly. Seconds later, there was a screech of tyres and another police car drew up. More uniformed officers emerged.

"You are not required to say anything..."

Bulman realized that he was being told his rights but the words didn't quite register. They were booming in his ears. He felt himself being picked up and propelled towards the car. A hand was placed on his head, to stop him banging against the door frame. And then he was inside, being driven away at speed. They even turned the sirens on.

An hour later, Bulman was sitting alone in a bare, brick interrogation room with a window set so high up it only showed a small square of sky. They had taken his fingerprints and a swab from the side of his mouth which, he knew, would be used to check his DNA. There were two new officers sitting opposite him. They were older and more experienced than the men who had made the arrest: thickset and serious. They had introduced themselves as Baker and Ainsworth. Ainsworth seemed to be the senior of the two, bald, with small, hard eyes and a mouth that could have been drawn with a single pencil line. Baker was younger and looked as if he had recently been in a fist fight. He was holding a file.

Bulman had been given a little time to collect his thoughts. He had worked out what he was going to say. "Listen to me," he began. "This is all a stupid mistake. The way you've treated me is outrageous. I am a well-known journalist and I'm warning you—"

"It's good to see you, Jeremy," Baker interrupted.

"That's not my name."

"Jeremy Harwood. Did you really think we wouldn't find you?" Baker laid the file on the table and opened it. Bulman saw a black and white police photograph. Once again he recognized himself. But it had this other name underneath it.

He drew a breath. "My name is not Jeremy Harwood. My name is Harold Bulman."

"Harold Bulman is dead."

"No."

"We've already analysed the blood we found on the knife in your briefcase. It's Bulman's. You killed him."

"No. You're making a mistake. This is all wrong." Bulman fought for control. How could this nightmare be happening?

Baker flicked a page in a file. There were fingerprints – five of them in a row – and a series of what looked like chemical formulae. "We've checked your DNA and your fingerprints, Jeremy. They all match up. So there's no need to pretend any more."

"You escaped from Broadmoor two months ago," Ainsworth said.

Broadmoor? Bulman blinked heavily. That was where they sent the most dangerous prisoners in the country, the ones who were considered criminally insane.

"Why did you kill Harold Bulman?" Baker asked.

"I ... I..." Bulman tried to find the answer but the words wouldn't come. Something had happened to his thinking process. He was aware that there were tears trickling down his cheeks.

"Don't worry, Jeremy," Ainsworth said. He sounded almost kind. "We're going to take you back. You'll be safe, locked up in your cell. You won't hurt anyone ever again."

"You'll be taken back to Broadmoor this afternoon," Baker added.

"No." The room was spinning in ever-increasing circles. Bulman gripped the table, trying to slow it down. "You can't..."

"We can. The arrangements have already been made."

The door suddenly opened and a third man came in. From the very start he didn't look anything like a policeman. He was more like a scoutmaster, someone you might expect to see umpiring a village cricket match. He was about forty with thinning hair and a face that was hurrying towards old age. He was wearing a suit that didn't match his brown suede shoes. "Thank you," he said. "I'll take over now."

He didn't exactly radiate authority but there was something in his voice, an edge of steel, that cut straight to the point. The two detectives stood up immediately and left. The man took their place at the table, opposite Bulman. His eyes were empty and cold.

"My name is Crawley," he said. Bulman was still crying. There were tears dripping off his nose. Crawley reached into his pocket and took out a tissue. "Use this," he suggested.

Bulman wiped his nose and ran a sleeve across his eyes.

"I work for the intelligence services," Crawley explained. "A branch of MI6."

And suddenly Bulman understood. It was like being slapped across the face. MI6! Who else could have twisted his life out of shape with such ease?

If he hadn't been so terrified, he would have been furious with himself. He should have expected something like this. "Alex Rider..." he rasped.

"I'm not saying I've ever heard of Alex Rider," Crawley responded. His voice was utterly flat. "But I am going to tell you this. I could snap my fingers now and a van would take you to a psychiatric hospital and lock you up, and that is where you would spend the rest of your life. Harry Bulman would be dead and you'd be the lunatic who killed him."

"But ... but..." Bulman couldn't talk. He could barely breathe.

"For that matter, I could eliminate you now myself," Crawley continued. "I actually know twenty-six different ways to kill you in a manner that will look completely natural. Some of them are quick. Some of them hurt." He paused. "But those are not my instructions. I've been told to give you another chance."

"You bastard..." Bulman was crying again.

"You can go home now. You can forget all about this. But if you ever go anywhere near Alex Rider again, if you approach any newspaper editor, if you so much as mention his name, we will hear about it and next time we won't be so generous. We will wipe you off the face of the earth. Do you understand me?"

Bulman said nothing. Crawley stood up.

"From now on, we'll be watching you, Mr Bulman," he said. "Every minute of every day.

Please believe me. This was just a warning. Next time, it'll be for real."

He left the room.

Bulman stayed where he was. Alex Rider. The two words thundered through his head. *Alex Rider.* He knew that he would never write his story. His hopes of a major scoop had been destroyed. He dragged himself to his feet. He was still trembling. Alex Rider. How he wished he had never heard the name.

He wiped his face one last time and set about finding his way out.

GREENFIELDS

The coach headed west down the motorway, turning off at Junction 15, near Swindon. It passed through the attractive town of Marlborough, then continued on towards the vast area of empty grassland that was Salisbury Plain.

There was nowhere quite like it in the whole of England. Three hundred square miles in area, it had been inhabited long before the Romans had arrived. Stonehenge stood on its southern edge. Traces of hill forts dating back to the Iron Age were still dotted around. The plain was used by the army, frequently shut down for night exercises using tonnes of live ammunition. And one small part of it had been leased out to Greenfields for a research centre that the authorities had decided was best kept hidden, in the middle of nowhere.

Alex Rider was sitting in the back of the coach next to Tom Harris and James Hale. There were forty students from Brookland on the trip, along with two teachers – Mr Gilbert and a prim, slightly nervous woman called Miss Barry, who taught music but who had been included to help with discipline. They had been driving for over two hours now and the initial excitement had long since faded away, replaced by the dull sense of endlessness that comes with any motorway journey.

Alex took out the postcard that had arrived the day before. It showed a picture of the Eiffel Tower in Paris. On the back someone had written a date – 22/5 – and a message:

> *Paris is beautiful and fortunately we didn't manage to get lost. I hope you have a great time.*

The signature was unreadable but Alex recognized Smithers' writing. He had been expecting the card and Smithers had told him how to use it. He slipped it away and turned to Tom.

"Can you do me a favour?" he said casually.

"Sure. What sort of favour?"

"While we're on this trip, I might have to disappear for a bit. So if there's any roll call, could you answer for me?"

Tom frowned. He spoke quietly so his voice wouldn't carry above the sound of the engine. "The last time you asked me to cover for you, we were in Venice," he said. "You're not doing that stuff again, are you?"

Alex nodded gloomily. He wasn't going to lie to his best mate.

"But I thought you'd finished with all that."

"Yeah. Me too. But it didn't quite work out that way." Alex sighed. "It's not anything dangerous, Tom. And it shouldn't take very long. I just don't want anyone to notice I'm missing."

"OK. Don't get yourself killed."

They had been following a series of minor roads through swathes of green countryside that stretched to every horizon. This wasn't the England of pretty fields and hedgerows. There was something ancient and untamed about Salisbury Plain. It seemed to be completely deserted with nothing – no buildings, no fences, no power lines, no people – for as far as the eye could see. There were a few clumps of trees huddled together on the hillsides, boulders and bits of debris thrown carelessly around. The wind was rippling through the grass, making strange patterns like silent music chasing ahead of them as they rumbled slowly towards the top of a hill.

"Here it is," James said.

He was right. The Greenfields Bio Centre had suddenly appeared in front of them concealed in a miniature valley. It was somehow shocking after so much emptiness, like a glass and steel city, or perhaps a prison, or even a colony on another planet. It certainly looked alien here, in the middle of Wiltshire. The complex was shaped like a diamond, completely surrounded by a fence with links so tightly meshed that it was almost like a metal wall, glinting in the sun. A single sliding gate, heavily guarded, stood at the end of the tarmac road. At least the guards didn't seem to be armed – but they looked threatening enough, even without weapons.

"What is this place?" James muttered, staring out of the window. "It seems a lot of fuss for a bunch of vegetables."

There were about twenty buildings on the other side of the fence. Many of them were greenhouses but they were enormous, taller and more solid than anything that might be found in any garden. The rest were offices, warehouses and factories, most of them low-rise but some five or six storeys high with radio masts, satellite dishes and tall, silver chimneys built onto the roofs. To one side, Alex saw what might have been a reception centre, sleek and white. A second building right next to the gate was square and solid with a sign marked SECURITY. But his eye was drawn to the construction at the very centre of the complex.

It was a huge dome, like something out of a science fiction film, filled with vegetation. He could make out the leaves of palm trees licking at the glass, twenty or thirty metres high. Creepers and knotted foliage hung down on all sides. It was connected to other buildings by four glass corridors, radiating out like points on a compass.

The biosphere, Alex thought. He didn't know where he had got the name from but it seemed right.

Greenfields looked brand new. There was a network of black tarmac roads separated by perfect rectangles of freshly mown grass. Or perhaps the grass had been genetically programmed to grow to exactly the right height. Silent electric vehicles were ferrying men and women from place to place. Some of them – presumably the scientists – were wearing white coats. Others were in suits. The guards wore green camouflage jackets as if to remind themselves that the environment was what this was supposed to be all about. And everywhere, on dozens of poles and on the sides of each building, arc lamps and sophisticated cameras gazed down from every angle so that if a single wasp or bee flew in, someone somewhere would know.

There was a loud whine inside the coach as Mr Gilbert turned on the intercom system. "Please don't be alarmed by all the security," he said. His voice, amplified and relayed through the speakers, didn't sound very confident. "A lot of work that they do here at Greenfields is sensitive. They have to protect themselves from competitors and journalists and that sort of thing, and some of the plants they grow here have to be contained. I'm afraid we are all going to have to be searched as we go in – but it shouldn't take long. Please remember to leave all cameras and mobile phones on the coach. They'll be perfectly safe but they won't be allowed inside."

There were general groans and protests but, as they drew closer to the gate, everyone began to open their backpacks, doing as they were told. They'd been on school trips before but they weren't used to blank-faced guards and body searches.

"I hope you know what you're doing," Tom muttered, glancing at Alex.

Alex didn't reply. *It's a very simple matter. Hardly worthy of your talents.* He remembered Blunt describing the job. Why should he be surprised by another lie?

The coach slowed down and stopped. They had reached the gate, which slid open slowly to allow them into a holding area. Someone rapped on the door and the driver opened it to allow a thin, unsmiling woman to step inside. Mr Gilbert stood up and held out a hand, but she ignored him.

"Good afternoon," she said. Her voice was clipped and somehow artificial. She sounded like a speak-your-weight machine. "May I welcome you to Greenfields Bio Centre. I am the supervisor here." She paused, running her eyes over the passengers as if committing the faces to memory. "My name is Dr Myra Bennett, and I will be looking after you during your visit."

It was difficult to say how old Dr Bennett might be. She was a severe, very masculine woman in a white coat which hung loosely from her shoulders and somehow defined her. There was so little emotion in her face that it was hard to imagine her doing anything that didn't involve books, Bunsen burners and bottles of chemicals. Her hair, bright blonde, was short with a fringe that cut diagonally across her forehead, the last strands touching her left eye. She wore circular, gold-framed spectacles that looked cheap and didn't flatter her. It was obvious that she didn't care about her appearance. She wore no make-up and no jewellery. She made no effort to be polite.

"We have not had a visit from a school before," she continued. "Any photography or recording is forbidden. When you leave this coach, every one of you will be searched. This was agreed with your school when you were invited. All mobile phones are to be left behind. You will follow me now, please."

"What a charming woman," Tom muttered.

"Yeah. I'm really glad we came," James agreed.

The supervisor had left the coach. The two teachers and the rest of the Brookland crowd followed her into the square building that had been kitted out exactly like a security area in an airport. There were uniformed men standing behind silver tables, X-rays for hand luggage and metal detectors that everyone would have to pass through.

Alex was one of the first to be searched. He watched as his backpack, with the pencil case inside, disappeared into one of the machines. At the same time, he was briskly patted down by a tight-lipped guard. The postcard that Smithers had sent him was in his inside jacket pocket and the guard pulled it out, glanced at the picture of the Eiffel Tower then handed it back to him. His backpack appeared on the other side of the machine, but before he could reach it, another security man picked it up.

"Is this yours?"

Alex nodded. "Yes." All around him his friends were being processed.

It was as if the guard sensed that something was wrong. He examined Alex, then opened the bag and looked inside.

"It's just my schoolwork," Alex said.

The guard ignored him. He riffled through the books, then removed the pencil case and opened that too. For a moment, Alex was certain that every alarm in the place was about to go off. The guard took out the rubber and turned it over between his fingers. But then, as if he had suddenly lost interest, he shoved everything back into the bag and handed it over.

"Next!"

Alex joined the others at the far end of the security hall. He noticed that Mr Gilbert was looking fairly disgruntled and he understood why. They were only on a school outing, but they were being treated as if they might all be terrorists.

Dr Bennett didn't seem to care. "We will now proceed into the main complex," she announced.

"Please stay together. Does anyone need to use the toilet?" There was silence. "Good. Then come this way." She led them to a final barrier and Alex noticed they were counted electronically as they passed through.

But at last they were inside Greenfields. Bennett gathered them in a group, standing in the open air with the great dome in front of them. Now that he was closer to the glass, Alex could see that there was an entire ecosystem contained on the other side. Exotic-looking trees sprouted in all directions like green fireworks photographed just as they went off. There were strange plants and bushes fighting for space, some of them carrying ugly, brilliant-coloured berries or fruit. It had to be hot inside. A thick layer of steam hung in the air and Alex noticed beads of moisture trickling down the panes. To his surprise, there was a movement inside the dome and a man appeared, covered from head to toe in a white protective suit, carrying a piece of measuring equipment. He paused briefly by the window. Then he was gone.

"You will be with us for two hours," Bennett began. She didn't sound pleased. Indeed, she was making it clear that this entire visit was an irritation. "We will start by looking at the laboratories, where you will see some of our techniques, including genetic transformation, cloning and the biolistic particle delivery system – we call it the gene gun – that fires new DNA into plants.

The gene gun was developed by our director, Leonard Straik. You will visit the greenhouses and storage facilities where we cultivate and keep fruits and vegetables, some of which have never before existed on this planet. After that you will be taken to our lecture theatre." She pointed at the white building which Alex had noticed from the brow of the hill. "There will be a discussion about the need for GM technology and the way that it can help the future of the planet.

"And finally" – she smiled so briefly that it seemed to be no more than a nervous twitch – "you are invited to our canteen for a cup of our own Greenfields Bio Centre Blend Coffee, which has been genetically modified to deliver a more satisfying flavour.

"Please do not at any time separate from the group. Some of the guards are a little nervous and I would be very sorry if any of you delightful young people were asked to leave. Also, do not touch anything. You will be standing close to many chemicals and plant specimens. Any of them could be dangerous. Are there any questions?"

"What's in there?" someone asked.

Dr Bennett turned round and looked at the central greenhouse. For a moment, her eyes seemed to flash behind the circular lenses. "We call that the Poison Dome," she explained. "For many years Greenfields has been researching natural poisons, toxins such as ricin and botulin which occur in nature but which can kill human beings. Inside the Poison Dome we grow some of the deadliest plants on the planet, including water hemlock, deadly nightshade, elephant's ear, death cap mushrooms and castor beans. The manzanilla tree has attractive fruit which you may choose to swallow. If you do so, it will kill you instantly. There is also a white resin dripping out of it which will blister your skin or blind you. The leaves of the ongaonga from New Zealand only need to touch you to produce hideous burns.

"It might interest you to know that the common nettle – *Urtica dioica* – which you may find growing in your garden injects you with five neurotransmitters when it stings you. The nettles inside the Poison Dome have been genetically modified so that they will sting you with five hundred neurotransmitters. I would like to describe to you the pain of such a death but, in truth, I do not have enough imagination."

She took out a tissue and touched it briefly to her lips.

"We are particularly interested in the way poisons interact," she continued. "So you will also find animal life in there, including specimens of the blue dart frog, which releases lethal toxins from its skin, the banana spider, the taipan snake and the marbled cone snail. A single drop of its slime will kill an elephant." She paused and looked around the group. "If any of you would like to visit the Poison Dome, please let me know. That visit will probably last about fifteen seconds before you die horribly."

Nobody spoke. Miss Barry had gone very pale.

"Very well. Let us head over to the laboratories. I will ask your teachers to take a roll call when we enter and again when we leave."

Tom Harris glanced at Alex, looking more doubtful by the minute. Alex shrugged. He was remembering what Blunt had told him about Philip Masters, how the whistle-blower had died. His body had been unrecognizable when it was found, and now Alex had a good idea what might have happened to him. Well, here was certainly one area of the bio centre he'd be careful to avoid.

They went into one of the taller buildings with a steel chimney rising above them and smoke trickling into the sky. Bennett let them in, using an electronic swipe card that she carried around her neck, and they passed into a clean, uncluttered corridor, where Mr Gilbert took their names. As they set off once again, Alex made sure he was lingering near the back. They passed a toilet. Quickly he nudged Tom, who nodded back, and without hesitating Alex ducked sideways, throwing his weight against the door and plunging inside. Suddenly he was alone, standing in a white tiled room with two sinks and two mirrors in front of him. He waited until he could no longer hear the voices or footsteps of his friends. Nobody had seen him leave. It was time to get started.

He took out the postcard with the view of Paris and went over to a sink. He ran a paper towel under the tap, then wiped it over the picture. The Eiffel Tower and its surroundings dissolved and disappeared. Underneath, there was an intricately drawn map of the Greenfields Bio Centre showing all the buildings and passageways with two tiny lights already blinking. One was red; one was green. They told him where he was and where he had to get to.

He listened for a moment, and when he was sure that there was no one near by, he slipped out into the corridor again, holding the postcard in front of him. According to the flashing display, the chief science officer – Leonard Straik – could be found in the building next to this one. The two of them were connected by a walkway, so Alex wouldn't have to go back outside. All in all, he didn't think he was in too much danger ... at least, not yet. He was wearing school uniform, part of an invited group. If anyone did run into him it would be easy enough to claim that he had simply lagged behind and got lost. And anyway, what was there to worry about? The research centre might look sinister and it might have poison at its heart, but nobody had suggested it was breaking any laws. He was here simply because one man, Straik, might be a security risk. His task was simple. And half an hour from now it would all be over.

Even so, his nerves were jangling as he made his way forward, the flashing light in the display signalling his progress. He had been heading in the same direction as the school party, but then he came to an open area where three corridors met at the foot of a concrete staircase up to the next floor. That was where the light seemed to be directing him. He went up the first few steps, then flattened himself against the wall as he heard foot-steps approaching. A man and a woman appeared, both of them wearing white coats, walking along one of the passageways below him. They were deep in conversation and didn't notice him. Alex waited until they were gone, then continued up.

The inside of the building was like a school or university. The whitewashed walls were mainly bare, with signs pointing towards different blocks. There were no decorations, just fire extinguishers and display boards full of safety notices. The first floor was identical to the ground, with doorways and interlinking corridors. Without Smithers' post-card Alex wouldn't have had any idea where to go, but he allowed it to lead him back on himself until he arrived at the glass bridge that led to the next building.

It was more dangerous here. The bridge was about ten metres long, exposed on both sides. From where he was standing, Alex could see electric vehicles passing each other on the road beneath. A couple of guards walked slowly past and Alex saw that unlike the others, these two were armed. He recognized the familiar shape of 9mm Micro Uzi sub-machine guns hanging lazily against their chests. It was a nasty surprise. Presumably the weapons had been kept deliberately hidden when the school party arrived.

To make matters worse, there were also several cameras pointing his way. Alex could wait until there was no one around, but he would still be spotted if he tried to cross the bridge. He opened his bag, took out the pencil case and found the calculator. Jamming the cameras might well advertise that something was wrong but he had no choice. He pressed the plus button three times, checked that the road was clear, then crossed the bridge.

He knew he was operating against the clock now. With the cameras down, security inside the complex would be heightened and it would be less easy to explain what he was doing if he was caught. He ran to the next corner, then jerked back as a door opened and a guard appeared, racing down a corridor in front of him. It was obvious that Alex had passed from an academic or administrative block into an area reserved for senior management and executives. Here the floor was carpeted, and there were pictures – highly detailed watercolours of different plants – on the walls. The lighting was softer and the doors were made of expensive wood. According to the navigation system concealed inside the postcard, Straik's office was near by, and Alex also knew its number: 225. That was the date Smithers had written above the message.

He found it at the end of the corridor round the next corner. As he approached, he heard a door slam somewhere downstairs and a voice called out. There were more footsteps ... someone hurrying. A telephone was ringing insistently. Nobody was answering it. They were only tiny details but Alex got the sense that something had changed inside Greenfields. The cameras were out of action and that had made them nervous.

Was there anyone in Straik's office? There was only one way to find out. Alex took a deep breath and knocked. This was the moment of truth. If someone called out for him to come in, the whole thing would have been a waste of time.

There was silence. Alex sighed. So far so good. He took the pencil case back out and removed the library card. He had noticed a card reader on the wall beside every door that he had passed and Straik's was no different. Alex swiped his card through the reader, then fed it into the slot at the bottom of his pencil case. He felt the whole thing vibrate in his hand as the machinery that Smithers had built into the secret compartment did its work. A few seconds later, the library card slid out again. Alex swiped it a second time. The card had been reprogrammed. There was a click and Straik's door swung open.

Alex hurried in, closing the door behind him. He found himself in a large, comfortable office with views over the perfect lawn outside the security block. That was where they had gathered when they had first arrived, and for a fleeting moment, Alex wondered if he had been missed yet. If there was a second roll call, would Tom be able to cover for him? He was beginning to see just how risky his plan had been – but it was too late now.

He looked around him. Straik had four or five potted plants which seemed to have been genetically modified to look artificial. There were half a dozen bookshelves, an antique mirror and a glass-fronted cabinet with a scattering of scientific awards. A picture had recently been delivered but not yet hung. It was still in bubble wrap, leaning against one wall. Two designer armchairs sat side by side, opposite an antique desk. Straik's computer was on the desk.

Alex made straight for it. He just wanted to get this over with and then rejoin his friends. Once he was back with the school group, he would be safe. Even if the security guards realized there was an intruder at large, they would never suspect him. He had to admit that Alan Blunt was right. Sometimes it did help to be fourteen.

Straik had a leather chair, a massive, swivelling thing that reminded Alex of the dentist's. He sat down and took out the rubber that had come with the pencil case. Some of the gadgets that Smithers had supplied him with over the past year had been ingenious but this one was very straightforward. He simply ripped the rubber in half, then pulled it apart to reveal the Memory Stick inside.

Straik's computer was already turned on, but Alex had no doubt that any important files would be encrypted and protected by a whole series of passwords. Fortunately that wasn't his problem. Alex found the USB port. There was already a Memory Stick there and he took it out, laying it on the desk. Then he plugged in his own.

Immediately the screen blazed into life, four columns of figures flickering and spinning crazily as the worm – or whatever was built into the Memory Stick – burrowed into the heart of the computer, sucking out its information. Alex thought he heard voices outside in the corridor and he felt the cold touch of the air conditioning against the sweat on his neck and brow. How long had Smithers said this would take? Half a minute. That was all. But the seconds seemed to stretch themselves in front of him as more and more files – thousands of them – appeared and disappeared, each one duplicated and stolen away.

And now someone really was approaching! He could hear two men talking. Were they walking past? No! Damn it! They had stopped outside. It had to be Straik. Alex could imagine him reaching for his wallet, taking out the magnetic swipe card that would allow him in.

The download still hadn't finished. Alex was tempted to snatch out the Memory Stick and do it all again later. But how much later? What would he do if Straik decided to spend the rest of his day in his office? How would he get back to the school group? The door was going to open any second now. Alex would be a sitting duck. Literally sitting in the leather chair behind the computer. Perhaps he could bluff his way out. Or he could run for it, try to find Mr Gilbert and the others. There was safety in numbers. Straik might shout at him or even have him arrested. But while there were witnesses, at least he couldn't be shot.

The Memory Stick completed its work. The computer screen went blank. The two men were still outside the door. Alex heard a faint bleep as the lock was activated. He grabbed the Memory Stick and dived forward, making for the one hiding place that he had seen inside the office. He had only just reached it when the door opened.

From where Alex was crouching, he could see Leonard Straik as he came in. The Greenfields director was reflected in the mirror, and with a sense of total shock, Alex realized that he recognized him. Silver hair rising up as if it had just been blow-dried. Heavy lips and jowls. Small, watery eyes. The two of them had met recently. But where...?

Then he remembered. Scotland. New Year's Eve. The man he had thought of as an accountant, playing cards with Desmond McCain. What had McCain called him? Leo. Of course! That was it. Leo was Leonard – Leonard Straik.

"Do you want something to drink? Tea? Coffee? We actually develop it ourselves, you know. But it still tastes disgusting."

"No. Not for me, thank you."

The other man came in, closing the door behind him. And that was an even bigger shock for Alex.

The second man was Desmond McCain.

HELL ON EARTH

"So is the shipment ready?"

Alex remembered McCain's voice so well: not loud but deep and powerful, brimming with confidence. And yet he'd had difficulty pronouncing that last word because it began with an *r*. His smashed jaw wasn't quite able to form it. He had taken one of the designer chairs and had his back to Alex, the silver crucifix in his ear just visible above his right shoulder. Meanwhile, Straik had taken his place on the other side of the desk. The two men had no idea that there was anyone else in the room.

It was fortunate that Straik liked big paintings. Whatever it was that he had bought for his office had provided Alex with his hiding place. He was squashed up behind it, in the triangular space between the picture and the wall. There certainly wouldn't have been room for a full-grown adult here and even he was cramped, the muscles in his thighs and shoulders already urging him to straighten up. He could make out a little of Straik and McCain, reflected in the antique mirror, but he didn't dare lean too far forward. If he could see them, they would be able to see him.

"Of course it's ready," Straik replied. He sounded irritated. "I gave you my word, didn't I?"

"So where is it now?"

"The bulk of it is at Gatwick Airport. It's being carried out in a commercial Boeing 757. Completely routine. But I thought it might amuse you to have a look at it, so I've kept a sample for you here." Straik slid open one of the drawers of his desk and took something out, but although Alex craned his neck, he couldn't see what it was. "It took a little while longer than expected. We had problems with mass production."

"How much of this did you produce?" McCain asked.

"Five hundred gallons. It should be more than enough. The main thing is to make sure that the temperature is kept constant when it's in the air. You have to remember, this stuff is alive. But that said, it's also fairly durable."

"How quickly will it work?"

"Almost immediately. You need to apply it in the morning. The process will start at once but it will take thirty-six hours to activate. There won't be anything to see, of course – not to begin with – but in about three weeks you'll have the attention of the entire world." Straik paused. "What about the shooting?"

"I'm sending Myra to Elm's Cross tomorrow. We're closing it down. That's all behind us now."

"Then it seems we're in good shape."

"My dear Leo. Didn't I always tell you? The Lord will reward you according to your works – as it says in the Book of Timothy."

"Well, yes, but—" Straik stopped.

And in the silence, somehow, Alex knew that something had gone wrong. Crouching behind the picture, he froze, afraid that the sound of his breathing or his heart beating would give him away.

"Someone has been in my office," Straik said.

"What?" The word came out like a whiplash.

"My desk..." Straik picked something up and, even without seeing it, Alex knew what it was. The Memory Stick that had been in the computer when he arrived. He had taken it out to insert his own – but he hadn't had time to replace it. "This was in my USB port when I came down to meet you," Straik said. "I loaded it myself. Someone's removed it."

"Are you sure?"

"Of course I'm sure."

"Your secretary could have been in."

"She's not here today."

Alex realized he couldn't hold his position much longer. He was desperate to straighten up, to allow his muscles to stretch. At least that was one good thing. The hiding place was so small that neither of the two men would suspect for a minute that he was still in the room. But he had to know what was going on. Very slowly he leant forward a few inches to catch a glimpse in the mirror. McCain was holding the Memory Stick. Straik was hunched over his computer, tapping furiously at the keyboard, his little eyes focused on the screen. Two pinpricks of red had appeared in his cheeks.

"This computer has been compromised," he announced.

"Compromised?"

"Someone has attempted to download documents and files from the main drive. For all I know, they may have succeeded."

Straik snatched up a telephone and dialled a number. There was a brief pause. Then he was answered.

"This is Leonard Straik," he said. "I want an immediate status report."

Another pause. Alex wondered what was being said at the other end of the line. It wasn't hard to guess. Then Straik spoke again.

"I want you to put out a double red alert," he snapped. "All security personnel to assemble immediately. This is not an exercise. We have a major security breach."

He hung up.

"What is it?" McCain demanded.

"We have an intruder. Ten minutes ago our entire surveillance system went down. Someone must be jamming the signal. This is what they were after." He nodded at the computer. "They must have left seconds before we arrived."

"What's a double red alert?"

"Any unauthorized person found wandering inside the bio centre will be killed – no questions asked."

Alex heard this in disbelief. What exactly had he stumbled on to? What could be so important that Straik would kill to keep it concealed?

"Don't you have a bunch of schoolchildren here?" McCain asked.

"I haven't forgotten that, Desmond. I'm not an idiot – whatever you may think. My staff have special instructions." He turned off the computer. "I'm going to the control centre. Are you coming?"

"Absolutely."

It struck Alex that McCain sounded more amused than alarmed. But that seemed to be his character. He was still in control. He didn't believe that anyone could get in his way.

The two of them stood up. Alex heard the swish of cloth as Straik came out from behind his desk. The door opened, then closed.

Gratefully Alex uncurled himself from behind the picture. For a moment, he stood where he was, trying to collect his thoughts. He was probably safe while he was in Straik's office, at least for the time being. They were searching for him – but this was the one place they wouldn't look. Even so, he couldn't stay here for ever. With an intruder on the loose, the school visit might be cut short and the coach sent back to London. Alex had to be on it. He couldn't be left behind.

But it was worse than that. Alex realized that his only chance of survival was to find Mr Gilbert and the others. There had been nothing accidental about the death of the whistle-blower, and no matter what Blunt might have said, there really was something seriously unpleasant going on at Greenfields. Why else would the director be so keen to have any intruder killed? Alex had to rejoin his class. No guard was going to fire at him when there were witnesses. Once he was back with the others he would be safe – just one bored student among many.

He headed for the door, about to leave, when he noticed a glass phial resting on Straik's desk. It was actually a test tube, sealed at the top, with a muddy grey liquid inside. This had to be the sample he'd heard the two men talking about. Alex still had no idea what it contained but five hundred gallons of it were on their way somewhere abroad. He still had the Memory Stick in his pocket but on impulse he went over and took the test tube too. Smithers would analyse it. And that would be the end of it. The liquid would surely reveal whatever was being planned.

He opened the door, checked there was no one in sight, then stepped outside. He had decided to head back the way he had come. He had no idea where his friends were and he was furious that he had no way of communicating with them. Normally he would have called Tom or James, but all their mobiles had been left on the coach. What had the woman, Dr Bennett, told them? The laboratories first. Then the greenhouses and storage centres. Finally the lecture theatre. Surely they couldn't be too hard to find.

Alex closed the door behind him and sprinted back through the building, his feet making no sound on the carpet. The glass bridge was ahead of him as he rounded the second corner, but even as he approached it he heard men running towards him and spun back, ducking into a storage cupboard a second before they appeared. There were three guards and they were all armed. Alex watched them run across the bridge and disappear down another passageway. Above his head he noticed a light flashing red. He gritted his teeth. This had turned into a cat and mouse game with only one mouse but an awful lot of cats.

The bridge was now clear and he crossed it into what he had thought of as the administrative block. He went back down the stairs but immediately realized that he had forgotten which way he had come – left or right. The trouble was that every direction looked the same. He tossed a mental coin and set off, knowing almost at once that he was lost. He still had the postcard with its guidance system in his back pocket but knew it couldn't actually help him now. All that mattered was to keep moving and not be seen.

"Stop!"

The guard had stepped out of nowhere, blocking his way. He had a machine gun dangling around his neck and he was already fumbling with it, bringing it up and round. Alex turned and ran, keeping his head low, ducking left and right. He had taken no more than ten steps when a neon light fitting exploded, sparks and broken glass flying out. At the same time, the wall showered plaster on him. Alex hadn't heard much more than a whisper but he realized that the guard was firing in his direction, that bullets were streaming close to his head. The gun had some sort of silencer attached to it – and of course, that made sense. These were the special instructions that Straik had issued. They couldn't risk the sound of gunfire, not when they had forty schoolkids on the site.

Alex hurtled down another corridor past a series of open doors. He passed a laboratory, surprisingly old-fashioned and cluttered with plant specimens on the work desks and bottles of different chemicals on the shelves. A woman in a white coat holding a Petri dish in the palm of her hand looked up and momentarily caught his eye. Behind her a man was taking a tray of flowers out of what looked like an industrial fridge. Alex wondered if his class had been here, perhaps a few minutes before. He was tempted to stop and ask. He could still pretend to be lost. He decided against it. Double red alert. He had so far been spotted by one guard, and the fact that he was a boy in school uniform hadn't made any difference at all. These people wanted him dead.

He heard shouting behind him. Out of the corner of his eye he could see another light flashing. Alex hadn't even slowed down. He saw a glass door ahead of him and raced towards it, palms out-stretched, praying that it wasn't locked. He pushed. It opened. He almost fell through as another blast of bullets fanned silently through the air, punching dotted lines across the wall beside him.

But now he was outside and running. He saw the sleek white exterior of the lecture theatre on the other side of the lawn but he couldn't reach it. More guards in electric vehicles were racing towards him, moving surprisingly fast. Alex felt a surge of despair. How could he have allowed Alan Blunt and Mrs Jones to talk him into this? He'd promised Jack he wouldn't get into trouble again. More than that, he'd promised himself.

Anger spurred him on. He reached one of the greenhouses and plunged in through two sets of doors. It had been cold outside but here the climate was subtropical. Hundreds of plants were arranged on shelves, some just a few inches tall, some bending against the roof high above. The greenhouses were actually more like glass factories, divided into dozens of different rooms, each one joined to another by a maze of interlinking corridors. Huge silver pipes and watering systems snaked across the ceilings. There were banks of machinery controlling the lights, temperature and humidity in each different area, ensuring perfect conditions for all this artificial life. Alex had to be safe here. The guards might have followed him in but there were too many hiding places. Provided he kept moving, there was no way they would be able to find him.

The next attack took him completely by surprise. The guards were firing at him from outside the greenhouse, a cascade of bullets that never stopped. They were on all sides, determined to kill the intruder even if it meant destroying the entire complex. He couldn't hear any gunshots, but inside the greenhouse, the noise of bullets smashing glass was deafening. Windows exploded all around him. Alex threw himself to the ground as shards of glass, thousands and thousands of them, sprayed in all directions. Inches above his head the plants were shredded, the very air turning green as it was filled with tiny cuttings of stalk and leaf. Terracotta pots exploded, earth showering out. Brightly coloured flowers tore themselves apart.

And still the bullets kept coming, hammering into the machinery, ricocheting off the metal pipes. Alex could just make out the dark shapes of the guards surrounding the building, destroying it.

He wondered if they had all gone mad. Or was it that the work at Greenfields was finished and nothing mattered any more so long as nobody was able to escape with its secrets?

He scurried forward on his hands and knees, trying to lose himself further inside the greenhouse. He came to a brick wall with another bank of machinery and crawled behind it, putting a solid barrier between himself and the gunfire. Nobody could see him here. He pressed his fingers against his forehead. When he examined them, they were stained with blood. None of the bullets had hit him. It must have been the falling glass. He brushed it out of his hair and off his shoulders. What must he look like? What would Mr Gilbert say if he ever turned up?

He had to find the school tour. Surely they must have heard all the racket, even if the guards were using silencers! Another corridor led into the distance, this one with mirrored tiles instead of glass. He set off, still keeping low. Suddenly he was surrounded by brickwork. He had entered some sort of equipment room with spades and wheelbarrows. He could have been in an ordinary garden centre rather than a top secret research institute, and there were even bags of fertilizer – as if he needed reminding of the sort of trouble he was in.

Somehow he had to find a way back outside so that he could cut back to the lecture theatre. At least he seemed to have lost the guards with their machine guns. Perhaps they were scouring through the wreckage, looking for a body. Alex checked the test tube that he had stolen from Straik's office. He had been carrying it in his top jacket pocket and fortunately it was still in one piece. He slipped it back in and set off again, heading for a set of solid-looking doors and a sign:

STRICTLY NO ADMITTANCE.
AUTHORIZED PERSONNEL ONLY.

The doors were locked and hermetically sealed but there was another electronic reader set in the frame. Alex still had the library card. He had reprogrammed it to open Straik's door and presumably Straik had access to every zone in the bio centre. So...

He tried it. It worked. The doors opened. Alex went in, smiling as they clicked shut behind him. It might well be that the guards were unable to follow him in here. How many of them, after all, would be authorized?

He only realized where he was when it was too late. The shape of the building, the intense heat, the moisture running down the glass panes – all that should have warned him. But the doors had already locked themselves and, looking back, he saw that there was no card reader on this side, no way back out. He stood where he was, feeling the heavy air on his cheeks and forehead. His clothes were already sticking to him. Something was buzzing loudly over his head. Alex closed his eyes and swore.

He had walked into the Poison Dome.

He looked around him. He had once visited the glasshouses at Kew Gardens in London, and in some ways this was similar. The building itself was very elegant, the great dome supported by a delicate framework of metal supports. The whole area was about the size of a circular football pitch, if such a thing could exist. But unlike Kew Gardens, there was nothing beautiful or inviting about the plants that grew here.

Alex examined the tangle of green in front of him, the trunks and branches criss-crossing each other, struggling for space. They all looked evil, the leaves either razor sharp or covered in millions of hairs. He remembered what Dr Bennett had said. These were mutant organisms. Touching just one of them would bring pain and death. Fruits shaped like half-sized apples hung over his head and rich, fat berries clung to the bushes. But they were all garish colours, somehow unnatural, warning him to stay away. He could hear droning. There were insects in here and they were big ones, from the sound of them. Bees, or perhaps something worse.

Alex's skin was already crawling but he forced himself not to move. The information that the Bennett woman had given them when they arrived might even now save his life. He couldn't brush against any of the plants here. They had been altered so that they were a hundred times more deadly than nature intended. And there weren't just plants. She had talked about the interaction of poisons. And so there were spiders and snails and, of course, bees. Why had Straik created this place? Hell on earth. What was he trying to prove?

Alex couldn't go back. He remembered the shape of the dome, with the glass corridors branching out like points of the compass. He had come in as if from the south. Now he had to reach the other side and one of the other three exits. Two in and two out – that had to be how it worked. The lecture theatre had to be directly in front of him. So all he had to do was walk straight. And at least there was a path – a boardwalk made of wooden planks stretched out ahead. And nobody would be looking for him in here: nobody would be stupid enough to follow him in. He might be stung, bitten, poisoned or scared to death but at least he wouldn't be shot.

There was no other way.

Alex moved forward very slowly. Touch nothing. And make no sound. If he was going to get out of here alive, he would have to take it literally one step at a time. Dr Bennett had mentioned snakes – the taipan. Alex knew it to be the most venomous land snake in the world, fifty times more toxic than the cobra. But it was also nervous. Like most animals, it wouldn't attack a human unless it was threatened. So provided he didn't brush against anything, touch anything, step on anything or alarm anything, he might come out of this all right. One step at a time.

He followed the boardwalk. The plants were horribly close to him. The nearest was an oversized thistle that seemed to be straining to break free and attack him, like an angry dog. Then came a squat, ugly tree corkscrewing out of the earth with green scalpel blades instead of leaves. The smell of sulphur rose in his nostrils. The path was crossing a bubbling pool. A creeper hung in front of him. He resisted the urge to brush it aside and bent low, contorting himself to avoid contact with it.

He was still forcing himself to move with extreme care. If he made one miscalculation, even so much as an inch, he might dislodge something and he knew that it could finish him. Everything here was his enemy. Something buzzed close to his head and he jerked round, unable to control himself. His sleeve brushed against a jagged-edged nettle but fortunately the material protected him from the bristling hairs – or neurotransmitters as Bennett had called them. Alex shrank into his jacket, pulling it around him. Every fibre of his being was concentrated on the way ahead.

Something slithered onto his foot.

Alex stopped. He was aware that he was no longer breathing. It was as if someone had drawn a wire tight around his throat. Trying not to panic, he looked down. He could already tell from the weight that this wasn't a snake. It was too small, too light. And it hadn't slithered; it had crawled. He couldn't see it at first and thought that perhaps, after all, he had imagined it.

He hadn't. It was almost worse than a snake. A glistening centipede, at least fifteen centimetres long, had settled on the top of his trainer. The creature could have been drawn by a demonic child: red head, black body, bright yellow legs that seemed to be writhing with anticipation. Alex knew what it was. He had seen something exactly the same once on television. How had the presenter described it? The red-headed centipede. Also known as the giant desert centipede. Unusually aggressive and extremely fast...

And this one had decided to stretch itself out on his Nike trainer. What if it decided to explore a little further, over his ankle and up his trouser leg, for example? Alex was standing as still as a statue. Without making any sound, he was screaming at the insect. *Go away! Go and explore a sulphur pit. Make friends with a marbled cone snail. But leave me alone!* Alex could see its antennae twitching as it made up its mind. He was aware of his bare flesh just inches away, above his sock. He couldn't bear it any more. He suddenly lashed out, using every muscle in his leg as he kicked at the air. He thought the centipede would cling on. It might get tangled in his laces. He was certain he was going to feel its bite. But when he looked down again, it was no longer there. He had managed to shake it free.

He needed a weapon ... anything to protect himself from whatever might come next. Why couldn't Smithers have built a flame-thrower into his Simpsons pencil case? Alex reached into his backpack once again. He had the two gel pens but the last thing he wanted to do in here was set off an explosion – it would advertise his presence to every living thing. That just left the pencil sharpener with the diamond-edged blade. He took it out and unfolded it three times, the plastic swivelling on concealed hinges. He was left with something that looked like a tiny axe or meat cleaver, barely three centimetres long. It might be useful for cutting through wire or even glass but it wouldn't be much good for anything else. Even so, Alex felt a little more confident, having it in his hand.

Where was the exit? The guards would still be looking for him and Alex knew he had to get a move on and find his way out of there as quickly as possible. But even so he didn't dare hurry. He took another step and his foot came down on a little cluster of mushrooms, crushing them. Pale yellow liquid, like pus, oozed out from beneath his sole. A moth fluttered briefly in front of him. It was hard to believe that he was in an artificially created environment, a greenhouse, and not lost in the jungle.

The pathway took him past a pool of boiling

mud, bubbles rising slowly and heavily to the surface. A tall, twisted tree with lianas trailing from its branches grew beside it. Alex looked up, then ducked back as a globule of milky white syrup splashed down, oozing out of the bark. It missed his face by millimetres and he knew that if it had hit his eyes he might well have been blinded.

The path curved round and Alex found himself in a slight clearing with a tiny river in front of him and a Japanese-style bridge. The pretty, hump-back structure looked ridiculous in this artificial jungle. Who could possibly want to come for a walk here among so much death? He could no longer see the glass windows that made up the outer walls of the Poison Dome and guessed that he must be at its very heart. Well, at least if he was halfway in, that meant he was also halfway out. Something buzzed past his head and he caught sight of a giant wasp, legs trailing, barely able to stay in the air as it struggled against its own weight. Alex waited until it had gone. He had to get out of here – now.

He stepped onto the bridge, still moving slowly. Silver water flowed beneath, but as Alex reached the middle it suddenly erupted in a frenzy. Some sort of fish life had detected his presence. Piranha – or something worse. Alex was beginning to wonder if the dome had really been built as a scientific experiment or if it wasn't just some huge toy, the fantasy of a sick mind. Straik might pretend to be studying poisons. In fact he seemed more interested in death.

He continued over and stepped off the other side of the bridge. That was when the man appeared.

It was a guard – or a gardener – dressed in a white protective suit that began at his ankles and continued all the way to his neck. His feet were weighed down by heavy-duty wellington boots and he was wearing gloves that doubled the size of his hands. His head was completely enclosed in the sort of helmet that a bee-keeper might wear, except that instead of a net, his face was covered by a plastic sheet. Alex was aware of two hostile eyes glaring at him and a mouth curled in a sneering smile. He was holding a machete. He was pointing it directly at Alex.

Alex stopped with the bridge behind him. "Hi," he said. "Are you the park attendant? Because if so, maybe you could show me the way out."

The man tightened his grip on the weapon. Alex knew what was about to happen and he was ready for it. As the machete swung through the air, the blade aiming for his neck, he dropped down, then threw himself forward, ducking underneath the man's arm. For just a second, Alex was behind him and he slashed upwards with his own, miniature blade.

The man didn't even feel it. He spun round and brought both his hands plunging down, using the handle of the machete as a club. It smashed into

Alex's shoulder and the pain ricocheted along his bones and muscles, all the way to his wrist. His hand fell open and the little knife dropped away.

The man came at him again, this time swinging the blade to force Alex away from him. Alex took one step back, then another. The machete sliced the air in front of him and at once he lashed out, his fist plunging into the man's abdomen. The protective suit absorbed much of the damage; Alex felt the hardened material take the skin off his knuckles. But the man had been winded and fell back. Alex lashed out with his foot, catching the man on his arm. The machete spun away and landed, point down, in a bed of earth.

The man charged straight at him, almost knocking Alex off his feet. Alex was terrified he was going to step on a nettle or fall backwards into one of the flower beds. The plants growing near the river were like porcupines, with huge spikes and bulging, overripe berries that could have been their disease-ridden eyes. For a moment, Alex lost his balance and he lifted an arm to steady himself. He touched a spider's web hanging from a branch. He hadn't even seen it but he felt it at once. A single strand of the web had wrapped itself across the flesh on the back of his hand. It burned into him like acid. Alex cried out. Behind his plastic mask, the man laughed.

The man reached for the machete, took hold of it again, and suddenly he was coming at Alex, chopping the air with a series of vicious blows. Alex looked left, right, then behind him. He had almost backed into another tree. The bark looked innocent enough but he didn't dare touch it. It might contain ricin or botulin or any other toxin that Bennett had forgotten to mention. How far away was it? Alex judged the distance carefully, then stood his ground. The man stumbled towards him. The heavy clothes he was wearing were slowing him down. The blade slashed towards his neck.

At the very last second, Alex ducked and, just as he had hoped, he heard the clunk as the metal bit into the tree. The man pulled at it but it was stuck fast. And that was when Alex twisted round and slammed his foot into the man's chest with all his strength.

The man was thrown backwards, slipped and fell on his back, landing in one of the beds of porcupine flowers. His suit should have protected him. But he hadn't realized what Alex had done. Before he had lost it, he had used the little pencil sharpener knife to make a slit in the fabric that ran all the way from the man's waist to the back of his neck. There was a gap which had allowed the spikes to penetrate. The man screamed. Behind the mask his eyes bulged and his entire body began to jerk, his legs kicking helplessly. Alex watched in horror as grey foam began to pour from his mouth. Then suddenly his arms shot out and he lay still.

Alex didn't stay a moment longer than he had to.

The noise of the fight would have disturbed whatever else was living in this nightmare place. If there were any other men working inside the dome, they would surely be on their way to investigate. He'd had enough. Still forcing himself not to panic, he pressed forward and was rewarded a few minutes later with the sight of another door. This one opened from the inside. Alex felt a great wave of relief as he swiped the card and passed through. The door swung shut. He had left the Poison Dome behind.

He examined the back of his hand. The web had left a white line running from one side to the other and the whole thing was swelling up. Well, he just had to be grateful that he hadn't actually met the spider. He rubbed the wound but that made it feel worse. He would have to try to ignore it until he could get medical help.

Where was he? The exit had led him into another greenhouse, this one filled with troughs of what looked like wheat. He wasn't safe yet, but at least he was away from the shooting. Maybe the guards thought he was already dead.

He found another door and made his way outside again. In the distance he could hear shouting, and two electric vehicles shot past, carrying more guards towards the noise. The lecture theatre – white and modern – was right in front of him. Alex didn't know if the cameras were still jammed but nor did he care any more. He was tired. His hand was hurting. There was still broken glass in his hair and he knew there must be cuts on his forehead and face. So much for double geography. The next time Mr Gilbert suggested a school trip, he would say he was busy.

He staggered forward, heading for the lecture theatre. Maybe the rest of his class were already inside. He would slip in without being noticed and join them. He could see himself dozing off during whatever talk was going on.

Then the doors opened. Two guards stepped out. They saw Alex at the same moment that he saw them.

It wasn't over yet.

Alex turned and ran.

EXIT STRATEGY

Tom Harris was getting worried.

Almost an hour had passed since Alex had slipped away, disappearing into a toilet like some superhero about to change into costume and save the world. Only it wasn't like that. Tom knew that Alex didn't really want to work for MI6. He had said as much when the two of them were together in Italy. So why had Alex chosen to go back to it all – and what could be so big a deal about a research centre that seemed to be spending most of its time designing the perfect tomato?

Once Alex had gone, the rest of the school party had been taken to one of the laboratories, where an earnest young scientist with a neatly trimmed beard had shown them the chemical process that put new DNA into a single plant cell. Tom had barely listened. He didn't find it easy to concentrate at the best of times; and anyway, he had already decided to drop geography and science after GCSE. He would drop school too, if he could.

What was the point? His parents had recently divorced. His father was living on his own in a bedsit in south London; his mother had started smoking again. They were both overachievers with a pile of A levels between them but what good had it done them?

As they moved from one laboratory to the next, Tom passed a window and found himself looking for Alex. There was nobody in sight. But during the next demonstration – something to do with plants freeze-dried in liquid nitrogen – he noticed a red light begin to blink discreetly in the corner of the room. Dr Bennett noticed it too. Tom saw her expression change, a look of concern creeping into her eyes. It was an alarm. He was sure of it.

And then, in the distance, he heard something. The sound of breaking glass – a lot of it. Everyone else was busy listening and taking notes. But Tom knew what it meant. Alex was on the run. Part of him was tempted to sneak out and join him.

It was lucky he didn't. As soon as the demonstration ended, Dr Bennett insisted on a roll call to check that everyone was there, and – as promised – Tom stood in for Alex, doing a reasonable imitation of his voice.

"Rider?"

"Here, sir."

Only James Hale, standing next to him, saw what was happening, and he glanced at him quizzically. Tom shrugged but gave nothing away.

And now they were in some workshop, two floors down, underground. Tom wondered if they had been brought here on purpose, to stop them hearing or seeing anything of what might be going on outside. Another scientist – this one young and Chinese – had arrived to show them the famous gene gun, developed, they were told, by the director of Greenfields. It was a rather ordinary-looking piece of equipment that resembled a small metal safe with a glass door. Nonetheless, this was at the heart of GM technology, the Chinese woman said. She opened the door and placed a round Petri dish inside.

"The gene gun is a very effective way to deliver new DNA into a plant," she explained. "This is done by a system known as biolistic particle delivery..."

As she continued, Tom noticed a guard, dressed in combat gear, steal into the room. He approached Dr Bennett and whispered urgently into her ear. Tom wasn't surprised when, a moment later, she stepped forward, interrupting the talk.

"I am very sorry, boys and girls," she exclaimed. "I am afraid we are going to have to end your visit to Greenfields. An emergency situation has arisen and you must return to your coach at once."

"Wait a minute..." Mr Gilbert began. His face was indignant. They had driven a long way to visit the centre and they had been here for less than an hour.

"There will be no argument," Dr Bennett snapped. "We will take the back staircase. Your driver has been instructed to meet you around the side of the building."

James moved closer to Tom. "This is about Alex, isn't it?" he muttered.

"Alex is standing right next to me," Tom replied.

James nodded slowly. "Yeah. Sure."

The class was already filing out and the two of them followed behind.

The guards had seen him. If they had been carrying Uzis, he would have been dead already. One of them was coming after him, catching up fast. The other had stopped to talk into his radio, alerting the others.

Alex was getting tired. He was in pain. As he reluctantly ran back towards the centre of the complex, he was aware of just two things. He had to drop out of sight. And – if it wasn't too late already – he had to find his way back to his friends. Safety in numbers. So long as he was part of Brookland School, inside the group, there was nothing that Straik or anybody else could do.

But where were they? There was no coach, no sign of anyone and definitely no other way out of the Greenfields Bio Centre. The fence was too high and he could see the gate, over on his right, firmly closed. The Poison Dome, which he'd managed to break out of just a few minutes ago, was now on his left. Well, one thing was certain. He wasn't going back in there.

Alex heard a whine and saw an electric car with three more guards speeding across the lawn towards him. He had the man with the radio to thank for that. The door of one of the brick buildings opened and more guards poured out. These ones were armed. For just a moment, Alex was tempted to hand himself over. He could still pretend he had lagged behind his class and got lost. What could they do?

Then he remembered the test tube in his top pocket. If they found it, they would know he had been into Straik's office. And he had left a dead man in the Poison Dome. Alex put the thought out of his mind. It was obvious what they could – and would – do if they got hold of him, and right now they were just seconds away. He had to move – and fast.

Ahead of him a wide tarmac driveway ran straight between what looked like two rows of factories. This was the only way with no guards, and it might lead him back to the block where the school visit had begun. A single white-coated technician stood in his way, but he was busy funnelling a steaming liquid from a steel cylinder into a heavily insulated container. Liquid nitrogen. It had to be. Alex had seen the same stuff – though in smaller quantities – at Brookland. And what were its properties? In physics class ... yes ... there was something he had been told.

The electric car was getting nearer. The guards

who were on foot had brought round their machine guns, preparing to fire. A single burst of silent bullets and he would be torn to shreds. Alex was already sprinting down the driveway. He barged into the technician and snatched the container and – in a single movement – spun round and hurled it behind him. The container hit the tarmac and the liquid nitrogen splashed out, immediately forming itself into marbles that bounced along the hard surface. At the same time, it began to evaporate, and suddenly there was a wall of white mist between Alex and his pursuers as the liquid reacted to the higher temperature and turned back into gas. The technician was shouting but Alex ignored him. It was time to disappear.

He raced over to the nearest door, using the library card to swipe his way in. With luck the guards would be unaware that he could open any lock and they would keep running. His eyes were watering and he could feel the nitrogen gas at the back of his throat. If he had thrown the liquid in a closed room, he would have killed himself, suffocating as the oxygen was swallowed up. He found himself in a bare industrial building with breeze-block walls and cement floors and ceilings. A series of furnaces, cold and silent, stood in front of him, none of them operating. A metal staircase twisted upwards. Alex was disappointed. He had hoped the building might offer more. Somewhere to hide. Some way of escape. Something. He took the stairs. He would go up to the roof. There was a communications system built into the pocket calculator that Smithers had given him. He would use it to call MI6. Hopefully they would respond before it was too late.

The staircase rose six floors. At the top he came to an old-fashioned door with a push bar. Even as he reached it, Alex heard the main door of the building crash open beneath him and knew that the guards had worked out where he had gone. He had to fight back a growing sense of hopelessness. There really didn't seem to be any way out of this mess. So what now? A fire escape. He would make his way back down again and find somewhere else to hide.

There was no fire escape.

Alex had gone hurtling through the door, which had slammed shut behind him. He was on a wide, flat roof covered with asphalt. A silver chimney rose about fifteen metres into the air, presumably to carry smoke from the furnaces that Alex had seen below. There were two air conditioning units and a water tank. But that was all. The roof had a low brick wall running all the way round the edge. The nearest building was ten metres away – too far to jump. Alex was six storeys up and he couldn't climb down. He was trapped.

He could imagine the guards already mounting the stairs, making their way towards him. Somehow he had to keep them at bay. There were a few pieces of scaffolding left over from building work lying on the ground beside the water tank. He snatched two of them up, ran back to the door and wedged them against the handle, slanting them into the ground. That would at least buy him a bit of time.

But he was still a sitting target. In a way, he had played right into their hands. They could leave him here all night and then pick him off at their leisure. Where were his friends? Alex ran back to the edge of the roof, skidding to a halt beside the parapet. And finally he saw them.

The coach was parked at the far end of the main driveway. The school visit must have ended early as it was already loading up. Even as he watched, he saw Tom Harris and James Hale climb on board, deep in conversation. He heard a couple of girls laughing. It seemed incredible that they could be unaware of what had been going on at Greenfields while they were being shown around. And there were Mr Gilbert and Miss Barry. Alex tried to catch their attention, tried to call out to them, but they were too far away and his voice was hoarse from the nitrogen. He could only watch in despair as the door hissed shut, sealing his friends inside.

He twisted round and looked the other way. Straik was determined to get rid of the school party as quickly as possible. The gate was already sliding open. The best Alex could hope for was one last roll call, perhaps delaying their departure by another few minutes. Then they would be gone.

He would be stuck here, on his own.

Already he was weighing up the angles. The coach would pass directly underneath him. Could he jump? No. He was far too high up. Even assuming he timed it properly and actually landed on the roof, he would break his arms, his legs and quite possibly his neck. Could he wave at the driver, somehow attracting his attention? Impossible. He wouldn't be seen at this height.

He heard the sound of fists pounding against metal. The guards had followed him up. A single door was all that was keeping them back, wedged shut by two pieces of scaffolding. Desperately Alex made a circuit of the roof. There were no ladders, no ropes, nothing. The coach engine had started. It was about thirty metres away at the end of the drive. At the other end, the gate was open with Salisbury Plain in clear view.

A cascade of machine-gun fire sent Alex diving for cover. The noise was deafening and very near. But they weren't shooting at him. One of the guards at the top of the stairs had opened up, spraying the door with bullets. Alex saw the metal bulging and blistering as it was hammered. Much more of this and it would be blown off its hinges.

The chimney...

Alex was already up and running as the idea took shape in his mind. The chimney was modern and silver; and as far as he could see, its outer casing was fairly thin. He didn't have time to work out the measurements but surely if it was horizontal, it might reach across to the next rooftop. He could use it as a bridge. And he had the means to bring it down.

Another burst of machine-gun fire. The door shivered in its frame. Feverishly Alex reached into his backpack and took out the red gel ink pen that Smithers had given him. Red was more powerful. It would do more damage. That was what Smithers had said. He glanced back at the door. It was being smashed out of shape, white smoke trickling through the cracks around the side. How much longer would it hold? Alex had the pen in his hand. He twisted the cap once – the shortest fuse – then pulled the little plunger up to activate it. He felt it click and slammed the pen against the base of the chimney, diving for cover behind one of the air conditioning units. The pen stayed in place, held magnetically.

The coach still hadn't moved. The guards were hammering at the door now, using the stocks of their guns to finish the job. There was a brief pause and then an explosion, louder than anything that had gone before. Surely the coach driver would hear it. He would have to stop and find out what was going on! Alex was crouching with his hands over his ears. He felt the blast sear across his forearms and the top of his head and looked up just in time to see the chimney topple like a felled tree, the metal close to the base grinding in protest as it was torn apart.

It crashed down; but even as it fell, Alex saw that his plan hadn't worked. The chimney was too short to reach the building opposite. It had fallen sideways, smashing into the low wall, which had acted as a fulcrum, tearing the metal skin a second time. The chimney ended up tilting down towards the main driveway. What had been its top end was now about ten metres above the road.

The guards fired again and this time the door couldn't take any more. It was blown out of the frame, the scaffolding falling away. Half a dozen men rushed out onto the roof.

The coach had started. It was picking up speed, roaring towards the gate as if desperate to get out of there. In a few seconds, it would pass directly beneath Alex.

One of the guards saw him and shouted. Alex stood where he was. The guard took aim. As the coach drew closer, Alex sprinted towards the edge, as if determined to throw himself off the side of the building. The guard fired. Bullets skidded across the roof, ripping up the asphalt.

The chimney had been sliced open by the edge of the wall and had almost broken in half. If it had, it would have fallen down to the road, blocking the coach's path. But it was being held in place by a small section of the metal skin resting on the wall and acting like a hinge. Alex dived head first into the opening. The chimney was just big enough for him with his backpack still strapped to his shoulders. It was like being inside a chute at a swimming pool. The round, shiny surface offered no resistance and Alex shot down.

In the end it was all about timing. If he had hit the road, he would have died. If he had started too soon, he might have missed the coach or been run over by it. But Alex had got it exactly right. He shot out of what had once been the top of the chimney at the very moment the coach passed beneath him. For a brief second, he saw the roof, a grey blur beneath him. He only had about three metres to fall but he knew that the impact was going to be painful.

It was worse than he imagined. The breath was smashed out of him. He was sure he had broken several ribs. He was rolling, spinning towards the edge, and even now he wondered if he had succeeded. If he fell off, he would be left behind and it would all have been for nothing.

Alex stretched out his arms and legs, spread-eagling himself, doing everything he could to stay in contact with the roof. He wondered why the driver hadn't stopped, but perhaps he hadn't heard anything above the noise of the engine.

The coach reached the security gate and passed through without slowing down. The guards must have seen what had happened but there was nothing they could do. They couldn't fire on a group of schoolkids. And anyway, the coach was already outside the complex, accelerating across Salisbury Plain.

Alex stayed where he was, allowing the cold air to wash over him. He was exhausted. Something felt wet against his chest and for a horrible moment he thought he had been shot. But it wasn't blood. The test tube had smashed. Smithers would just have to use whatever liquid he could separate from the fibre of Alex's jacket. Surely there would be enough of it to analyse.

He couldn't travel all the way back to London on the coach roof.

Just before they reached the main road, Alex crawled over to the edge and lowered the top half of his body so that he was hanging upside down outside the window where he had been sitting. He was lucky. Tom Harris saw him, his eyes widening in disbelief. Alex made a sign with one hand. Tom nodded.

About one minute later, the coach stopped and Tom got out. Alex watched him rush behind a tree and pretend to be sick. He used the opportunity to slide to the edge and lower himself down. He limped over and joined his friend.

"Alex!" Tom looked horrified. "What happened to you?"

"Things didn't quite go as planned."

Alex followed Tom back to the coach. The two of them had to pass Mr Gilbert, who was sitting at the front. The geography teacher was even more shocked than Tom. He had only seen one boy leave the coach. So how was it possible for two of them to be returning?

"Rider!" he gasped. "What are you doing out of the coach? What happened to you?"

Alex didn't know what to say. He could only imagine what he must look like.

Tom came to his rescue. "He fell out of the window, sir. It's lucky we stopped."

"I don't believe a word of it! The windows don't even open..."

"It was the back door."

"Well..." The geography teacher was out of his depth. He just wanted to get back to London. "You'll see the headmaster first thing tomorrow morning," he snapped. "Now get back to your seat."

Alex and Tom continued to the back of the coach past forty staring faces. Everyone would be talking about this at school the next day – but that was Alex Rider. Somehow, any strange behaviour was to be expected. As for Alex, he still had the Memory Stick with its precious download, and the sample from the test tube was an added bonus. He had completed his part of the bargain and had come out of it more or less in one piece. And as he hadn't heard a word from Harry Bulman, he assumed that MI6 had kept their promise too.

He sank down into his seat, reflecting that his part in all this was over. He might never find out what McCain and Straik had been planning – but what did it really matter? It was none of his business and he was just glad that he would never see either of them again.

Desmond McCain was back in Straik's office and for once it was clear that he had lost his composure. He was sitting, legs crossed, one hand clenching and unclenching on his knee, and the crack that divided the two halves of his head seemed to have somehow widened as the damaged muscles in his jaw attempted to chew over what had happened. Even the silver crucifix earring had lost its shine.

"This intruder must have been in here, in the room, when we were talking," he growled.

"That's right, Desmond." Behind his desk Leonard Straik licked his lips. He was blinking repeatedly.

"But where?" McCain's grey eyes slid slowly round the office. "Behind the picture!"

"I wouldn't have thought there was room."

"Where else?" McCain paused, deep in thought. "What did he hear?"

"I don't think he could have heard anything very much, Desmond," Straik faltered. "We were only in here a couple of minutes. It's just lucky I noticed the Memory Stick."

"He will have copied the contents of your computer."

"All the files are encrypted. And even if he manages to break into them, they won't give much away."

"What about the test tube?"

"I don't think that matters either. Of course, it's bad news. He'll have the sample analysed, but it won't tell him very much. I don't think anyone will be able to guess its significance."

"You don't *think*." McCain's fist came pounding down on the side of his chair. Straik heard a dull crack as the arm of the chair broke in two. "Five years' work and hundreds of thousands of pounds! We're just a few days away from Poison Dawn and you don't *think* we've been compromised! Obviously this intruder came in here on the back of your blasted school visit. Why did you allow it in the first place?"

"We had no choice. We only rent this facility: the land and the buildings. We have to do what the government tells us, and they insisted we had a couple of schools in. They said we had to educate children about GM technology."

"So it was a government agent who broke in?"

"I don't know, Desmond." Straik took out a handkerchief and wiped his brow. "But I don't think it was a coincidence that the cameras packed in when they did."

"Did any of the guards see the intruder?"

"Quite a few of them did. And they're insisting it was a boy – a teenager."

"If it was a child, then the whole thing could have been ... I don't know ... a prank!"

"He blew up a chimney on the recycling unit.

And he killed a guard in the Poison Dome."

"Then who was he? What was he doing here?"

There was a knock at the door and Myra Bennett came in carrying a file, her white coat flapping behind her. There was something military about the way she walked, like a soldier delivering news of a defeat. "I have the photographs," she announced.

"I thought you said the cameras weren't working," McCain said.

"They were jammed for about forty minutes." Straik took the file. "But they were working when the coach arrived and I thought it might be worth our while examining who exactly came here today."

Desmond McCain went over to the desk. The file that Bennett had brought contained a dozen photographs, taken by the camera closest to the gate. They were grainy, in black and white, but Mr Gilbert and Miss Barry were clear enough, stepping down from the coach with the rest of the school group following behind. Straik and Bennett were both leaning forward, studying the pictures, when McCain suddenly stabbed down with his finger.

"Him!"

"Who is it, Desmond?" Straik asked.

"Don't you recognize him, you idiot? I don't believe it! It's impossible. But there's no doubt about it. It's the boy from Scotland."

"What boy?" Then Straik realized. "The boy from the card game."

"Alex Rider." McCain uttered the name with

undisguised hatred. "That was what he called himself."

"I heard that name during the roll call," Dr Bennett muttered. "But he never left the group."

"Somebody must have answered for him," McCain said. His finger was still pressing down on Alex, as if he could squash him like a bug. "It's definitely the same boy. This is the second time he's crossed my path."

Myra Bennett stared at the picture in dismay. "I thought we'd dealt with him, Desmond. He was the boy in the car with the journalist..."

"Evidently we failed." McCain twisted away. "How is this possible? We always thought someone might take an interest in us after that business with Masters, the so-called informer. But a child barely out of short trousers? Who is this Alex Rider? Why is he interested in us?"

"We can find out," Straik muttered.

McCain nodded. "We have contacts. We need to use them. It doesn't matter how much it costs. Someone must know something about this boy; he clearly wasn't working alone." McCain took one last look at the photograph. With an effort he broke free. "We'll locate him and we'll bring him back here."

"And then?"

"And then we'll find out what he knows."

FEELING THE HEAT

Henry Bray had been the headmaster at Brookland for seven years and assistant head at another comprehensive for five years before that. He didn't often find himself lost for words, but right now that was exactly how he felt. Once again he examined the boy in front of him while he tried to work out how to proceed.

Alex Rider was different from all the other pupils at Brookland. He knew that. The unfortunate death of his uncle in a car accident almost a year ago had clearly sent him off the rails. That was understandable. But Alex had barely been in school since then, missing week after week because of so many different illnesses that in the end – Mr Bray hadn't told anyone he'd done this – he had actually written to the doctor, suspecting that something might be going on. He had received a short note back. Alex had viral problems; his health was very delicate. The doctor – his name was Blunt – wouldn't be at all surprised if Alex had to miss a lot more school in the future.

Alex didn't look ill now. He looked as if he had been in a fist fight. There were a number of small cuts on his forehead and the side of his cheek and, from the way he was standing, Mr Bray guessed he had hurt his shoulder. He was here because of a report sent in by his geography teacher, Mr Gilbert. But Alex didn't give any sign of being ashamed or nervous about what might follow. He just seemed angry.

Mr Bray sighed. "Alex. You made a very good start in Year Nine. All your reports said the same. And I am well aware of your personal circumstances. I imagine you were very close to your uncle."

"Yes, sir."

"It doesn't help that you've had a lot of time off school ... all these illnesses. Obviously I've made allowances for you. But this business yesterday – frankly I'm appalled. As I understand it, the coach had an emergency door which you opened and you managed to fall out. Is that correct?"

"Yes, sir."

"I'm amazed you could be so irresponsible. You could have seriously hurt yourself. And there were other young people on the coach too. Didn't you stop to think that you might cause an accident? I can't imagine why you would do such a stupid thing." Mr Bray took off his glasses and laid them on his desk. It was something he always did when he was about to pronounce sentence. "I hate the idea of your missing any more lessons but I'm afraid I am going to have to make an example of you. I'm giving you one day's exclusion from school. You will go home straight away; I've written a note for you to take with you."

Half an hour later, Alex crossed the schoolyard with a sense of injustice burning inside him. He had survived poisonous plants and insects, hand-to-hand combat and machine-gun fire. He had downloaded the contents of Straik's computer and stolen a sample of whatever he was brewing at Greenfields. Jack would already have delivered them to the MI6 offices in Liverpool Street. And what was his reward? To be treated like a naughty schoolboy and sent home with a note.

The first lesson had already begun and nobody noticed Alex as he made his way out of the gates and down the road. As he walked, he found himself going over the events of the day before. The appearance of Desmond McCain had completely thrown him. What was the head of an international charity doing in a GM research centre in Wiltshire? He was planning something with Leonard Straik. That much was clear. The two of them had talked about shipping five hundred gallons of liquid – and they had said that it was alive. But what was it and what was it for? The more Alex thought about it, the less sense it all made.

This was all about McCain. He had been to prison once in his life and it seemed he hadn't changed his spots. Alex was certain now – not that he had ever really doubted it – that his near death in Scotland, along with Sabina and her father, had been no accident. McCain had tried to kill them. He was prepared to do anything to protect himself. MI6 had wanted to investigate Leonard Straik because he might be a security risk. In fact it was McCain who was using Greenfields – and it was for something much bigger than anyone suspected.

And then Alex remembered something he had overheard while he was in Straik's office. McCain was going to send the Bennett woman somewhere the following day – today. A place called Elm's Cross. The name rang a faint bell. Alex continued walking until he arrived at an Internet café not far from Brompton Cemetery. The place served disgusting coffee but it only charged a pound for half an hour on one of its ancient computers. At least it had broadband.

Alex paid and chose a computer at the very back, away from the window. The owner glanced at him briefly, then returned to a crumpled copy of *The Sun*. Alex googled Elm's Cross and waited for the page to come up on the screen. The result was disappointing. There was a packaging company with that name in Warminster, a restaurant in Bradford and a film studio in west London that had apparently closed down last year. None of them could possibly be connected. Except...

What about the shooting?

Straik to McCain. When Alex had heard them, he'd automatically assumed that they were talking about guns. But suppose they had actually meant shooting *film*? Alex looked for more information about the studio. It was on the other side of Hayes, not far from Heathrow Airport. According to an old news report, a raft of British comedies had been shot there back in the fifties, but the increasing noise of aircraft, along with the decline in British film production, had combined to put it out of business. There was talk of the land being developed: affordable housing and more office space. The last film that had been shot there was an advertisement for the shopping chain Woolworths. It seemed appropriate. A few weeks later, Woolworths had gone bust too.

Alex had made his decision. Jack wouldn't be expecting him, and even if the school had contacted her, she wouldn't be too worried if he took his time turning up. He would have to be careful. He was still in school uniform and that would certainly attract attention, being out on the street in the middle of the day – but he doubted there would be many policemen around where he was going.

He caught the Tube from Fulham Broadway and a taxi the rest of the way. Elm's Cross was in a strange derelict area that had somehow been forgotten by the housing estates, industrial zones and soulless retail parks that surrounded it. As Alex paid the taxi driver, there was a sudden roar and he looked up to see the underbelly of a 747 as it lurched out of the sky towards the main runway of Heathrow. In the distance he could make out the M4 motorway, raised up on concrete spurs, injecting London with a never-ending stream of cars and trucks.

The driver looked at him suspiciously. "Shouldn't you be in school?" he asked.

Alex tipped him generously. "I'm on a school project," he replied. "We're writing about air pollution."

The lie had come easily. Alex could actually taste the exhaust fumes in the air and he couldn't imagine what it would be like to live with it day in, day out. He wondered what he was doing. Less than twenty-four hours ago he had been congratulating himself on a mission accomplished. MI6 had what they wanted. So why was he here, quite possibly putting his head back in the noose?

He was angry. But that wasn't the whole reason. Alex knew it was more than that. He couldn't deny it any longer. There was a part of him that needed to investigate, to uncover the answers. That part had been deliberately cultivated by MI6 and his uncle. Using him wasn't enough. They had turned him into someone who *wanted* to be used.

Alex hoisted his backpack onto his good shoulder and set off. He had given the taxi driver an address about a quarter of a mile from his true destination, just in case he took it upon himself to call the authorities and warn them about a boy bunking off school. He passed through an empty area with a wide expanse of dirty, litter-strewn grass on one side and what looked like a reservoir on the other. A wire fence stretched out ahead of him. Now he had to be careful. McCain had said Bennett was coming here today. If she happened to drive past, Alex would stick out like a sore thumb and this time there were no witnesses.

ELM'S CROSS STUDIOS

PRIVATE

WARNING: 24-HOUR SURVEILLANCE

The sign hung on the fence outside the main gate but Alex wasn't sure he believed it. How could there be round-the-clock surveillance when there were no cameras? There were no guards in sight either. The paint on the sign had faded, with rust speckling through. And the gate itself was open, inviting him in.

Alex could see a tarmac road leading down to a cluster of buildings, most of them low-rise with long, narrow windows running horizontally just beneath the roof. They might once have been surrounded by lawns but the site had become overgrown with long grass and shrubs running rampant. In the middle of it all, there was a row of three hangars, big enough to house planes ... although they would long ago have ceased to fly. The whole place looked sad and abandoned.

He walked in. If any security men appeared, he would just have to bluff it out. With a bit of luck, nobody here would know what had happened the day before. And although the guards at Greenfields had been armed, it was very unlikely that they would be toting guns right next to a major international airport.

Nobody stopped him. There were definitely no cameras. Alex passed a couple of skips, filled to overflowing. A lot of the contents were household rubbish – old cartons and broken pieces of furniture. But there were also oddities: a plastic cactus, a swordfish, a scaled-down replica of the Statue of Liberty missing the hand holding the torch. He thought he saw a car parked on the other side of some shrubs and was about to duck out of sight, when he realized it was a black BMW saloon, left over from the forties, burnt out and resting on bricks instead of tyres. He was surrounded by the remnants of old films that had been made, seen and forgotten. Elm's Cross had once been a dream factory but the machinery had long since shut down.

He came to the first of the hangars, the words

STUDIO A stencilled in yellow letters on the corru-
gated iron wall. The huge sliding doors were open
but there was nothing inside apart from a puddle of
oily water and a pile of broken wood. Cables hung
down from the ceiling. A pigeon cooed somewhere
in the rafters, the sound amplified by the empty
space. The second hangar was the same. Alex was
beginning to think he was wasting his time. There
was nobody here. And what would someone like
Desmond McCain want with an abandoned film
studio anyway? He must have been referring to a
different Elm's Cross after all.

Alex looked at his watch. Quarter past eleven.
Jack would be on her way home. He took out his
mobile phone, thinking he would ring her. There
was no signal.

"It's ready, Doctor..."

"Then I'll leave you to it."

Alex heard the voices and crouched behind a
low brick wall – in fact made out of painted card-
board and wood, another old piece of film scenery.
He had already recognized the voice of Dr Myra
Bennett; and a moment later, there she was, walking out of the third studio, dressed in a raincoat
which she had tied tightly around her waist. There
were two men with her. Alex looked around for
anyone else but it seemed they were alone.

Bennett nodded at the men. "I'll see you back at
Greenfields," she said.

For the first time, Alex noticed a couple of cars

parked in the narrow driveway between Studios B and C. Bennett got into one of them and drove off. The two men went back into the studio. What could they possibly be doing there? Alex knew that he'd already been in enough trouble. Jack would kill him if she found out he'd come here. But he couldn't just back out now. He had to know.

Alex crept over to the studio entrance, worried that the two men might re-emerge at any moment. He peered inside. There was no sign of them but it seemed that this studio was still in use. He could make out powerful lights on the other side of a huge screen, stretched over a metal frame. The screen was a barrier between Alex and whatever was happening but at least it was dark on this side. He could hear the two men talking in the distance and knew that, for the time being, he was safe. He slipped inside.

"Some of this stuff must be worth a fortune."

"You heard what she said. Leave it!"

The two voices carried easily in the enclosed space. Alex made his way along the back of the screen, keeping close to the outer wall. McCain was closing this place down. That was what he had said in Straik's office. Perhaps Mr Bray had done Alex a favour after all. If he hadn't been excluded from school, he might never have had the opportunity to find out what was going on.

Then the two men appeared round the side of the screen. But for the darkness, they would have seen Alex at once. Alex slipped behind a pile of boxes, crouching low. The men walked straight past him, so close that he could have reached out and touched them. He watched them disappear the way he had come. Good. Now he was on his own.

The sound of the door slamming shut echoed all around him like a gunshot. Alex twisted round but he knew already there was nothing he could do. He heard the rattle of a chain being drawn through the handles, followed by the snap of a padlock. The men had finished here. They had left the lights on, but they had locked and bolted the main doors. He heard their footsteps as they walked away and, a moment later, the sound of a car engine starting up. He would just have to hope there was another way out.

Alex straightened up, then moved round the side of the screen. And suddenly he was no longer in London, no longer in a grubby industrial area near Heathrow Airport.

He was in Africa.

Alex had never actually been to Africa but the scene that surrounded him was unmistakable. He was in the middle of a cluster of mud huts, half a dozen of them, with no windows and roofs made out of straw. They had been constructed close to each other in a dusty enclosure, surrounded by a wooden picket fence. An assortment of clothes, old but brightly coloured, hung on a washing line between two stunted acacia trees. To one side, there was a well with a few objects – pots, pans, some tin plates – scattered around it. A shield, shaped like a leaf, and two wooden spears had been propped up against one of the doorways as if guarding the entrance.

It was only when he looked up that the illusion was broken. Electric arc lamps blazed down from a network of walkways high above. Together they were creating the heat and light of an African summer's day. The giant screen was actually a cyclorama, made out of a bright green fabric. Alex understood enough about film technology to know that a computer could insert anything into the green background. A flick of a switch and the village could be in a jungle, a desert, beneath a clear blue sky.

But what sort of film was being made? With a shudder, Alex realized that the village was populated – but not with anything that resembled life. There were three dead cows lying on their sides, their legs rigid, their stomachs bloated, their eyes glassy and empty. They had to be made out of plastic. There was no smell, no flies swarming over them as there would have been in reality. But that didn't take away any of the horror. From the look of them, if these animals had been real, they would have died in pain.

They weren't alone. As Alex moved further into the set, drawn in almost against his will, he saw what had once been a large bird, perhaps an eagle, now a crumpled heap of bone and feathers lying in the dust. It was only when he reached the edge of the village that he came upon the first human being. A little black boy, maybe two or three years old, was lying curled up, one matchstick arm drawn across his eyes. Alex felt sick. He could tell that it was just a dummy, not a real child. But who would create something like this? And why?

He had seen enough. He could work out the reason for all this later. He just wanted to be back out in the fresh air. Alex looked around for a way out and saw a second door, set in one of the walls of the hangar. He tried it but it was locked too. There were no windows. He looked up. He could see two barred skylights in the roof but there was no way he was going to be able to reach them, even if he climbed up to the lighting platforms. A rectangular air conditioning shaft ran the full length of the hangar, suspended from the ceiling by a series of metal brackets. He might be able to reach the skylights if he climbed on top of it – but even then, how would he cut his way through the bars?

Perhaps he could blow them up. He still had the second gel ink pen that Smithers had given him. He was about to take off his backpack, when he remembered. He had left the pencil case with the pen and the pocket calculator beside his bed. He checked his mobile again. Still no signal. So it looked as if he was going to have to wait here until someone came back.

And then the whole world burst into flames.

Alex didn't know what was more shocking – the fact it was so silent, or so unexpected. The ground simply erupted, tongues of fire shooting upwards, as if powered by hidden pipes below. He could have been in the middle of a minefield. About half a dozen bombs, incendiaries perhaps, were being set off, one after another. Alex was thrown off his feet. He knew that if one of the devices went off directly underneath him, he would be killed. He threw his arm across his eyes, protecting them from the heat.

Now he understood what Dr Bennett and the two men had been doing. Closing this place down meant destroying it. The three of them must have just finished laying the explosive charges when he had come across them. They had been set off either by timer switches or by remote control. It made no difference either way to Alex. The flames were roaring all around him. He had only minutes to break out of here. Very soon he would be unable to breathe. And if he passed out, that would be the end of him. Everything in here would burn. Including him.

The green screen had caught light. Alex saw it dissolve like a huge sheet of paper, turning black and then orange and red as the flames burst through. His eyes were streaming now. It was difficult to see, almost impossible to think. The doors were locked. The skylights were out of reach.

The walls were metal. His mobile was dead. He had nothing with him. There was no way out.

The air conditioning shaft.

It was a rectangular tunnel hanging underneath the ceiling, plugged into the wall. It brought air into the building. So it had to lead outside. The silver shaft was big enough to crawl through and Alex thought he could make out an access panel. He wiped a sleeve across his eyes. All the clothes on the washing line were ablaze. One of the huts had vanished, consumed by a whirlpool of fire.

Suddenly all the lights blinked out. The main electric cable must have melted. Now the hangar was an intense red, lit only by the inferno that was destroying it.

Coughing, forcing himself to suck in the hot air, Alex started forward. Without knowing quite why, he grabbed hold of the shield and carried it over to the ladder. It would make it more difficult to climb but somehow he had a feeling he would need it. He reached out and grabbed the first rung. It was already warm. In a minute's time it would be too hot to hold.

Dragging the shield with him, he climbed up to the walkway. The air conditioning shaft was directly above him, running about thirty metres to the far wall. He was going to have to climb into it and then crawl with the flames roaring underneath him. Alex stared at the distance across the studio with a sense of despair that made him weak.

It was going to be like feeding himself into an oven. If he didn't move fast, he would roast before he reached the other end.

But would there even be a way out? There had to be. There was no other choice.

The access panel to the ventilation shaft was fastened with four nuts and bolts and Alex was lucky. They turned in his hand. But even this wasn't easy. The smoke was blinding him. There was a foul chemical smell – many of the props must have been made of synthetic materials – and as he dragged at what little air remained, he felt sick. Finally the fourth bolt came free and the panel fell away, bouncing off the walkway and spinning down below. Alex watched it disappear into the flames. There was nothing but fire now. The entire studio was being devoured.

He pulled himself up into the open shaft, sliding the shield in front of him. Now he was glad that he had brought it. Even as he crouched in the rectangular tunnel, he could feel the metal underneath him heating up. The shield would at least protect his hands. Quickly, moving with difficulty in the confined space, he tore off his backpack and dropped it behind him. Then came his jacket. He folded it under his knees as a cushion against the heat. He was already sweating. He could see the air rippling in front of him. He fixed his eyes on the end of the tunnel. There was a square of daylight: another access panel. That was what he had to reach.

He set off.

He could no longer see the flames but he could imagine them stretching out, licking the metal surface directly beneath him. He was shuffling forward as quickly as he could, his hands resting on the shield, his knees on the jacket. But there wasn't enough room to move properly. For just one moment, he lost his balance and his palm and five fingers landed on the metal. He winced. The surface was already too hot to touch. He wasn't going to make it. The end was too far away.

Push the shield. Draw in the knees. Push the shield. Draw in the knees.

His head was swimming. There was almost no air left in the tunnel. And the jacket wasn't thick enough. Most of his weight was on his knees and he could feel the heat coming through. There was a dull clang behind him and he glanced back to see that the access panel was filled with smoke and the metal was buckling. There was certainly no way back. It occurred to him that the entire shaft could come free, that the brackets holding it up could melt or break loose and that the whole thing could plunge down, smashing into the studio floor and the roaring fire below.

His knees were hurting now and he'd had to move his hands to the very edge of the shield, gripping the sides. It was fortunate that the African shield seemed to be the real thing. If it had been made of plastic, it would already have melted. Alex could hear someone grunting and realized it was him. Every movement was an effort, fighting the heat, fighting to breathe, forcing himself not to give up. He was over halfway. He could see the exit – a metal grille – ahead of him. He wouldn't have time to turn any screws, even assuming there were any. What if the grille was welded into place? No. Don't even think it. Alex shuffled faster and faster.

Draw in the knees. Push the shield.

The last ten metres were the worst. Alex's vision was blurred. He could feel tears streaming down his face. But then he was there. The grille was in front of him. He reached out and grabbed hold of it, curling his fingers over the metal slats. It didn't budge. He shook it. Something whispered behind him and he turned round to see a ball of fire rolling in slow motion from the far end towards him.

There was only one thing to do. He slid the shield behind him then somehow manoeuvred himself right round so that he was lying on his back with his feet in front. His shoulders screamed at him. The metal was too hot. He lashed out with both feet, smashing them into the grille. Nothing.

The fireball was getting closer, floating in space, already halfway down the shaft. He kicked a second time and the grille swung open. Still on his back, Alex drew himself forward using the balls of his feet. He hooked his heels over the edge of the wall and somehow spilled out into the open.

He was falling. How high up was he? Had he done all this just to break his neck when he hit the concrete below? But he was lucky. The ground rose up at the back of the studio and he hit soft cold grass, the slope of a hill. He rolled over several times, then came to a halt. There were flames above him, shooting out of the little square that had just provided him with an exit. Although the metal walls were keeping most of it contained, smoke was seeping through the cracks and rising into the air. Alex heard the glass shatter as the skylights broke and thicker smoke began to billow out. Coughing, wiping his eyes, he got to his feet. He knew that he had been lucky. It had all been incredibly close.

The first fire engines arrived ten minutes later, followed by the police. A pilot coming in to land at Heathrow had seen what was happening and had radioed the authorities. By the time the firemen bundled out and began uncoiling their hoses, the whole of Studio C was a raging inferno. Not a single piece of evidence from the film set would remain inside.

The firemen did what they could but in the end it was easier just to let the building burn. Meanwhile, the police checked the rest of the complex, making sure there was no one else around. None of them had noticed the single schoolboy limping along the main road, looking for a taxi to take him home.

Q&A

"Alex Rider is an agent working for the Special Operations division of MI6. I know that's hard to believe, but I promise you it's true. He lives in Chelsea, just off the King's Road, with a housekeeper who acts as his guardian. She's called Jack Starbright. He has no relatives that I know of. His uncle, a man called Ian Rider, was also a spy but he was killed. That was when the kid got recruited."

Harry Bulman unwrapped a stick of chewing gum, rolled it carefully between his finger and thumb and slid it into his mouth. He was sitting in a Portakabin that stood on the edge of a building site in London, not far from King's Cross. There was a cheap desk, three plastic chairs and a fridge with a kettle and coffee mugs on top. The walls were covered with architects' drawings. Outside, work had finished for the day and it looked as if everyone had gone home. There were two men with him. He recognized one of them. Desmond McCain had been in the papers often enough for his face to be familiar. He was dressed entirely in black, one leg crossed over the other, his hands resting in his lap. Bulman could see his own reflection in the brightly polished leather of McCain's shoe. The other man had been introduced as Leonard Straik. He was older than McCain, with silver hair sticking up over his forehead. He looked nervous.

Bulman was also dressed smartly. He had put on a suit and tie for this meeting and his briefcase, with all his notes, was at his feet. But something had gone out of him since he had turned up at Alex's house. His confidence and swagger had been replaced by a dull sense of resentment. He was a man who had been injured and it showed. He talked slowly, measuring his words, and the hatred in his voice was unmistakable. Even the way he chewed the gum had a mechanical quality. He could have been chewing paper.

After he had been released by the police, Bulman had gone home. He had opened a bottle of whisky and drunk half of it, staring at the wall. He had been terrified. In a matter of hours his entire life had been stripped away from him and – this was the worst part – it could happen again at any time. The man called Crawley had made that absolutely clear. They could snap their fingers and he would vanish off the face of the earth, spirited away to some mental hospital where he would be left to rot. They were probably watching him even as he sat there. He wondered if the flat was bugged. Almost certainly. For the first time in his life, he realized how powerless he would be if the system – society, the government, whatever – turned against him. They had given him a warning and it had struck him in the heart.

Harry Bulman was many things but he wasn't stupid. He knew there was going to be no story about Alex Rider, no front page headlines, no publishing deal. Even if he dared try again, there wasn't an editor in town who would go anywhere near him. The Internet? Despite what he had told Alex, he knew there was no point in posting the story in cyberspace. It would do nothing for him. And it might kill him.

But what rankled him most wasn't Crawley. It wasn't MI6. It was that he had been defeated by a fourteen-year-old boy. Mr Alex Bloody Rider. The kid was probably laughing at him even now. The whisky tasted sour as Bulman worked his way through the bottle. He couldn't even get drunk. It was as if he had no feelings left.

And then, a few days later, the telephone had rung. It was one of Bulman's contacts, the ex-soldier who had put him on to the story in the first place. The moment Bulman heard the voice, he was tempted to hang up. Fortunately the man didn't mention Alex Rider. He simply said that something interesting had turned up and wondered if Bulman would like to meet at the usual place.

The usual place was the Crown in Fleet Street. Bulman used his old commando training to make sure he wasn't being followed but he still insisted on them both walking to a second pub on the other side of the river before he said a word. And even then, he chose a back room with the music turned up loud and nobody else in sight.

And that was when he heard that someone was asking questions about Alex Rider, that they were prepared to pay good money for information. It was all being done very discreetly. The friend didn't even know who they were – but the money involved had a lot of zeros and there was a telephone number he could pass on if Bulman was interested.

Bulman took twenty-four hours to come to a decision. Every instinct told him that Alex Rider had an enemy and that they weren't doing this to buy him a surprise present for his birthday. There was a risk putting himself forward. He could be walking into a trap. But even as he mulled it over, two thoughts stayed in his mind. The first was the money, which he needed. The second was the possibility that he could do Alex serious harm. In the end he made the call.

He had been passed from one anonymous voice to another. There had been three different people asking him questions before he had finally been told to come here, and he was fairly sure that his own background, everything about him, would have been checked. But the way that it was all being handled reassured him. Whoever these people were, they were afraid of being found out, just like him. And the more careful they were, the safer he would be.

Eventually the time and place for this meeting had been set. According to the signs on the street, this was the site of a new hostel for the homeless, being built by the international charity First Aid. Even so, Bulman was astonished to find himself face to face with the Reverend Desmond McCain. He remembered the story of the Tory MP who had gone bad, the building that had burnt down and the false insurance claim. He'd heard that McCain had reformed and for the past five years had been devoting himself to charity projects. Well, maybe he wasn't quite as saintly as people thought. It had already occurred to Bulman that there might be another story in all this, but of course he kept the thought to himself.

There had been no pleasantries. No offers of tea or coffee. So far, the other man hadn't spoken. After Bulman had sat down, McCain had opened the meeting as if he really were a vicar addressing his congregation.

"I appreciate your coming here today, Mr Bulman. May I introduce my colleague, Leonard Straik. We understand you have information about a boy called Alex Rider. Please would you be good enough to tell us everything you know."

And Bulman had done just that. Once he had

started, he found it all pouring out of him, every-thing he had learnt during his research. It had been difficult to stop.

"They recruited a child!" McCain had listened in silence but now he turned to Straik. "'For they are a wicked generation, children who have no faith.' We should have been warned by the Book of Deuteronomy, Chapter 32."

"He's been incredibly successful," Bulman said, although it annoyed him to have to admit it. "I have notes on his last three assignments and there may have been others."

"You have his address?"

"I've actually been to his house. I know where he goes to school. I've written it all down for you. There's a whole file in my case. I can tell you everything you want to know." Bulman didn't want to push his luck but he couldn't resist asking a few questions of his own. It was too good an opportu-nity to miss. He began innocently. "What is this place? You're building a hostel..."

"It's a dreadful thing, the number of young homeless people in London," McCain said. "Out on the streets with no food or shelter! First Aid was given this land by one of the city's most prominent developers, and I'm happy to say that we have raised enough money to build somewhere they can be looked after and given food and warm clothes."

"You do a lot for charity."

"I have made it my life's work."

It was the moment to ask what Bulman really wanted to know. "So why are you interested in Alex, Reverend McCain?" he continued casually. "I have to tell you, whatever you do with that kid is fine with me. But I would be interested to know..."

"I'm sure you would, Mr Bulman." The grey eyes settled on him and for a moment Bulman shuddered. "You are a journalist, I understand."

"That's right."

"I would hate to think that you might be tempted to write about this meeting."

"That depends how much you're going to pay me."

"We've already agreed the price," Straik replied. "Ten thousand pounds, in cash."

Bulman licked his lips. He could taste the mint from the chewing gum. "I agreed that price before I realized that the Reverend McCain was involved," he said. "But I thought, in the circumstances, that we might renegotiate."

"I agree with you," McCain said. "That's exactly what I've decided to do."

He took out a gun and shot the journalist three times: once in the head, once in the throat and once in the chest. Bulman's last gesture was one of surprise. His eyes widened even as his hands flew up and his body jerked in the chair. Then he slumped back. Blood trickled down from the three bullet holes, spreading across his shirt.

"Was that completely wise?" Straik asked.

"It was unavoidable," McCain replied. He slipped the gun back into his pocket. "He wasn't going to keep quiet. A week or a year from now he would have made himself a nuisance."

"I'm sure. But are we safe?"

"I would doubt very much that he told anyone he was coming here. There's nothing to connect him with you or me. He was a journalist. Now he's a dead journalist. Who really cares about the difference?"

"And what about Alex Rider?" Straik asked. "We can't go ahead, Desmond. Poison Dawn is finished—"

"No!" McCain hadn't raised his voice but the single word was dark and thunderous. The two of them had known each other for years, but at that moment Straik wondered if he fully understood what went on inside the other man's head. There was a sort of madness there. He wouldn't listen to any argument.

"We have been planning this too long," McCain said. "We've spent too much time and too much money. Everything is in place."

"But it looks as if MI6 have been on to us from the start..."

McCain got up and went over to the window. He made a signal and, a moment later, there was the sound of an engine starting up. "They can't have been," he said. "It's impossible."

"They sent the boy. First to Scotland and then to Greenfields..."

"I'm not so sure." McCain turned round and glanced at Bulman, as if he'd forgotten that he had just shot him and was expecting him to make some comment. "When Alex Rider came to Kilmore Castle, he was a guest of another journalist, Edward Pleasure. There was a teenage girl too. When he came to Greenfields, he was with a school party. The two events were quite unconnected. I don't know what's going on here but it may not be as cut and dried as it seems."

"Even so..."

McCain held a hand up for silence. "We are not cancelling Poison Dawn," he said. "Not until we've had our conversation with Master Rider."

"You think he'll just walk in here?"

"I have something else in mind." McCain stood up. "We are about to make an unimaginable amount of money," he said. "A hundred million pounds. Maybe more. But that means we have to take risks. More than that, we have to make sure that we move one step ahead of the opposition. And that's exactly what we're going to do."

He reached forward and grabbed Harry Bulman by the front of his jacket. The journalist had never been a small man and now he had become, in every sense, a deadweight. Even so, McCain pulled him effortlessly to his feet and dragged him over to the door. Still holding him, he stepped outside. A mechanical digger had started up while he was talking with Straik and it was waiting for him on the other side of the door with its metal arm raised. There was a driver sitting behind the wheel, smoking. McCain threw down the body and the driver revved the engine and trundled forward. There was a crunch of machinery as the arm was lowered and the dead man was picked up. Then the digger reversed, carrying Bulman towards the muddy excavation that would soon be his grave.

McCain watched him go. "Well, it looks as if Mr Bulman finally got what every journalist wants," he said.

Straik glanced at him.

"A scoop."

McCain had made his decision. He set off, avoiding the puddles so that he wouldn't get his shoes dirty as he made his way towards his car.

"So what exactly do you think is going on?"

Even as Alan Blunt posed the question, a waiter approached their table with the main course: steak and kidney pudding for him, a tuna salad for Mrs Jones. The two of them fell silent as the plates were positioned and the wine was poured. They were having dinner at Blunt's club, the Mandarin, in Whitehall. And although all the waiters had received security clearance, they preferred not to talk while there was any chance of their being overheard. A great many members of the Mandarin were either politicians or intelligence chiefs and it was said to be the most unfriendly place in London. Nobody trusted anybody. Members very rarely spoke to each other at all.

That afternoon, Blunt and his deputy had been given a full briefing by the chief science officer at MI6, a fiercely intelligent woman called Redwing. She had analysed the liquid that had seeped into Alex Rider's jacket after the test tube he had stolen had smashed. Her report – she was always thorough – had begun with wool, polyester and apple juice. The first two, of course, were the materials of the jacket itself. The third had perhaps been a spill during school lunch.

But the rest of the ingredients had been more interesting. According to Redwing, the test tube had contained something which she called *Bitrites infestans*. This was essentially a biological soup that seemed to have been developed from a variety of different mushrooms. It was too soon to say exactly which mushrooms had been used, but preliminary tests were surprising. The liquid was completely harmless. It even had a nutritional value. Although it would taste disgusting, it could be consumed by humans or animals with no side effects.

Redwing had eaten once or twice at the Mandarin and had concluded by saying, "They could serve it at your club, Mr Blunt, and you might not even send it back. Quite why they're making so much of it is a little puzzling. Five hundred gallons? Is that what your agent said? Well, I can't tell you what they're going to do with it but I can assure you that the worst it would give you is indigestion..."

Alex had told Jack what had happened at Greenfields and she had in turn informed MI6. The appearance of Desmond McCain, the chase through the complex, the Poison Dome, the escape from the roof – they knew all of this. But, like Alex, they still had no clear idea what was going on.

The waiter retreated and Mrs Jones tried to answer Blunt's question. "I'm not surprised that McCain is up to no good," she said. "He has a criminal record, after all."

"Didn't he convert to Christianity?"

"So he claimed – and to be fair, his charity, First Aid, has done some very good work. But after what Alex has told us..."

"Of course." This time, Blunt was going to believe everything Alex had said. After all, as much as it embarrassed him to admit it, the boy had been right in the past and MI6 had been proved wrong. "Is there any business link between McCain and this man Leonard Straik?" he asked.

"None that we've been able to find."

"What do we know about McCain's movements in the past five years?"

"I'm having a report prepared. It'll be on your desk tonight."

Blunt broke the crust on his pudding and examined the contents. The food at the Mandarin Club was not good but the members liked it that way. It reminded them of school. "I have to say, I'm quite worried about all this," he said. "I always had a feeling that the department would have to turn its attention to GM food one day. There are people out there doing things that half the world doesn't even understand."

"We are what we eat." Mrs Jones had gone off her tuna salad. She put down her knife and fork.

"That was why I was interested in Mr Straik. And if he's working hand in hand with McCain, that's certainly alarming. We need to know what the two of them are up to."

"What about Alex?" Mrs Jones asked.

"As usual, Alex has done an extremely good job. We really are going to have to make sure we recruit him full-time after he finishes university. He's already shown himself to be more resourceful than a great many of our adult agents." Blunt stuck his fork into the pudding and pulled out a piece of rather fatty meat covered in thick brown gravy. "But as far as this business is concerned, he's no longer involved. Maybe you should drop him a note, Mrs Jones. We've treated him badly in the past but perhaps we could send him a brief thank you. And maybe we should enclose a bag of sweets."

Alan Blunt began to eat his dinner. He was still puzzled about the mushroom soup but his department would work on it. That was the important thing. In the meantime, Alex Rider was already out of his mind.

SPECIAL DELIVERY

Alex could tell that Jack was in a bad mood. She had made the breakfast as she did every morning: boiled eggs for him, fruit and muesli for her. There had been a freshly ironed jacket waiting for him in his room. But she was stamping around the kitchen in silence, and when she loaded the dishwasher, she slid the plates in as if she had a personal grudge against them.

He knew what had upset her. "Jack," he said. "I'm sorry."

"Are you?" She lifted up the toaster and wiped away imaginary crumbs.

"I am. Really."

Jack turned round and let out a sigh. She could never stay angry for long and they both knew it. "I just don't understand you sometimes," she said. "We both agreed that Greenfields wasn't your business. You did what you were told and you were lucky to get out alive. So what on earth did you think you were doing, sneaking into this film studio?"

"I don't know." Alex thought for a moment. "I just felt angry being told off by Mr Bray. And I thought if I could find out what McCain was doing..."

"But what exactly *is* he doing?" Jack sat down at the table. "You say there was a film set, an African village. But why? What's the point?"

"I've been thinking about that. McCain runs a charity. First Aid. They have appeals all over the world. Maybe that's his plan. He wants to raise money for something that hasn't happened."

"A fake charity appeal."

"Exactly. He shows a film of some village that doesn't exist. People send in money. He gets to keep it."

Jack shook her head. "It wouldn't work, Alex. These days everything is on TV or in the papers. People would soon find out if it wasn't true."

"Can you think of anything else?"

"No. But maybe we should tell MI6 and leave it to them this time." She glanced at him. "Is that OK?"

Alex smiled. "That's what I'd already decided," he said. "Do you mind going back?"

"Of course not," Jack replied. "I'm beginning to wonder where this will end. You go to a party in Scotland and you end up at the bottom of a loch. A school visit almost lands you in hospital. And now this!" She took one of Alex's Marmite soldiers and bit it in half. "The trouble is, you've got too much of the spy in you. It's your uncle's fault. And your father's. Maybe even your grandfather's. For all we know, he was probably a spy too."

Alex looked at his watch. It was quarter past eight. "I ought to be on my way to school," he said.

"Yes." Jack nodded. "Let's not get into any more trouble with Mr Bray."

Alex ran up to his room, collected his books and put on his jacket. He had lost his backpack at Elm's Cross but he had a spare shoulder bag which he'd dug out of the wardrobe. He was about to leave, when he noticed the black gel ink pen that Smithers had given him, lying on his desk. On an impulse he slipped it into his inside pocket. He knew that Tom Harris would get a kick out of seeing it. And if Mr Bray told him off again, maybe he would set it off outside the staffroom.

He hurried back downstairs and out through the hall, calling out a last goodbye as he went.

"Don't forget your scarf!" Jack called back.

She was too late. It was cold outside but dry and there was no wind. Alex hoisted his bag over his shoulder and made his way along the back streets that would lead him to the King's Road. This part of Chelsea was full of elegant town houses standing side by side and expensive cars parked in the residents' bays. In a few months the trees would blossom and the wisteria would tumble down the brickwork. Ian Rider had liked being here because it was quiet and private but still in the middle of the city. He'd always had a hatred of the suburbs. *Too many children and vets.* Alex could still hear his slightly cryptic remark.

There was a FedEx van at the end of the street, badly parked across the corner, and two men dressed in overalls were examining a clipboard which they held between them. They were obviously lost and as Alex approached, one of them came over to him.

"Excuse me, mate," he said. "We've got a delivery for Packard Street. You wouldn't know where that is, would you?"

Alex shook his head. "There's no Packard Street around here."

"Are you sure? That's what it says here..." The man held out the clipboard, inviting Alex to take a look.

It was the empty van that alerted him.

The doors of the van were open, and if they were making a delivery to an address in Chelsea, why was there nothing inside? Alex jerked back but it was too late. The two men had manoeuvred Alex between them so that they were perfectly placed, one in front of him, one behind. He heard the clipboard hit the pavement. It was just a prop; they didn't need it any more. Alex felt himself being grabbed by the throat. He twisted round, trying to break free. At the same time, he saw something that sent a chill up his spine. The second delivery man had produced a hypodermic syringe. They weren't here to kill him. They were here to take him. The van was for him.

Alex put everything he had ever been taught into action. He knew that it would be almost impossible even for two grown men to drag him into the van – unless they made contact with the needle. That was what he had to avoid. So he didn't waste energy trying to break free of the neck lock. It was too strong anyway. Instead he used the man's own strength against him, levering himself back, raising both legs off the ground and lashing out. The man with the syringe had been looking for somewhere to plant it, and with a smile of satisfaction Alex saw the soles of his shoes smash into it, breaking it against the man's chest. If they'd been planning to knock him out, they could forget it. Now it would be twice as hard to make him disappear.

So far, no more than about ten seconds had passed since the attack had begun and Alex knew that time was on his side. The streets of Chelsea might be quiet but it was eight thirty in the morning and people would be on their way to work. He couldn't call for help; he was still being strangled. But someone would see what was happening. They had to.

Sure enough, a figure turned the corner and Alex was overjoyed to see the blue and silver uniform of a police officer. He felt the man behind him loosen his grip as the officer ran forward and he gratefully sucked in air.

"What's going on here?" the police officer demanded.

"They—" Alex began and stopped as he felt something stab him in the back, just above his waist. A second needle! The man who had been holding him must have taken it out of his pocket. But surely...?

The policeman wasn't doing anything, and even as the strength drained out of him and his legs buckled, Alex understood. The delivery men weren't real. Nor was the police officer. They were all in it together. Alex had been tricked and there was nothing he could do as whatever drug had been pumped into him coursed through his system. He saw the street tilt and then turn sideways and knew that the only reason he wasn't lying flat on the pavement was because the delivery men had caught hold of him.

He was angry with himself. Only a few minutes ago, Jack had been worrying about him. He could have died at Elm's Cross and she would never have known what had happened to him. He had promised her he would stay out of trouble. And now this. In a few hours the school would report him missing. She would think he had betrayed her again. If he died, she would never know the truth.

This was all his fault. He shouldn't have gone to the film studio. He should never have got involved with Desmond McCain in the first place. He wished he could call Jack and tell her. But it was too late.

He tried to find the strength for one last move. If he could lash out with a leg or even call out for help...

But it was already too late. Barely conscious, unable to struggle, he was bundled into the back of the van. He didn't even hear the doors slam shut.

Alex opened his eyes.

Someone was doing something to his head. A lock of fair hair twisted, falling in front of his eyes. At the same time, he heard the snip of scissors.

He was sitting in a chair in what looked like a hotel room. There was a window covered by a blind and, at the very corner of his vision, an unmade bed. No carpet. The two delivery men were standing over him. They were cutting his hair. They hadn't tied him up but they didn't need to. He was still drugged and couldn't move. He'd been taken out of his school uniform and dressed in an ill-fitting tracksuit. His feet seemed to be resting on some sort of metal shelf but he didn't have the strength to look down.

The two men were talking but their voices were distant echoes and he couldn't make out what they were saying. One of them noticed he was awake and grabbed his head, squeezing his cheeks between thumb and fingers. More of his hair tumbled down into his lap. He could feel the cold air touching his scalp.

"He's back," the man said.

"Good..."

A woman appeared from nowhere – she must have been standing behind him – and Alex recognized Myra Bennett. Bizarrely she was dressed as a nurse, complete with a starched white hat and a watch dangling from her front pocket. The diagonal fringe of yellow hair looked more severe than ever, as if it had been sliced with a single sword stroke. Her eyes, behind the round, gold glasses, were slightly mad. Alex's mouth was dry and he was feeling sick but he managed to swear at her, a single, venomous word.

"We'll do it now," she said.

They took hold of his arm and rolled up his sleeve. Alex winced as they gave him another injection, a long needle sliding into the flesh just above his wrist. But this time they didn't remove it. Bennett taped it in place and Alex saw there was a tube connecting it to a plastic box about the size of a cigarette packet which they taped to his arm.

"The box will continue to give you a timed injection of the drug we are using over the next few hours," Bennett explained. "You will not be able to move or speak. There will be other side effects. Try to breathe normally."

Alex felt a wave of nausea. He was completely helpless. And whatever these people were planning, it wasn't going to end in this room.

The men rolled his sleeve back down, hiding the plastic box. Alex knew that it was pumping its venom, drip by drip, into his bloodstream. He tried to jerk his arm but he had no strength at all. He swore at Bennett a second time but his voice was no longer working and all that came out was an inarticulate grunt.

Bennett leant over him and pressed a pair of glasses onto his face. Alex tried to shake them off but they were tight-fitting, hooked over his ears.

"You can take him out now," she said.

He was in a wheelchair! Alex didn't realize it until one of the men spun him round and pushed him out of the door. They turned into a long corridor.

"Wait a minute," Bennett said. She crouched beside Alex so that her face was close to his. "What do you think?" she asked with a thin smile.

There was a full-length mirror at the end of the corridor. Alex stared at himself in shock and disbelief. His hair had been cut so badly that he looked two years older than his true age and completely pitiful. The tracksuit was a nasty shade of purple. It was one size too big and covered in stains, as if he was unable to feed himself. His skin was pale and unhealthy. The glasses he had been given were deliberately ugly: black plastic with thick lenses. They hung slightly crookedly on his face.

The drug had attacked his muscles, paralysing him and somehow changing the shape of his entire body. His jaw was hanging open and his eyes were glazed. Alex knew exactly what they had done. They had turned him into a foul parody of a disabled person. They had made him look brain-damaged ...

but, worse than that, they had stripped away his dignity too. In a way, it was a brilliant disguise. People might glance at him in the street but they would be too embarrassed to look twice. Bennett was taking their prejudices and using them to her own advantage.

She gave a signal and Alex was wheeled down the corridor and round to a lift. After that the extra drug must have kicked in, because his world seemed to skip and jump.

He was in the street, being lifted into the van.

He was in the van.

He was at Heathrow Airport! Hadn't he been in exactly the same terminal with Sabina and her parents? The lights hurt his eyes and – just as he had suspected – he saw people staring briefly at him before looking away, ashamed of themselves. He tried to call out for help but the low, pathetic mumbling that came out of his lips only made people turn away. They had no idea what was going on. They wouldn't even begin to guess that he was being kidnapped, spirited away in front of their eyes.

Passport control. They had provided Alex with fake documents, of course, but it seemed to him that the official didn't look too closely. A boy in a wheelchair accompanied by a nurse. The two men had stayed behind.

"Jonathan loves flying on big planes. Don't you, Jonathan!" Bennett was talking to him, addressing him as if he were six years old.

"I'm not..." Alex wanted to tell the passport officer his real name. But nothing resembling a word came out.

And now he was in some sort of lounge.

Now being wheeled down a corridor.

On the plane. A seat had been taken out to make room for the wheelchair. Other passengers were passing him, carrying their hand luggage. He saw them glance in his direction. Each time, the reaction was the same. Puzzlement, the realization that something was wrong, then pity, and finally a sense of embarrassment. The drug was making his knee twitch. His hand, resting on the knee, was doing the same.

"Try to get some sleep, Jonathan," Bennett said. "It's a long flight."

Where were they taking him? And why? Did they really think they could get away with this, whisking him out of the country with a fake ID? Jack would know by now that he was missing. The school would have rung her and she would have alerted MI6. They would be looking for him. Every airport would be watched.

Except...

What day was this? He could have been kept drugged for a few hours or a week. Or a month. Alex had no control over his body but his mind was intact. Sitting in the wheelchair, waiting to take off, he considered his situation. He didn't look anything like himself. He hardly needed the glasses and the badly cut hair. He was paralysed and travelling with a nurse. But it wasn't completely hopeless. Everything led back to Desmond McCain. MI6 knew what had happened at Greenfields. Jack would have told them about Elm's Cross. They would track down McCain and that would lead them to him.

They were in the air. How was that possible? Alex couldn't remember taking off. How long had they been flying for? He tried to work out where they might be going. It had been light when they were on the runway and it was still light now. If they had been in the air for a while, that would suggest, at the very least, that they weren't heading east. The different time zones would have brought the night in faster. South then? He couldn't turn his head – the muscles in his neck refused to work – but as the other passengers had filed past, he had noticed that many of them were black, dressed in clothes that were too brightly coloured for the UK. They could be going home. If so, he was on his way to Africa.

Food was served – but not to him. The stewardess smiled at him sadly as if understanding that he couldn't feed himself. Dr Bennett brought out some baby food and tried to force it into his mouth with a spoon. Using all his remaining strength, Alex kept his mouth shut. He wasn't going to be humiliated by her any more than he had been already.

They were on the ground.

The doors were open.

And then Alex was being wheeled through an arrivals hall and a poster on the wall answered the question he had been asking himself for the past ten hours. A brightly dressed black woman with a huge smile, holding a basket of fruit. And a caption.

SMILE! YOU'RE IN KENYA

Kenya! Vaguely Alex remembered something that Edward Pleasure had told him. *He's the part-owner of a business somewhere in Kenya.* The words might have been spoken a century ago and on a different planet. Had he really once been in Kilmore Castle, dancing with Sabina? What would she say if she could see him now?

The plastic box was still taped to his arm and he felt the whole thing vibrate as the timing mechanism clicked in, sending another spurt of the liquid into his veins. He felt unconsciousness returning and didn't even try to fight it. He was thousands of miles from home. He had fallen into the hands of a ruthless enemy and nobody knew where he was. Ahead of him a set of automatic doors swung open and Alex was wheeled into the dark.

A SHORT FLIGHT TO NOWHERE

Movement returned, one twitch at a time.

Alex had no idea how long he had been here but he guessed that it was at least twenty-four hours. He had watched the sun rise, not out of the window but through the cloth that made up the wall. He was lying on his back on a comfortable bed in what seemed to be a cross between a luxury hotel room and a large tent. The floor was made of polished wood. The walls were made of canvas. The windows consisted of two flaps, fastened closed from the outside. There was an expensive-looking wardrobe, a carved wooden table and two chairs. A fan hung from the ceiling above his head, turning continuously. He was completely enclosed by a mosquito net which rippled in the breeze.

Where exactly was he? From the sounds that surrounded him – the chatter of monkeys, the occasional bellow of an elephant, the constant whoops and screams of exotic birds – it seemed that he was somewhere in the bush.

That tied in with his memories of the journey here, even if they were still confused. There had been the poster he had seen. SMILE! YOU'RE IN KENYA. As if he had felt remotely like smiling! After that the drug must have kicked in again. They had driven through a city but he had barely seen any of it. It had been night-time. Nairobi? And then there had been a second, smaller airport and another plane, this one a four-seater with a single propeller. They had bundled him in, leaving the wheelchair behind. And then...

He had woken up here, on his own. It was dark, evening or night. But they had left two little battery lights on. At least he could see, even if he couldn't yet move. The plastic box had been removed from his arm and a dirty plaster stuck over the puncture where the needle had gone in. That was the first thing he noticed – and he was grateful for it. With the drug no longer pumping into his system he began to recover. He could lift his hand. He could turn his head from side to side, taking in the sweep of the room. Eventually he stood up and tottered on unsteady legs into the bathroom, behind the bed, separated by a screen. He was sick and that made him feel better. Then he took a cold shower, the water washing away some of the horror of the past two days.

He was still too weak to make his way outside. He decided he would wait for the sun. Once again he fell asleep, but this time more naturally.

And now it was morning. Alex rolled off the bed and stood up. He had slept in his shorts. The tracksuit that they had dressed him in was lying on the floor, a crumpled heap. He noticed that his school uniform had been brought over from England. It seemed somehow strange to see it but of course he had been wearing it when he was kidnapped. He went over to it, feeling in the inside pocket of his jacket.

Yes. It was there. The black gel ink pen that Smithers had given him. Nobody had thought to remove it. It wasn't as powerful as the device that had brought down the factory chimney, but it might still be useful. Anyway, it gave Alex hope. McCain had made his first mistake.

They had used a powerful drug on him but it had left his system completely. Just to be sure, he forced himself to do twenty press-ups, then had another shower. He got dressed in his own trousers and shirt, leaving off the jacket. Although it was early morning, it was already warm. He could feel the sun beating through the walls of the tent and the fan was having to fight against the sluggish air. He slipped the gel ink pen into his trouser pocket. From now on he would make sure it never left him.

The front of the tent was sealed. There was a large flap with a zip running round the side. Well, if this was his prison, it was a very flimsy one. Alex went over and unzipped it. At once he saw the green of the jungle, confirming what he had believed. He was in the bush. But the way was blocked by a guard, a black man dressed in jeans and grimy shirt, a rifle strapped over his shoulder. Alex realized that he must have been there all night.

The guard turned round and scowled. "You stay inside." That seemed to be the limit of his English.

"What time do you serve breakfast?" Alex asked. He had already decided he wasn't going to let these people think he was scared.

"Inside..." The guard brought the rifle round.

Alex raised his hands and retreated. There was no point starting a fight. Not yet.

Breakfast came half an hour later: tea, tinned orange juice, two slices of toast, carried in by a second guard. Alex wolfed it down. It had been a long time since he had last eaten and his stomach couldn't have been more empty. There was a bottle of water in the tent and he drank that too. He had no idea what was going to happen to him. He would take any food or water he could get.

Why had they brought him here? Alex almost admired McCain. The man had nerves of steel, kidnapping him in broad daylight and smuggling him out of England through one of the world's busiest airports. But, what was the point? McCain must have identified him as the intruder at Greenfields. He would have remembered their meeting at the castle in Scotland. Maybe he had decided to take revenge. After all, he had already tried to kill

Alex once. And yet somehow Alex didn't believe it. Whatever McCain was planning, the stakes were too high. This wasn't personal. This was business. McCain needed Alex for a reason.

And now Alex was completely in his power. It was probably best not to think too much about what might lie ahead.

Instead Alex thought about Jack. What would she be doing now? And what about MI6? Once they'd realized he had gone, they'd have spared no effort. Every intelligence agency in the world would be looking for him. Surely someone would remember a teenage boy being taken through passport control, even if he was in a wheelchair. The trail would lead to Kenya and they had to know that McCain had a base here.

Except that McCain would have covered his tracks. He knew exactly what he was doing. Alex was going to have to rely on his own resources to get himself out of this mess. He would just have to wait for an opportunity and take it when it came.

The tent flap suddenly opened and Myra Bennett stepped inside. She had changed once again, and was wearing a safari outfit – a loose shirt and long trousers in different shades of brown. The clothes made her look more masculine than ever. She was carrying what looked like a leather cloth.

She wasn't alone. A third guard had come with her, this one in dirty jeans and a black string T-shirt with no sleeves. Alex noticed the knotted muscles of his arms and the machete hanging from his belt. He had narrow, mean eyes. He was looking at Alex as if the two of them were lifelong enemies.

"I heard you were up," Bennett said. "How are you feeling?"

Alex wasn't sure what to say. Just seeing her made him feel sick again. "I've never been better," he muttered.

"The serum that we injected you with was my own invention and I'm very pleased with the way it worked. It was derived from the water hemlock which we cultivate at Greenfields. The effect is not dissimilar to a bad snake bite, only far less permanent. Can I trust you to behave yourself? If not, we can always inject you with some more."

"What do you want with me?" Alex asked.

"You'll find out in good time. For the moment, let me introduce you to Njenga." She gestured at the guard. "He's a Kikuyu tribesman, as are all the guards here, and they will do anything we tell them. There are no other jobs, you see. You might like to know that the Kikuyu once fought against the British with a ferocity that made them a source of great terror. One of their tricks was to impale their victims with a spear up their backside, and then leave them to die slowly on the side of a hill. Of course, they're rather more civilized now. But even so, you might think twice before you do anything to annoy them."

"Nice to meet you, Njenga," Alex said.

Njenga's scowl deepened.

"Where's McCain?" Alex demanded.

"The Reverend McCain won't be here until later today. It is very likely that your friends in MI6 are watching him, so he's had to take a more roundabout route. But he's hoping to have dinner with you this evening. In the meantime, I thought you might like to come with me."

"Where are we going?"

"Oh, nowhere in particular." Dr Bennett smiled, her lips barely moving. "A short flight to nowhere." She lifted the piece of leather and Alex saw that it was a flying helmet. "You don't mind another plane?"

"Do I have any choice?"

"Not really. This way..."

She led him out of the tent.

He was in a safari camp. The tent where he had spent the night was one of a dozen, each one surrounded by a wooden veranda and built into the embrace of a wide river that swept round them. Alex looked at the silver water rippling past, a tangled wall of green rising in a steep bank on the other side. This really was a beautiful spot. He heard chattering above him and looked up to see a family of grey monkeys leaping from the branches of a juniper tree, using their hands and tails. Some of the mothers had tiny babies clinging to their chests.

"The monkeys are a nuisance," Bennett snapped. She barked out an order in another language and one of the guards standing beside the path lifted his rifle and fired. A dead monkey plunged out of the tree and crashed to the ground. The others scattered. "The guards are equally accurate with guns and spears," she went on. "They keep the population down."

"What is this place?" Alex asked. He was careful not to react to what he had just seen. He knew it had been done for his benefit.

"This is Simba River Camp, a business that belongs to the Reverend McCain. I take it you know which country you're in?"

"Kenya."

"That's right." Another hint of a smile. It was as if she had forgotten how to do the real thing. "We're on the edge of the Rift Valley. Simba River Camp was once a world-class safari lodge with visitors from America, Europe and Japan. Brad Pitt once stayed here. Unfortunately it became a victim of the global recession. The visitors stopped coming and the business went bust."

Looking around him, Alex could see it for himself. His was the only tent that looked habitable. The others were empty and falling into disrepair. The path that they were following had been neglected, weeds and wild grass breaking through. They passed a swimming pool but it had no water and the cement was cracking. All around, the vegetation was tumbling over itself, out of control. If the camp was left to itself for much longer, it would be swallowed up, disappearing into the bush, and nobody would know that it had ever existed.

They came to a beaten-up Land Rover with dirty windows and wires poking out of the dashboard. Njenga climbed into the driving seat with Bennett next to him. Alex went in the back. He was moving completely normally now and he was glad of it. Even on this short journey, he might get a chance to break away.

"It's seventy miles to the next camp and I doubt that you'd ever find it," Bennett said. She must have seen what he was thinking. "So please don't entertain any foolish ideas. The Kikuyu are also excellent trackers. They would be able to follow your trail in the darkness, even in the pouring rain. I'm afraid Njenga would enjoy hacking you to pieces. That's the sort of person he is. If I were you, I wouldn't give him the opportunity."

They rumbled along a dirt track for a couple of minutes, passing through a wire fence with a rusting gateway and leaving the camp behind them. Almost at once they came to an airstrip – a dusty, orange runway that had somehow been cut through the long grass. A dilapidated wooden hut stood to one side with a windsock hanging limply from a pole. This must have been where Alex had landed when he was brought to Simba River Camp, although he had no memory of it.

There was a plane parked on the grass, next to a line of about thirty oil drums. It was like an oversized toy with two seats, one behind the other, three wheels and a single propeller at the front. It had no cabin or cockpit. A slanting window protected the pilot but any passenger would be sitting outside, feeling the full force of the air currents. A single wing on struts stretched out over the plane and Alex saw a series of rubber tubes running all the way to the tips. These were connected to two plastic drums lashed to the side of the plane just behind the passenger seat.

It was a crop duster, but a very old one. It should have been in a museum. Alex wondered if it could really fly.

"This is a Piper J-3 Cub," Bennett told him. She had taken off her glasses and was putting on the flying helmet, fastening it under her chin. She was also wearing a leather jacket which she had brought from the Land Rover. Alex noticed she wasn't offering him anything to keep warm. "Twenty-two feet long. Sixty-five horsepower engine. They used them for training during the war. Please, get in..."

Njenga was staying with the car. Alex was feeling increasingly uneasy but he did as he was told. There was a metal lever between the seats, connected to a control box with two sets of wires running towards the wing. When he sat down, it was right in front of him. There was almost no room for his feet. Myra Bennett climbed into the front and made a few checks. She produced a pair of goggles and slipped them over her eyes. Then she flicked a switch and the propeller began to turn.

It took a full minute for the propeller to blur and then come up to speed. Alex could feel the high-pitched buzz of the engine in his ears and knew that from this point on there would be no more conversation. That suited him. He had nothing to say to the woman. Njenga pulled the chocks out from under the wheels. Alex clicked on his seat belt. The Piper rolled forward.

They taxied all the way to the end of the runway, bumping up and down on the uneven surface. At least Dr Bennett seemed to be an experienced pilot. She spun the plane round, then raced back again, the engine straining like an overworked lawnmower. Alex wondered if they had enough speed to get into the air, but then one last bump and they were up, the wind rushing past and the ground sweeping away below.

Alex looked back. He could see Njenga standing on his own beside the Land Rover and behind him, separated by a line of brush, Simba River Camp, the water now a silver ribbon twisting over it. The far bank rose steeply then sloped down again, opening onto a great savannah that fanned out to the horizon. He saw a herd of antelope, startled by the sound of the engine, racing across the plain as if it were a bed of hot coals, their hooves barely touching the grass. The flat African landscape, with its burnt-out yellows and browns, had a true majesty. The sun was shining. The sky was a brilliant blue.

Dr Bennett had taken the Piper Cub to a height of perhaps one thousand feet, at the same time tilting away from the river, heading north. Alex could see the compass on the control panel in front of her. He studied the landscape, holding up a hand to protect his eyes from the slice of the wind. They were flying over a sprawl of green, but there were hills ahead of them, grey and rocky, rising up to the east and west, then closing together to form an upside-down V. In the far distance was something that looked like a man-made wall, but it had to be a very big one if he could see it from here. Over to one side he noticed a track winding up into the hills, and an electricity pylon. Had Bennett been lying when she said there was no one around for seventy miles? There seemed to be signs of civilization much closer than that.

They flew over a wheat field. The entire valley between the hills had been planted with the crop, which looked almost ready to harvest. Alex could see thousands of golden blades bending in the breeze. He wondered how it could possibly grow out here in this heat, and a moment later he got his answer. The wall he had seen was a dam, built into the neck of the valley. The plane flew over it and suddenly they were above water, a huge lake stretching out to the mountain range on the far shore. The water must somehow flow into the river. It would also be used to feed the crops.

Bennett manœuvred the joystick and the Piper

Cub performed a tight circle, the whole continent tipping on its side. Alex felt his ears pop and he was glad he was belted in. For a few seconds he had almost been upside down, and in a plane like this it would be easy enough to tumble out. They were flying back exactly the same way they had come. For a second time, they passed over the lip of the dam. The wheat field lay ahead of them, less than a quarter of a mile away.

Bennett turned round and called out to him. Behind the goggles her eyes looked enormous. "When I tell you, I want you to pull the lever."

Alex could barely hear what she was saying. She repeated herself, stressing each word. He nodded.

Pull the lever? What was this all about? Alex wondered if he might be about to eject himself, if this hadn't all been some cruel and horrible trick. But he had no choice but to play along; and anyway, if he refused, it would be easy enough for her to reach back and do it herself.

They swept in low over the wheat and Bennett signalled with one hand. Alex pulled the lever. At once, there was a gurgle. Alex felt the rubber pipes swell as liquid rushed through them, and seconds later a spray began to burst out from beneath the wing, spreading out in the air and falling evenly onto the crop. He wondered why he should have been even remotely surprised. The plane was a crop duster and that was what they were doing. Dusting the crops.

They flew over the field four times before the liquid ran out. Alex could only sit there, watching the artificial rain, completely mystified. At last Bennett turned round again. "Now we can go back!" she shouted.

It took them just a few minutes to return to the runway. Njenga was still waiting for them, leaning against the Land Rover in the heat of the sun. Alex saw his head turn slowly as they approached. He had been smoking a cigarette. He dropped it and ground it out under his foot.

They landed. The plane rattled back to the grass and came to a standstill. Myra Bennett flicked off the engine, then took off her goggles and cap and climbed down. Alex followed her. He was glad to have his feet back on the ground. He stood there, waiting for her to explain herself.

"Did you enjoy that?" she asked.

"What was it all about?" Alex demanded. Suddenly he was angry. "Why don't you stop playing games with me? I don't know what you're doing but you've got no reason to keep me here. I want to see McCain. And I want to go home."

"The Reverend McCain will be here this evening and he will explain everything to you, including the purpose of our little flight today. But I'm afraid I have to tell you, there's no chance of you going home."

"Why not?"

"Because we're going to kill you, you silly boy.

Surely you must have realized that? But first we're going to hurt you. You see, there are things we need to know. I'm afraid you do have a very unpleasant time ahead of you. If I were you, I'd get as much rest as you can."

She unhooked her spectacles and put them back on. Then, with a brief laugh, she walked back to the waiting car.

WOLF MOON

Alex heard Desmond McCain arrive later that afternoon. He came in a plane that was larger than the Piper, with a deeper, more solid-sounding engine. Alex didn't actually see it – he hadn't been allowed out of his tent since the flight with Myra Bennett – but he heard it land.

He had been on his own all afternoon. Only once, a Kikuyu guard had come in, carrying a meagre lunch on a tray: a couple of overripe bananas, bread and water. Alex refused to think about what the Bennett woman had told him. He had been threatened before and he knew that part of her plan was to weaken him, to sap his strength psychologically.

Instead he used the time to collect his thoughts. It seemed likely that the crop duster had been carrying the liquid that had been developed at Greenfields. But what was the point of spraying a single field in Kenya and why had Bennett made such a big deal of it? Alex tried to join the dots. An international charity, a dead African village mocked up in a film studio, his own kidnapping, the wheat field. The more he thought about it, the more unsettled he became; and in the end he pushed it out of his mind and dozed off. He would let McCain explain himself when the time came.

But the sun had set and darkness fallen before Bennett returned to the tent.

"The Reverend McCain would like you to join him for dinner," she announced.

"That's very kind of him." Alex swung himself off the bed. "I hope it's nicer than lunch."

Once again, they left the tent.

Simba River Camp looked better at night than it had in the day. There was a full moon and the pale light softened everything and made the river sparkle. A few lights were burning in the camp, but they were hardly needed when the sky was so full of stars. The air smelled of perfume. Cicadas were already at work, grinding away in the shadows.

Alex followed the woman to what was clearly the centre of the camp, a circular clearing with the river on one side and acacia trees on all the others, the wide branches stretching out as if to form a protective screen. Two buildings made partly out of wood stood opposite each other. One was a reception and administrative office; the other combined a bar, lounge and restaurant. It had a thatched roof that was much too big for it, as if thrown over it like pastry on a pie. There were no windows or doors – in fact no walls. Alex could imagine the guests meeting here for iced gin and tonic after their long day spotting game, except the tables were piled up in the corner and the bar was closed.

He noticed a satellite dish mounted on the roof of the first building and realized there must be a radio somewhere inside. Might it be possible to reach it and send a message? He doubted it. There were yet more guards patrolling the area – there must have been a dozen of them altogether – armed with spears which they carried as if they'd had them from the day they were born. Guns and spears. It seemed a strange combination in the twenty-first century, but Alex guessed that in the hands of the Kikuyu they would be as dangerous as each other.

"Over here, Alex..."

There was a raised platform close to the river with a bonfire burning low to one side. The embers were glowing bright red and the smell of charcoal crept into the air. A table and chairs had been placed on the platform with two white china plates and two crystal wine glasses, but only one set of silver knives and forks.

"You're not joining us?" Alex asked.

Dr Bennett added a couple of branches to the fire. "The Reverend McCain hasn't invited me."

"Well, you can do the washing-up."

"Still making jokes?" She glared at him. "We'll see if you find this all so amusing tomorrow."

She spun round and left him. It occurred to Alex that she might be annoyed that she hadn't been invited. He still hadn't worked out what her part in all this was. What had persuaded her to throw in her lot with Desmond McCain?

Alex sat down. A bottle of French wine, already opened, stood next to a jug of water. He helped himself to the water. His eye fell on one of the knives. It looked sharp, with a serrated edge. Would anyone notice if it was missing? He glanced around, then slid it off the table and into the waistband of his trousers. The blade against his skin felt strangely comforting. He would use his bread knife when it was time to eat.

He looked over at the river, wondering what animals might gather there at night. There was no fence, no barrier between them and the camp. He had seen monkeys and antelope. Might there be lions too? Despite everything, he had to admit that this was a memorable place, with the river sweeping around, the fire blazing, the African bush with all its secrets. He looked up at the night sky packed with so many stars that even in the vastness of the universe they seemed to be fighting for space. And there, right in the middle of them, huge and pale...

"They call it the wolf moon."

The voice came out of the shadows. Desmond McCain had appeared from nowhere, walking up to the table in no particular hurry. Alex wondered how long he had been standing there, watching him. McCain was dressed in a grey silk suit, black polished shoes and a T-shirt. He was carrying a laptop, which seemed to weigh nothing in his hand. His face gave nothing away. He sat at the table and laid the computer down. Then he unfolded his napkin and looked at Alex as if noticing him for the first time.

"American Indians call it that," he went on. "But I have heard the name used here too. With the coming of the moon, the breezes will begin to blow from the north east. I have been waiting for them. The moon is the start of it all. The moon is important to my plans."

"There's a name for people with an interest in the moon," Alex said. "They're called lunatics."

McCain laughed briefly but without making any sound. "The late Harold Bulman told me a great deal about you," he said. "I was impressed by what I heard, but I have to say I am even more impressed now. Any other boy who had been through what you have been through would be a snivelling wreck. Far away from home. Transported in a manner that cannot have been agreeable. And you're still brave enough to trade insults with me. At first I was disinclined to believe that the British intelligence services had recruited a fourteen-year-old child. But I'm already beginning to see why they chose you."

"Bulman is dead?" Alex wasn't sure what else to say.

"Yes. He told me what I wanted to know and

then I killed him. I enjoyed doing so. If you have learnt anything about me, Alex, it won't surprise you that I have a strong dislike of journalists." McCain picked up the bottle. "Will you have some wine?"

"I'll stick to water."

"I'm glad to hear it. You're too young to drink." McCain poured himself some wine. Alex saw the swirl of red against the side of the glass. "Did you have a good day?" he asked. "Did Myra look after you?"

"She took me for a ride in the crop duster."

"Do you know that she taught herself to fly? She never had a single lesson. She merely had a complete understanding of the laws of physics and worked it all out. She is a remarkable woman. When this is over, she and I plan to get married."

"I'd say you were made for each other." Alex drank some of his water. "I can't think what to buy you."

"I'm afraid you won't be invited, Alex." McCain still hadn't tasted his wine. He was gazing into the glass as if he could see his future in it. "The meal will be brought over very shortly. Have you ever eaten ostrich?"

"They don't serve it at school."

"The meat can be quite tough and you will need a sharp knife to cut it. I notice that yours is missing. Can I suggest you return it to the table?"

Alex hesitated. But there was no point denying

it. He took out the knife and placed it in front of him.

"What were you going to do with it?" McCain asked.

"I just thought it might come in useful."

"Were you planning to attack me?"

"No. But that's a good idea."

"I don't think so." He raised a hand and almost at once, something whipped past Alex's head and buried itself in a tree. It was a spear. Alex saw it quivering in the trunk. He hadn't even seen who'd thrown it.

"It would be a great mistake to try anything unwise," McCain continued, as if nothing had happened. "I hope I have made myself clear."

"I think I get the point," Alex said.

"Excellent."

"Are you going to tell me why I'm here?"

"All in good time." McCain turned his head and for a moment the flames were reflected in his silver crucifix. It was as if there were a fire burning on the side of his face. "I am sure you will have worked out that I risked everything bringing you here. Of course, your disappearance has not been reported in the English news but I have no doubt that the police forces of the world are united in the search for you. But I am playing for an enormous prize, Alex. It is a little bit like the poker game that first brought us together. All gamblers know the greater the reward, the greater the risks."

"I suppose you want to take over the world," Alex said.

"Nothing as tiresome as that. World domination has never seemed particularly attractive to me. But dinner is served. We can talk further as we eat."

Two guards had appeared, carrying the dinner. They laid the food down on the table and disappeared. Alex was served with barbecued meat, sweet potatoes and beans. McCain had a bowl of brown sludge.

"We have the same food," McCain explained. "Unfortunately I am no longer able to chew." He took a small silver straw out of his top pocket. "My meal has been liquidized."

"Your boxing injury..." Alex muttered.

"It wasn't so much the injury as the operation that I underwent afterwards. My manager decided to send me to a plastic surgeon in Las Vegas. I should have known it would be a botch job. His clinic was above a casino. I take it you are familiar with my past."

"You were knocked out by someone called Buddy Sangster when you were young."

"It happened at Madison Square Garden in New York, two minutes into the middleweight championship. Sangster destroyed not only my hopes of becoming third time world champion but my career. He made it difficult for me to speak and impossible to eat. Since then I have only taken liquids, and every time I sit down for a meal I remember him.

But I had my revenge."

Alex remembered what Edward Pleasure had told him. A year later, Sangster had fallen under a train. "You killed him," he said.

"Actually, I paid to have him killed. An international assassin known as the Gentleman did the job for me. He also took care of the plastic surgeon. It was very expensive and, in truth, I would have preferred to do it myself. But it was too dangerous. As you will learn, Alex, I am a man who takes infinite care."

Alex wasn't hungry but he forced himself to eat. He knew he'd need all his energy for what was to come. He tried a mouthful of the ostrich. It was surprisingly good, a bit like beef but with a gamier flavour. He would just have to do his best not to picture the creature while he ate. Meanwhile, McCain had leant down and was busily sucking. His brown porridge entered his mouth with a brief slurping sound.

"I am going to tell you a little about myself," McCain went on. "This is the third time you and I have encountered each other, Alex. We are enemies and tomorrow, I'm afraid, we are going to have no time for idle chat. But I am a civilized man. You are a child. Tonight, under the wolf moon, we can behave as if we are friends. And I welcome the opportunity to tell my story. I've often been quite tempted to write a book."

"You could have the launch party back in jail."

"I would certainly be arrested if I were to make public what I'm about to tell you – but there is no chance of that happening."

McCain put down his straw and dabbed at his lips with his napkin. His mouth was slanting the wrong way as if it had been further dislodged by the food.

"I began my life with nothing," he said. "You have to remember that. I had no parents, no family, no history, no friends, no anything. The people who fostered me in east London were kind enough in their own way. But did they care who or what I was? I was just one of many orphans that they took in. They were do-gooders. This was my first lesson in life. Do-gooders need victims. They need suffering. Otherwise they cannot do good.

"I grew up in poverty. I went to a tough school, and from the very first day, the other children were cruel to me. I can assure you that it is not a good start in life to be named after a bag of frozen food. I was bullied unmercifully. My colour, of course, was also against me. If you had ever been a victim of racism, Alex, you would know that it goes to the very heart of who you are. It can destroy you.

"I soon came to understand that only one thing would keep me safe and separate me from the herd. Only one thing would make a difference. Money! If I was rich, people wouldn't care where I came from. They wouldn't tease or torment me. They would respect me. That is the way modern life works, Alex. Look at self-satisfied pop stars or greasy, semi-literate football players. People worship them. Why?"

"Because they're talented—"

"Because they have money!" McCain almost shouted the words. His voice echoed across the clearing and a couple of the guards turned towards him, checking that everything was all right. "Money is the god of the twenty-first century," he continued, more quietly. "It divides us and defines us. But it is no longer enough to have enough. You have to have more than enough. Look at the bankers with their salaries and their pensions and their bonuses and their extras. Why have one house when you can have ten? Why wait in line when you can have your own private jet? From the age of about thirteen, I realized that was what I wanted. And, very soon, that is what I shall have."

McCain had forgotten his food. He still hadn't tasted the wine but held it in front of him, admiring the colour, balancing the glass in the palm of his hand as if afraid of smashing it. Once again Alex was aware of the power of the man. He could imagine the huge muscles underneath the silk suit.

"I had little education," McCain went on. "The other children in my class saw to that. I had no prospects. I was, however, strong and fast on my feet. I became a boxer, a path which has seen more than one working-class boy rise to riches and success. And for a time, it looked as if the same might happen to me. I was known as a rising star. I trained in a gym in Limehouse and I threw myself into it. Sometimes I would go there for ten hours a day. This was in many respects the happiest time of my life. I loved the feel of my fist smashing into an opponent's face. I loved the sight of blood. And the sense of victory! Once, I knocked a man out. I thought for a moment I had killed him. It was a truly delicious sensation.

"But, as I have explained to you, my dream came to an end. My manager dropped me. The press, which had once fawned over me, forgot me. I returned to London with no money and no job. I had to move back in with my foster-parents but they didn't really want me. I was no longer a poor little boy that they could feel good about helping. I was a man. There was no room for me in their life.

"My foster-father managed to get me a job in an estate agency and that was how I found myself in the world of property. It was an area in which I had almost immediate success. I liked the company of estate agents. At that time, it was easy to make a fast profit and I began to do well. People noticed me. You could not be a successful black person in Britain without standing out, and as I moved up the ladder, more and more businessmen wanted to be seen with me, to pretend that they were my friends. People liked inviting me to dinner parties. They thought of me as a bit of a character –

particularly after my brief fame in the boxing ring.

"I made a large donation to the Conservative Party, and as a result I was asked if I would like to become a prospective member of Parliament. I accepted and was duly elected, even though the seat had been Labour for as long as anyone could remember. Success followed success, Alex. I became a junior minister in the department for sport. I would often find myself on the terrace outside the House of Commons, sipping champagne with the prime minister. The entire Cabinet came to my Christmas parties, which became famous for their fine vintage wine and macaroni cheese. I gave talks all over the country. And, thanks to my property empire, I was getting richer than ever. I still remember buying my first Rolls-Royce. At that point I couldn't even drive – but what did I care? The next day, I went out and hired a chauffeur. By the time I was thirty, I had a dozen people working for me."

He spread his hands. "And then it all went wrong again."

"You were sent to prison for fraud."

"Yes. Isn't it amazing how quickly people desert you? Without a moment's hesitation the British public turned their backs on me. I was thrown out of Parliament. Journalists jeered and mocked me,in a way that was every bit as bad as the boys I had once known at school. In prison I was beaten up so often that the hospital reserved a bed for me. Other men would have chosen to end it all, Alex – and there were times when even I considered dashing my head against a concrete wall. But I didn't – because already I was planning my comeback. I knew that I could use my disgrace as just one more step on the journey I had been born to make."

"You didn't convert to Christianity," Alex said. "You just pretended."

McCain laughed. "Of course! I read the Bible. I spent hours talking to the prison chaplain, a pompous fool who couldn't see further than the end of his own dog collar. I took a course on the Internet and got myself ordained. The Reverend Desmond McCain! It was all a sham, but it was necessary. Because I had worked out what I was going to do next. I was going to be rich again. A hundred times richer than I had ever been before."

Alex had left most of his food. One of the guards came over and took the plates away, removing McCain's unfinished food. Another brought over a basket of fruit. In the brief silence, Alex listened to the sounds of the night: the soft murmur of the river as it flowed past, the endless whisper of the undergrowth, the occasional cry of some animal far away. He was sitting in the open air, in Africa! And yet he was sharing a table with a madman. He knew it all too well. McCain might have suffered hardships in his life but what had happened to him had nothing to do with his background or his colour. He had been a psychopath from the start.

"Charity!" McCain said. "A very wise man once defined charity in the following way. He said it was poor people in rich countries giving money to rich people in poor countries." He smiled at the thought. "Well, I have been thinking a lot about charity, Alex – and in particular how to use it for my own ends." He looked up at the night sky, his eyes fixed on the full moon. "And in less than twenty-four hours, my moment will come. The seeds have already been sown ... and I mean that quite literally."

"I know what you're doing," Alex interrupted. "You're faking some sort of disaster. You're going to steal the money for yourself."

"Oh – no, no, no," McCain replied. He lowered his head and gazed at Alex. "The disaster is going to be quite real. It's going to happen here in Kenya, and very soon. Thousands of people will die, I'm afraid. Men, women and children. And let me tell you something rather disturbing. I really want you to know this.

"I can see the way you're looking at me, Alex. The contempt in your eyes. I'm used to it. I've had it all my life. But when the dying begins, just remember. It wasn't me who started it."

He paused. And somehow Alex knew what he was going to say next.

"It was you."

ALL FOR CHARITY

The guards had served coffee and McCain had lit a cigarette. Watching the grey smoke trickle out of the corner of his mouth, Alex was reminded of a gangster in an old black and white film. As far as he was concerned, the habit couldn't kill him quickly enough.

McCain stirred his coffee with a second silver straw. The night had become very still, as if even the animals out in the bush had decided to listen in. There was no breeze. The air was heavy and warm.

"There are two ways to become rich," McCain began again. "You can persuade one person to give you a lot of money – but that means finding someone who is wealthy and stupid enough in the first place, and it may involve criminal violence. Or you can ask a great many people to give you a little money. This was the thought that obsessed me while I was in prison and it was there that I came up with my idea. It was easy enough to fake my conversion to Christianity. Everyone likes a sinner who repents. And it certainly impressed the parole board. I was released a long time before I had completed my sentence and I immediately set up my charity, First Aid. The aim, as I described it, was to be the first organization to respond to disasters wherever they took place.

"I would imagine that you know very little about international charity, Alex. But when a catastrophe occurs – the Boxing Day tsunami is a good example – people all over the world rush to respond. Old-age pensioners dip into their savings. Five pounds here, ten pounds there. It soon adds up. At the same time, banks and businesses fight to outdo each other with very public displays of generosity. None of them really cares about people dying in underdeveloped countries. Some donate because they feel guilty about their own wealth. Others, as I say, do it for the publicity—"

"I don't agree with you," Alex cut in. He thought of Brookland School and the money they had collected for Comic Relief. There had been a whole week of activities and everyone had been proud of what they had achieved. "You see the world this way because you're horrible and insane. People give to charity because they want to help."

"Your opinions mean nothing to me," McCain snapped, and Alex was pleased to see that he was annoyed. The anger was pricking at his eyes. "And if you interrupt again, I'll have you tied down and beaten." He leant forward and sucked at his coffee. "The motives are irrelevant anyway. What counts is the money. Three hundred million was raised for the tsunami in the UK alone. It's very difficult to say what a charity like Oxfam raises internationally over a period of twelve months, but I can tell you that last year they reached the same figure – three hundred million in Great Britain. That was just one country. Oxfam also has branches in a dozen other countries and sub-branches in places like India and Mexico. You do the maths!"

McCain fell silent. For a moment, his eyes were far away.

"Millions and millions of pounds and dollars and euros," he murmured. "And because the cash comes so quickly and in such large amounts, it is almost impossible to follow. An ordinary business has accountants. But a charity operates in many countries, often in appalling conditions – which makes it much harder to pin down."

"So basically you're just a thief," Alex said. He knew he was treading close to the line but he couldn't resist needling McCain. "You're planning to steal a lot of money."

McCain nodded. Surprisingly he didn't seem offended. "I am a thief. But you underestimate me, Alex. I am the greatest thief who ever lived. And I do not need to take the money. People will give it to me willingly."

"You said you were going to create a disaster…"

"I'm glad you were listening. That is exactly what I am going to do – or perhaps I should say, it is exactly what I have done. The disaster is already happening, even as we sit here in this pleasant night air."

He stubbed out his cigarette and lit another.

"People need a reason to give money, and my genius, if you will forgive the word, has simply been to work out that the reason can be created artificially. I can give you an example. A serious accident took place last summer at the Jowada nuclear power station in Chennai, South India. That was a fairly simple matter, a bomb carried into the plant by one of my operatives. I have to say that the results were disappointing. The full force of the blast and the resulting radioactivity were contained and did less damage than I had hoped.

"But even so, First Aid were the first on the scene and received more than a million pounds in donations. Some of it, of course, we had to give away. We had to buy large quantities of some sort of anti-radiation drug and we had to pay for advertising. Even so, we made a tax-free profit of about four hundred thousand pounds. It was a useful dress rehearsal for the event I was planning here, in Kenya. It also helped us with our operating costs."

"And what are you planning here? What did you mean when you said I started it?"

"We'll come back to you in a minute, Alex. But what I am planning here is a good old-fashioned plague. Not just in Kenya but in Uganda and Tanzania too. I am talking about a disaster on a scale never seen before. And the beauty of it is that I am completely in control. But I don't need to describe it to you. I can show you. I am, as you will see, one step ahead of the game."

McCain opened his laptop and spun it round so that Alex could see the screen. "When the disaster begins, a few weeks from now, other charities will rush to the scene. In a sense, all charities are waiting for bad things to happen. It is the reason for their existence. We need to be faster than them. The first on the ground will scoop the lion's share of the money. So we have already prepared our appeal..."

He pressed ENTER.

A film began to play. Slowly the camera zoomed in on an African village. At first everything seemed normal. But then Alex heard the buzz of flies and saw the first dead bodies. A couple of cows lay on their sides with bloated stomachs and rigid, distended legs. The camera passed an eagle which seemed to have crash-landed, slamming into the dust. And at the same time, he heard a voice speaking in a soft, urgent tone.

"Something terrible is happening in Kenya," the commentary began. "A dreadful plague has hit the land and nobody knows how it started. But people are dying. In their thousands. The oldest and the youngest have been the first to go..."

Now the camera had reached the first child, who stared up with empty eyes.

"Animals are not immune. African wildlife is being decimated. This beautiful country is in the grip of a nightmare and we urgently need money now, to save it before it's too late. First Aid is running emergency food supplies. First Aid is already on the ground with vital medicine and fresh water. First Aid is funding urgent scientific research to find the cause of this disaster and bring it to an end. But we cannot do it without you. Please send as much as you can today.

"Call us or visit our website. Our lines are open twenty-four hours a day. Save Kenya. Save the people. How can we ignore their cry for help?"

The final image showed a giraffe stretched out in the grass, part of its ribcage jutting through its side. A phone number and a web address were printed over it with the First Aid logo below.

"I am particularly pleased with the giraffe," McCain said. He tapped the keyboard and froze the picture. "Many people in the First World just look away when a child or an old woman begs in the street. But they'll weep over a dead animal. A great many giraffes and elephants will die in Kenya in the next few months. It should double the amount we receive."

Alex sat in silence. Everything that McCain was saying sickened him. But it was worse than that. He knew exactly what he was looking at. The African village on the screen. He had been there. He had stood in the same village when he had broken into the Elm's Cross film studio. The only thing that was different was the backdrop. The green cyclorama had gone, replaced by swirling clouds and forest.

"You've made it all up," he gasped. "It's all fake. You built the village. It's a set..."

"We are merely preparing ourselves for the reality," McCain explained. "As soon as the first reports of the Kenyan plague hit the press, we will come forward with our television appeal. There will be posters and advertisements in all the newspapers. This will happen not just in England but in America, Australia and another dozen countries. And then we will sit back and wait for the money to flood in."

"And you're going to keep it! You're not going to help anyone!"

McCain smiled and blew smoke. "There's nothing anyone can do," he said. "Once the plague begins, there will be no stopping it. I can tell you that with certainty because, of course, I created it."

"Greenfields..."

"Exactly. I wish my good friend Leonard Straik was here to explain the science of it, but I'm afraid he met with an accident and won't be joining us. You could say he choked on a snail. Except the snail in question was the marbled cone variety and deadly poisonous. I have a feeling that Leonard's heart exploded before I forced it down his throat."

So McCain had murdered Straik. Presumably he

didn't want to share his profits with anyone. Alex filed the information away. He had to find a way to contact MI6.

"It works like this," McCain explained. He was enjoying himself and he didn't try to hide it. "You don't seem to have spent a lot of time at school, Alex, but can I assume you've heard of genes? Every single cell in your body has about thirty thousand of them – they are basically tiny pieces of code that make you what you are. The colour of your hair, your eyes and so on. It's all down to the genes.

"Plants are made up of genes too. The genes tell the plant what to do, whether to taste nice or not, for example. Now, what Mr Straik and his friends at Greenfields were doing was changing the nature of plants by effectively adding a single gene. Plants are more complicated than you might think. The information required to make a single stalk of wheat would fill a hundred books with a thousand pages each. And here's the remarkable thing. If you added just one paragraph of new information – the equivalent of an extra gene – you would change the entire library. Your wheat might still look like wheat but it would be very different. It might not be quite so tasty, for example, if eaten with milk and sugar for breakfast. It might, in fact, kill you.

"Do you see where I'm going with this? I'm talking about taking something very ordinary and agreeable and turning it into something lethal.

And this happens in every kitchen in the world almost every day of the week! Let me try to explain it to you.

"I'm sure you enjoy potatoes. Boys like you eat them all the time as chips and crisps. It probably never occurs to you that you are in fact eating a poisonous plant. Not many people realize that the potato is closely related to deadly nightshade. Its leaves and flowers are extremely toxic. They won't kill you but they will make you very sick indeed. What you actually eat is the tuber, the bit that grows underground.

"The tubers, of course, are delicious – but they can also harm you. If you leave them out in the sun, even for one day, they turn green and taste bitter. If you eat them after that, you will be sick. And why has this happened? There's a gene – a genetic switch – hidden inside the potato. It's completely harmless and almost invisible, but the sunlight seeks it out and turns it on. And once that happens, the tuber behaves differently. It goes green. It becomes poisonous. You have to throw it away.

"For the last five years Greenfields Bio Centre has been supplying seeds to grow wheat to several African countries. The wheat has been genetically modified to need less water and to produce extra vitamins. But what nobody knows is that Leonard Straik used his particle delivery system to add an extra gene to the package. Like the potato gene I just told you about, it's harmless. A loaf of Kenyan bread made out of home-grown Kenyan wheat will be fine. But once the genetic switch has been activated, although the wheat will look exactly the same, it will begin to change. It will quietly produce a toxin known as ricin. Ricin normally grows in castor beans and is one of the most lethal substances known to man. A tiny pellet will kill an adult. And very soon it will be growing all over Africa."

"That stuff I found in Straik's office," Alex muttered. "In the test tube..."

"You're very quick," McCain said. "The more I get to know you, Alex, the more I admire you. Yes. That is our activating agent. It is a sort of mushroom soup. And this is very important. It's not a chemical, it's a living organism – which is to say, it can reproduce itself.

"Again, I can explain this to you by taking you back to the kitchen. If you place an ordinary mushroom on a piece of paper and leave it overnight, you'll notice a blackish sort of dust covering the surface the next day. What you are looking at are spores. If they are released outside, spores will spread – a little bit like the common cold – travelling from one field to another. It may interest you to know that the Irish potato blight of 1845, which led to the death by starvation of almost a million people, was caused by a spore attacking the potato crop.

"I can see from your face that you're beginning to understand the exact purpose of the flight which you took this morning. You were kind enough to help Dr Bennett by pulling a lever inside the Piper Cub, and when you did this, you sprayed a single field of genetically modified wheat with the activating agent. Leonard Straik told me that it would take thirty-six hours for the reaction to occur. So, at sunset tomorrow, the genetic switch will be thrown and the wheat in the field will begin to produce ricin. But that will only be the start of it. This is the season of the wolf moon. Very soon the wind will carry the spores to the next field and to the one after that. Nothing will be able to stop them. Nothing will stand in their way.

"The birds will be the first to die. A little peck of poisoned wheat and they'll look like the plastic eagle you saw in that film. Then it will be the turn of the people. It's hard to believe that a loaf of bread bought from the local baker or wrapped in plastic on a supermarket shelf will contain enough poison to kill an entire family. But it will. It will have become a slice of death. Animals will die too. It will be as if God has passed judgement on the whole of Kenya.

"Except that it won't stop at the borders. Greenfields has sold millions of seeds to Africans in Uganda, Tanzania and all around. Soon the contamination will have spread across half the continent."

"They'll realize," Alex said. "People will know that the wheat is poisoned and they'll stop eating it. They'll burn the fields."

"That's exactly right, Alex. It will all be over very quickly. It won't even make a great economic difference to Kenya. They only grow two hundred and twenty-five thousand tonnes of wheat a year and a lot of their food is imported. But that's why First Aid has to act fast. It'll be in the initial panic, the first weeks, that we'll make our billions. People will rush to give money without thinking. And what do you imagine they'll do when they discover that it's only the wheat that has mysteriously developed this sickness, that the plague can be contained? Do you think they'll ask for their donations back? I doubt it.

"And anyway, it will be too late. By then I will have married and moved to South America. I already have a new identity waiting for me. I will have plastic surgery ... this time, I think, more successfully. I will re-emerge as a slightly mysterious billionaire businessman but I don't think people will ask too many questions about who I am or where I've come from. I discovered that when I was supporting the Conservative Party. When you are rich, people treat you with respect."

McCain fell silent. He had completed his explanation and sat back, waiting for Alex to respond. There was a sudden hiss as one of the logs in the fire collapsed in on itself and a flurry of sparks leapt into the night air. The guards had disappeared from sight but Alex knew they would be watching and would come in an instant if they were needed. He felt sick. It had been a final twist, a little act of extra cruelty, to make him pull the lever that had released the spores. There had been no real reason for it. It was just how McCain and his fiancée got their kicks.

"So what happens next?" he asked. "What do you want with me?

"Is that all you want to know? Haven't you got anything to say about my plan?"

"I think your plan is as sick as you are, Mr McCain. I'm not interested in it. I'm not interested in you. I just want to know why I'm here."

Perhaps McCain had been expecting applause or at least some sort of reaction from Alex but he was clearly disappointed, and when he spoke his voice was sullen. "Very well," he said. "I might as well tell you."

He had finished his second cigarette. He ground that out too.

"I have been thinking a great deal, Alex, about how you managed to cross my path on two occasions. The first time was at Kilmore Castle in Scotland. You were with the journalist, Edward Pleasure. Why were you there?"

"I'm a friend of his daughter's." Alex couldn't see any harm in admitting the truth. "He invited me."

"So it was just a coincidence?"

"That's right."

McCain considered this for a moment. "I was concerned about Pleasure," he continued. "I had been warned that he might be dangerous and I wondered how much he knew about me. I only agreed to be interviewed by him because to have refused might have raised his suspicions. And then, when I heard the two of you talking about genetic engineering..."

"You thought he was talking about his article?" Alex almost wanted to laugh. "I was telling him about my homework! He'd asked me how I was doing at school!"

"I believe you, Alex. But at the time, I couldn't take any chances. If Pleasure had found out about my involvement with Greenfields, he would have put this entire operation in jeopardy."

"So you decided to kill him. You got one of your people to shoot out his tyre."

"Actually, Myra did it for me. She was there too that night. Of course, there was a certain risk attached. But as you already know, I am something of a gambler. Perhaps that's why I allowed myself to lose my temper when you managed to beat me at cards."

He lifted a hand and waved. It was a signal. Two guards, both carrying rifles, began to approach the table. Dr Bennett was with them.

"The first time we met may have been a coincidence as you say," McCain said. "The second time most definitely was not. You were sent to Greenfields by MI6. There is no point in attempting to deny it. You were carrying equipment that allowed you to jam the surveillance cameras and you also exploded a chimney on the recycling unit roof. It is therefore absolutely critical for me to discover how much the intelligence services know about me and in particular about this operation. In short, I need to know why you were at Greenfields. How much of my conversation with Leonard Straik did you overhear? What were you able to tell MI6?"

Alex was about to speak but McCain held up a hand, stopping him. Bennett and the two guards had reached the table. They were standing behind Alex, waiting to escort him back to his tent.

"I do not want to hear any more from you tonight," McCain said. "It is already clear to me that you are brave and intelligent. It is quite possible that you would be able to deceive me. So I want you to consider the questions I have asked you. I will ask them again in the morning.

"But the next time I put them to you, it will not be over a pleasant dinner." McCain leant forward and Alex saw the ferocity in his eyes. "'Behold, I have the keys of hell and of death,' as it says in the Book of Revelation. Tomorrow I intend to torture you, Alex. I want you to sleep tonight in the knowledge that when the sun rises, I am going to inflict terror on you such as you have never known

315

in your life. I am going to strip you of your courage and your bravado so that when you open your mouth and speak to me, you will tell me everything I want to know and won't even contemplate lying. Over this table you have made some jokes at my expense, but you will not be making jokes when we meet again. You must be prepared to shed tears, Alex. Leave me now. And try to imagine, if you will, the horror that awaits you."

Alex felt the two men grab hold of his arms. He shrugged them off and stood up.

"You can do what you like to me, Mr McCain," he said. "But your plan will never work. MI6 will find you and they'll kill you. I expect they're already on their way."

"You're right about one thing," McCain replied. "I can do anything I like to you. And very soon I will. Goodnight, Alex. I'll leave you to your dreams."

Alex was taken away. The last thing he saw was Myra Bennett, standing behind McCain, massaging his shoulders. McCain himself was leaning forward with his elbows on the table, his hands in front of his face. He looked very much as if he was at prayer.

PURE TORTURE

The sun rose all too soon.

Alex watched the sides of his tent turn grey, silver, then finally a dirty yellow as the morning light intensified. He had lost his watch and had no idea of the time but, being so close to the equator, he suspected that it was earlier than he thought. When would they come for him? Exactly what sort of torture did McCain have in mind?

He lay back and closed his eyes, trying to fight off the demons of fear and despair. The fact was, he was completely in McCain's power. And McCain wasn't taking any chances. There had been guards – two Kikuyu tribesmen – outside his tent all night. He had heard them murmuring in low voices and had seen the occasional flare of a match as they lit cigarettes. Once, he thought he had heard a plane flying low overhead, but apart from that there had been nothing except for the usual, eternal sounds of the bush and Alex had been left entirely on his own, completely unable to sleep. Right now, he was close to exhaustion. He could see no way out.

The sun was getting stronger by the minute. Alex thought of it beating down in the Simba Valley, just two miles to the north. The wheat would be growing taller, turning gold. And the deadly spores that he himself had released would be activating themselves. Before nightfall they would be ready and then the winds would come and spread them all over Africa. Alex's eyes flickered open and suddenly he was angry. Why was he wasting time and energy worrying about himself when, in a few hours, half a continent might begin to die?

Eventually the flap of the tent opened and Myra Bennett stepped inside, dressed in white with a round, straw hat – the sort of thing a schoolgirl might have worn a hundred years ago. She had clipped two dark lenses over her spectacles to protect her eyes from the sun's glare. They made her look less human and more robotic than ever.

She was obviously surprised to see Alex lying on the bed, seemingly relaxed. "How did you sleep?" she asked.

"I slept very well, thank you," he lied. "Have you brought my breakfast?"

The woman scowled. "I think you will find you *are* the breakfast." She gestured at the exit. "Desmond is waiting. Let me show you the way..."

It was another beautiful day, with just a few wisps of cloud in an otherwise perfect sky. There was a familiar chatter above Alex's head and he looked up to see that at least one monkey had dared to come back, staring down at him with shock-filled eyes as if it knew what was about to happen. Birds with long tails and brilliant plumage hopped along the pathways. There was a time when tourists would have woken up to this scenery and thought themselves in heaven. But one sight of the glowering guards reminded Alex. McCain had turned it into his own peculiar version of hell.

"It's not very far," Bennett said. "Please, follow me."

She led him out of the camp, away from the open area where he had eaten the night before, and past the landing strip. Alex was still wearing part of his school uniform – the shirt, trousers and shoes. Even with his sleeves rolled up he was still too warm, but they hadn't bothered to give him any fresh clothes. He had just one crumb of comfort. The gel ink pen was in his trouser pocket. Even now he might get a chance to use it. He had no other surprises left.

With two guards behind him and Bennett a few steps ahead, he was taken down a path that followed the curve of the river. The camp disappeared behind them and in the far distance Alex saw a family of elephants washing themselves in the sparkling water. It was an extraordinary sight but he couldn't enjoy it. Not when it might be the last thing he ever saw.

Desmond McCain was waiting ahead of them,

dressed comfortably in a well-tailored safari suit with a white silk cravat. It seemed they had arrived at their destination. Alex looked around him. He didn't like what he saw.

A steep slope ran down to a stretch of sandy shingle, a narrow beach at the very edge of the water. There was a stepladder, three or four metres high, standing on the beach, and above it a metal pipe that had been fastened to the branch of a tree. The pipe ended with two handles and reminded Alex of a periscope in a submarine. A wooden observation platform had been constructed at the top of the slope. This was where McCain was standing.

Alex had already worked out what might be going on here and was making calculations. If he walked down to the beach and climbed the ladder, he would be able to reach the handles. Then the ladder could be taken away and he would be left hanging from the pipe. He would be close enough to the platform to be able to talk to McCain and to hear what he had to say – but not close enough to reach him. Because the pipe was rigid, he wouldn't be able to swing back and forth. In other words, he would simply have to stay there until his arms grew tired and he dropped.

The question was – why? What was the point?

"This will not take very long, Alex," McCain said. He had watched Alex taking everything in. "I will talk to you a little bit and then, I'm afraid, we will begin. As I have already told you, I need most urgently the answer to the questions which I put to you last night. What was it that brought you to Greenfields? Why did MI6 send you? And how much do the intelligence services know about Poison Dawn?"

Alex had already decided what he was going to say. "You don't need to play your sadistic games, Mr McCain," he said. "I'll tell you what you want to know anyway..."

McCain held up a hand. "I don't think you were listening to me during dinner. Of course you will tell me what I want to hear. That is the point I'm trying to make. You will tell me anything to protect yourself. But I have to be one hundred per cent certain that you are telling me the truth. There cannot be even the tiniest margin of doubt."

"And you think torturing me will achieve that?"

"Normally, no. There are many horrible things I could do to you, Alex. We have electricity here, and wires attached to various parts of your body would produce excruciating pain. My Kikuyu friends could take you far beyond the limits of endurance using only their spears, perhaps heated first in the flames of a fire. We could cut pieces off you. We could boil you alive. And do not think for a single minute that I would hesitate to do any of this because you are only fourteen. MI6 clearly do not think of you as a child, so why should I?"

"Is part of the torture boring me to death?" Alex asked.

McCain nodded. "Bravely spoken, Alex. Let us see how brave you are ten minutes from now." He took out a handkerchief and wiped his brow. The sun was beating down on his bald head and beads of sweat were standing out. "The pain that you are about to experience is going to be all the worse because you will inflict it on yourself. You will, as it were, cooperate with your torturers. And you will do so to escape the terror that lies below." He took out a gun, an old-fashioned Mauser with a shortened barrel and a white ivory grip. It looked like something out of a museum. "I would like you now to go down to the river," he explained. "If you refuse to do so, if you attempt to run away, I will shoot you through the knee."

Alex stayed where he was. Bennett was smiling properly for the first time and he realized that she knew what to expect, that she had seen this all before. The two guards were covering him with their rifles. If McCain missed with his pistol, they would certainly shoot him before he'd taken a single step. He glanced at the beach and the river. There was nobody else down there. He had a nasty feeling he wasn't going to be alone for long.

"I'm waiting, Alex," McCain said.

Without speaking, Alex made his way down the slope. Now McCain and the others were directly above him, looking down from the protected height of the observation platform. Alex was reminded of a Roman emperor and his entourage. They were in the imperial stand. He was the gladiator, about to entertain them. What about the ladder and the steel pipe? He was beginning to see their purpose too.

"This is part of the River Simba," McCain explained. "It runs all the way up to the Simba Dam and Lake Simba beyond. It is the water from this river that feeds my wheat field, Alex. And as you are about to learn, it is infested with crocodiles."

"Here comes one now!" Bennett crowed.

Crocodiles.

Alex turned to see a dark shape on the opposite bank dart forward and launch itself into the water, followed quickly by a second. There was something strikingly evil about the way they moved. They twisted and sliced through the water like two knife wounds and somehow they managed to swim – or slither – very quickly without seeming to be in a hurry. Alex realized that they would cross the river in less than a minute. They somehow knew he was here. But of course – they had been fed this way before.

Alex looked up. Bennett was gazing at him with her mouth open, and he could see the saliva glistening on her lips and tongue. McCain was next to her, his gun held loosely, watching with interest. Alex glanced back. The crocodiles were halfway across the river. He wanted to run but he knew he would be gunned down if he tried. Nor would he be allowed onto the safety of the platform. Everything had been carefully arranged. There was only one way of escape.

Sick with himself, knowing that he was doing exactly what McCain wanted, Alex stepped onto the ladder. He was trying not to panic but his every instinct was driving him up, out of harm's way. As he drew nearer to the top he felt the whole structure tremble beneath him, and for one terrible moment he thought he was going to fall. Somehow he managed to steady himself. He neared the top even as the first crocodile heaved itself out of the water and began to crawl towards him.

Alex turned back and looked at it. It was a mistake. In an instant he felt the terror that McCain had promised him, the deep-rooted fear of this ancient monster that had to be hot-wired into every human being. The crocodile that had just emerged was almost twice his own size from the ugly snout to the writhing tip of its tail. Its great jaws were open, two lines of ferocious white teeth waiting to snap shut on his arm or leg. That was how they operated, of course, clamping down on their victims and then dragging them back into the water. And only when the bones were loose and the flesh had begun to decompose would they start their feast.

But worst of all were the eyes, midnight black, snake-like and swollen on the sides of its head, surely too small for its body and filled with hatred. They really were the eyes of death. Alex had heard it said that crocodiles wept as they attacked their prey, but there would be no pity in those eyes. They were part of a machine that existed only to kill.

The second crocodile was a little smaller and much quicker. Alex saw it overtake the other, scuttling over the shingle on its short, squat legs all the way to the foot of the ladder. He climbed the last few steps, using his hands to steady himself at the top. If he fell... He could imagine it. Smashing into the shingle. Perhaps breaking an ankle or a leg. And then being torn apart by the two animals as they fought over him. There could be no more horrible death.

The crocodile threw itself at the ladder and the whole frame shuddered. How many people had McCain terrorized in this way? Alex looked up. He still wasn't level with the observation platform. He knew what he had to do. With dreadful care he balanced himself on the highest step. The handles at the end of the pipe were directly above him. Swaying, using his arms to steady himself, he reached up and grabbed hold of them. His fingers closed around them even as the larger crocodile reared up, hurling its entire weight against the ladder. The whole thing came crashing down. Alex was left dangling in space.

And now he saw how McCain had arranged this.

He was facing McCain, the two of them level, about a metre and a half apart. The crocodiles were directly underneath Alex, climbing on top of each other, snapping at the air. For the moment, he was safe. But he was stretched out, hanging in space, clinging to the pipe by his fingers. His wrists and arms were already feeling the strain as they supported his entire body weight, and the burn of lactic acid was building up in his shoulders. It was just as McCain had said. He was the one causing himself the pain – and it would get worse the longer he hung there. In the end, of course, he would have to let go. And that was the horror of it. Once he dropped, there would only be more pain and then death. How long did he have?

"The longest anyone has ever remained where you are is eighteen minutes," McCain said. He spoke slowly and evenly. He didn't have to raise his voice to make himself heard. "The man in question lost his sanity before the end. He was giggling as he fell. But you, Alex, you have one hope, one chance of survival. My men can shoot at the crocodiles and scare them away. But first you have to answer my questions, and I have to believe you. If you can make that happen, then you will be safe..."

Alex swore. It was difficult to speak. All his concentration was fixed on his hands, the increasing pain in his arms, the need not to let go.

"I dislike that sort of language, Alex," McCain said. "I am, after all, an ordained priest. Would you like me to go away for five minutes and come back when you're in a better frame of mind?"

One of the crocodiles lunged towards him. Instinctively Alex pulled his legs up, tucking his knees in towards his stomach. The movement put extra strain on his arms but he actually heard the jaws of the animal snap together and he knew there could only have been inches between its teeth and his ankles.

"No!" he shouted. His voice was strangled. He didn't sound like himself. He had to get this over with. "Ask me what you want..."

He had been hanging for less than a minute. It felt longer. He would never manage another five, let alone another seventeen. In his desperation he found himself twisting. His arms crossed and he had to jerk his body back round to bring himself face to face with McCain.

"The first question, then." McCain paused. He was speaking deliberately slowly. He knew that every second only added to the torture. "Why were you at Greenfields?"

"It was a school trip."

"You're still lying to me, Alex. I'm going to leave you for a little while..." McCain turned his back on Alex and walked away. At the same moment, Alex heard a strange piglike grunting and looked down. Below, on the beach, the crocodiles were writhing together in a frenzy of claws and scales and black eyes and teeth.

"It's the truth!" Alex shouted after him. His

hands were sweating, making it even more difficult to keep his grip. "It was a geography project.
But then MI6 asked me to help them. They weren't
interested in you. It was Leonard Straik."

McCain turned back. "Go on."

"There was someone in Greenfields. An informer..."
What was his name? Alex thought back desperately.
"Philip Masters. He'd gone to the police and then
he got killed. That was why they wanted to find out
about Straik."

"You broke into his computer."

"They gave me a Memory Stick. That was all they
asked me to do."

"What about Poison Dawn?"

"They never said anything about Poison Dawn.
They never even mentioned it to me. I'm telling
you, they only knew about you and Straik when I
told them I'd seen you together."

"That was very unfortunate. What else did you
tell them?"

"I told them I'd heard the two of you talking – but
you didn't say anything that made any sense. I gave
them the stuff I found in Straik's office." To Alex, it
was as if his arms were being torn out of his shoulders. He didn't dare look at the crocodiles below.
"But I never even spoke to them again. I don't know
what they know. They don't know anything..."

McCain let him dangle in silence. Ten seconds
dragged to twenty and then to half a minute. Alex
felt every one of them. He could feel his bones

wrenching in their sockets and knew that McCain was doing this on purpose. He was staring straight into Alex's eyes as if trying to read what was going on inside his mind. Alex tried to ease his grip but his palms were so slippery that the smallest movement could make him fall. Dr Bennett had edged closer to him. She was breathing heavily, watching Alex struggle with evident delight. He could see himself reflected in the dark circles of her glasses.

The silence stretched out. Alex could smell the crocodiles, a deep, sickly odour of stale fish and decaying meat that rose up and crept into his nostrils. He was finding it difficult to breathe. The pain was getting worse and worse. All the muscles in his upper body were burning.

"I believe you," McCain said at last. "You are telling the truth."

"Then get rid of them..." Alex jerked his head towards the crocodiles. They had been silent and utterly still, watching him with something like a smile, as if they had all the time in the world. But the moment they made eye contact they seemed to sense it, and they both leapt up again, launching themselves at Alex's feet; and if he hadn't immediately coiled himself into a ball, drawing his knees up, they would have had him. The crocodiles fell back and lay still again, one across the other. They knew it was only a matter of time before they got what they wanted.

Another long pause. Alex's arms screamed.

"I'm afraid I've changed my mind," McCain said.

"What?" Alex shouted the word.

"You have annoyed me very much, Alex. I nearly killed you when you were in Scotland, and it would have been a lot better if I had. Your activities at Greenfields very nearly brought an end to an operation that has taken me five years and a great deal of money to develop. Thanks to you, my name is now known to MI6 and that will make my future life more difficult. And, added to that, you are a very troublesome boy, and all in all I think you deserve to die." He turned to Myra Bennett. "I know you enjoy this, my love, so you can stay to the end. I'll be interested to know how many minutes he manages to hang on before he falls. I somehow doubt that he'll beat the record."

The woman took out her mobile phone. "I shall take photographs for you, Dezzy."

McCain took one last look at Alex. "I hope you die painfully," he said. "Because although you have not lived long, I really think you deserve an unpleasant death."

He signalled to the guards and the three of them walked away. But he had given his gun to Dr Bennett. She was holding it in one hand, the mobile phone in the other. Behind him, Alex heard a splash. A third crocodile had launched itself into the river and was already wriggling its way across.

"Four minutes." The woman glanced at her watch. "I do not think you will make five."

And she was right. Everything was pain, and with every second the pain was getting worse. Alex couldn't swing himself to safety. He couldn't climb. He couldn't move. He could only fall.

He closed his eyes and knew that very soon he would do just that.

RAW DEAL

Seven minutes. Maybe eight minutes. Alex wasn't even sure why he was hanging on any more. His whole body was racked with pain and blood was pounding in his ears and behind his eyes. With every second that passed, the strength was draining out of his arms. He tried to accept what was about to happen: his fingers slipping off the handles, the short fall down to the riverbank, the jarring impact and then the final horror as the crocodiles attacked.

Myra Bennett leant over. "Do you have any last words?" she asked. "Any goodbyes you want to make? I can record them for you." She held out her mobile phone.

"Go rot in hell." Alex's eyes felt as if they were swollen shut but he forced them open, staring straight at her.

"You are the one on the way to hell, my dear," she said.

Her eyes widened. She took a step towards him

as if something had surprised her. Once again she opened her mouth and Alex thought she was about to speak, but instead a stream of blood poured over her lower lip. A moment later, she pitched forward and fell, and Alex glimpsed the hilt of a knife jutting out of her back. Desperately clinging on to the handles, he corkscrewed round and looked down.

The woman had landed in the middle of the crocodiles. She was still alive. He heard her scream as she was torn apart, her arms and legs being pulled in three directions. He turned away. He couldn't watch any more.

He was going to join her. His own strength was gone. He felt his grip loosening. But then suddenly there was a man on the observation platform, leaning out, reaching towards him, and even as Alex wondered where the man had come from he knew that he had seen him somewhere before.

"Alex!" the man whispered. "Take my hand."

"I can't reach..."

"One last effort. You can make it."

The distance was too great. Alex would have to let go with one hand and throw himself sideways, reaching out with it. If he miscalculated or if the man was tricking him, that would be it. The crocodiles would get a second feed.

"Now!" The man couldn't shout. They were too close to the camp. His voice was an urgent whisper.

Alex did as he was told, stretching as far as he

could, using every muscle to propel his body away from the handles. The man was leaning out. And somehow, just when Alex was certain he would fall, they managed to lock together, wrist in hand and hand over wrist.

"OK. I've got you. I'll take your weight..."

Alex let go of the other handle. He felt the man pull him towards the platform. Even so, there was one dreadful moment when he was sure they had overbalanced and they would fall together. He came crashing down. But he was right on the edge of the platform. He clawed at the wooden planks and managed to find some purchase. His legs were dangling below him but then he pulled himself forward and rolled over onto his side. He was lying next to the man who had just rescued him. He was safe.

For a few seconds he lay in silence, recovering his breath and waiting for his jangling nerves to calm down. Then he looked up. The man was Asian, young, with very dark skin and close-cropped hair, dressed in camouflage khakis with a harness for three knives strapped across his chest. One knife was missing.

Alex knew him at once. With a sense of astonishment he remembered where they had met before. It was the man from Loch Arkaig, the driver of the white van who had appeared from nowhere when he had crawled out of the freezing water. He had driven Alex, Sabina and Edward Pleasure to hospital. And now he was here! What sort of guardian angel was he, operating on two sides of the world?

"Who are you?" Alex asked.

"My name is Rahim," the man said. "But now we must leave. When they find the woman is missing, they will come looking for her. Here – give me your shirt."

Alex didn't know what the man was thinking but this was no time for an argument. He stripped off his school shirt and handed it over. Rahim took out a second knife and cut the shirt to shreds, then tossed it down to the crocodiles. There were now only two of them on the beach, fighting over what was left of the woman. The third one had returned to the river, dragging part of her with it.

The pieces of Alex's shirt fluttered down onto the riverbank. "It may fool them," Rahim said. "It may not. Let's go."

"Go where?"

"I have a camp."

Alex followed Rahim off the platform and away from the river, heading into the bush. He was alarmed to see that Rahim was limping badly and that the back of his jacket was covered in sweat. The man had a fever. Alex had also seen it in his eyes. He was clearly a soldier of some sort, extremely fit. But he was also hurt. It was only willpower that was keeping him going.

Even so, they maintained a fast pace for the next

fifteen minutes, finally arriving at a clearing dominated by a huge *Kigelia africana* – a sausage tree – with its strange black pods hanging down from the branches. This was where Rahim had set up a makeshift camp. Alex saw a backpack, a few tins of food and – at least this answered one of his questions – a parachute made of black silk, bunched up and tucked under a bush. A very sophisticated-looking gun was leaning against the trunk of the tree. It was a Dragunov SVD-59 gas-operated sniper rifle, built in Russia but used extensively by the Indian army.

Rahim went over to the backpack and took out a spare T-shirt. He threw it to Alex. "Here. You can wear this." He opened a water bottle and drank, then offered it to Alex. Alex took a swig. The water was warm and tasted of chemicals.

"You were in Scotland," Alex said.

"Yes." Rahim was exhausted. The sweat was pouring down his face and he was breathing heavily, fighting against the fever. Now Alex saw that one of his legs was bleeding. It was probably bandaged underneath the trousers but the blood was seeping through. Rahim sat down and began to untie his shoelaces. He was wearing heavy combat boots.

"How safe are we here?" Alex asked.

"Not safe. The Kikuyu will be able to track us. Maybe McCain will think you are dead. But he is already nervous. He will not take any chances."

"You're hurt." Alex handed back the water bottle. "What can I do to help you?"

"I was unlucky." Rahim drank a second time. "I parachuted in last night." Alex remembered hearing a plane. It had passed over the safari camp, flying close to the ground. "I landed badly in a thorn bush and cut my leg open. The wound has become infected. But I have taken antibiotics and I will recover. There is nothing you can do."

"You've told me your name but you haven't said why you're here."

Rahim didn't reply but Alex had already worked it out for himself.

"You were at Kilmore Castle, so you must be interested in McCain."

Rahim nodded.

"Who are you working for?"

Rahim took a deep breath and shifted his position. The movement caused him pain. "I know who you are," he said. "You are Alex Rider. You are a part-time operative working with the Special Operations division of MI6. They are looking for you. They have put out the call to every intelligence service, including mine."

"But you didn't come here looking for me."

"I did not expect to find you here, Alex." Rahim smiled, and at that moment Alex saw how young he was, perhaps only twenty-three or four. There might be less than ten years between them. "I was sent here for one reason only. It was the same reason that I was sent to Kilmore Castle, and this is now the second time you have got in my way. I am here to kill Desmond McCain."

"Why?" There were so many questions Alex wanted to ask and he was aware of the clock ticking, The guards could come looking for them at any time. But at least the rifle might put the odds more on their side.

Rahim took a plastic bottle out of his pocket. "I will tell you," he said. He tipped two pills into the palm of his hand and dry swallowed them. He grimaced. "I am a spy like you, Alex. I belong to a division of the Indian secret service called RAW. It stands for Research and Analysis Wing and it deals in counter-terrorism, foreign affairs and covert action. My own department goes further than that. Our activities often come under a single word. Revenge."

"This is about the nuclear power station," Alex said. "The one that McCain tried to destroy."

Rahim nodded. "The Jowada facility in Chennai. We know that he bribed a man by the name of Ravi Chandra to carry a device into the building. It was a lamentable lapse in security, but the security at Jowada was in general a disgrace. Unfortunately we were unable to question Chandra, because he died in the initial explosion. McCain took a great deal of care. There were a number of connections between him and the man who paid Chandra, but we investigated and in the end we found a link with First Aid. Suddenly everything made sense. Even so, we cannot prove the case against McCain but nor do we need to. Sometimes RAW deals with its enemies in a simpler and more direct way. I was sent to Scotland to kill him there and I was checking out the castle when your car went off the road and into the loch. That was fortunate for you. And it is even more fortunate that I should be here a second time. That business with the crocodiles..." Rahim gave Alex the ghost of a smile. "I have never seen anything like that."

"How were you going to kill him?" Alex asked.

"I was planning to shoot him but, as I discovered last night, that will not be as easy as I thought. He is well protected by his guards. However, I have come prepared. I can also blow up his plane."

"You have plastic explosive?"

"Of course." Rahim gestured at his backpack. "McCain flies a four-seater Cessna 172 Skyhawk."

Alex nodded grimly. "That must have been what brought me here."

"I will blow it up in mid-air. In a way, that is the better option. It is part of my brief that RAW should not be seen to be involved. A bomb, I think, will be more anonymous than a bullet."

"I'm afraid you're going to have to think again, Rahim." Alex went over to the Indian agent and sat down next to him. His thoughts had already raced ahead. "I have to contact MI6," he said.

"You want to let them know you are safe."

"More than that. Do you have a radio?"

"I have a laptop equipped with a demodulator. It will produce a baseband output signal that can be picked up by satellite. Do you have an address?"

"No." It only occurred to Alex now. In all the missions he had undertaken for MI6, they had never once given him an email address or a phone number. On the other hand, he'd been supplied with gadgets. What about the calculator with the built-in communications system? It was a shame it hadn't been in his pocket when he was snatched.

"It's not a problem," Rahim said. "We can contact the Intelligence Bureau in New Delhi. They will pass on any message to Liverpool Street. What is it you want to say?"

Quickly Alex told Rahim everything that he had learnt from Desmond McCain the night before: the genetically modified wheat crop, the spores, the plan to poison half the continent. "We have less time than you thought," he said. "And killing McCain right now isn't going to do anyone any good. We have to go north to the Simba Valley. It's only three miles from here..."

Rahim shook his head. "I'm sorry, Alex. I don't have enough explosive to blow up an entire wheat field."

"That's not my idea." Alex was weighing up what McCain had told him, and what he had seen for himself when he was in the crop duster. "There's a place called the Simba Dam," he explained. "It's on the edge of a big lake. I saw it from the plane. If we could blow it up, we could flood the valley. We could put the whole crop underwater before it has a chance to do any harm. But we have to do it today. Right now. McCain said that the spores would start working at sunset. It must be early afternoon now."

"Alex, I know this dam," Rahim said. "I studied the whole area before I parachuted in. It is what is known as a double curvature arch dam – it curves against the side of the valley and also against the valley floor, making it doubly strong. I have just one kilogram of plastic explosive. That would not be nearly enough even to make a crack in the wall."

"There must be some sort of pipe or valve..."

"There will be a whole series of pipes carrying the water down the hill. The Simba Dam is used for irrigation purposes but there are also two hydro-electric turbines." Alex was impressed. Rahim had clearly done his homework. "It might be possible to attack the bottom outlet valve or the scour valve that is next to it. Either of them would release enormous amounts of water." He shook his head. "But it cannot be done."

"Why not?"

"Because I cannot do it. My leg is infected. I was barely able to limp to the river. The Simba Dam is over three miles from here."

"I could go on my own."

"That I will not allow."

Alex thought for a minute. "You parachuted in," he said. "How were you planning to leave?"

"McCain has a crop duster as well as the Skyhawk. I imagine he used it to spread this spore of his that you described." Alex nodded. He remembered all too well the moment when he had pulled the lever. "I can fly," Rahim went on. "I was intending to steal it."

"Then you could fly me to the dam?"

"There is nowhere to land. I might be able to slow the plane to as little as thirty-five miles per hour and fly low over the water to allow you to jump, but even so the chances are high that you would be killed."

Alex lost his temper. "We can't just sit back and do nothing!"

"No, Alex. We can contact the Intelligence Bureau as I have already suggested. They will, in turn, speak to the British authorities. Together they will know what to do." Rahim went on quickly, before Alex could interrupt him. "I have my instructions. I am here to kill McCain. I was acting improperly when I decided to rescue you and I can assure you my superiors will not be amused when I make my report." He broke off. He was sweating again and his eyes were unfocused. "My laptop..." Rahim pointed at the backpack. He was too weak to go over himself.

Alex stood up. He went over to the backpack and opened it. Everything was packed very neatly inside. There was the laptop, a map, a compass, ammunition for the Dragunov, medical supplies, spare clothes and food. Much of the space was taken up by a silver box about the size of a car battery with two switches and a clock set behind glass. Alex knew at once what it was. Rahim was planning to conceal it in the Skyhawk's hold.

"Bring it to me," Rahim said.

Alex left the bomb and carried the laptop over. Rahim opened it, booted it up and then handed it across. "It will be easier if you do it," he said. "But I suggest you don't take too long. We will have to move from this place before the Kikuyu come looking for us and I need to break into the Skyhawk and prepare it for its last flight."

Alex crouched down. It felt weird to be tapping away at a keyboard sitting in the dust in the middle of the African bush. He wondered what either the British or the Indian authorities would be able to do. Another five hours and it might be too late. He briefly outlined the location of the valley, the crop that McCain was growing there, his plan to bring famine and disease to Kenya. Finally he added a PS.

Please let Jack Starbright know where I am and tell her I'm all right.

If there was one good thing to come out of all this, it was that Jack would know he hadn't been hurt. He quickly read the page over and pressed SEND.

He looked up. Rahim had slumped forward. Alex went over and examined him. The RAW agent was unconscious, breathing heavily. He had been knocked out – either by the fever or by the medicine he had been taking to fight it. Alex eased him gently to the ground, then looked back in the direction of the camp. Everything was silent in the bush as even the animals slept in the afternoon sun. It was very hot but at least Rahim was tucked away in the shade of the sausage tree.

What would London do when they received the news?

Alex had visions of Alan Blunt and Mrs Jones conferring with the appropriate ministers at Downing Street. A new government had recently been voted in. They probably wouldn't even know he existed, so they would have to be persuaded he was reliable, that his information was accurate. And then they would have to make a decision ... but what exactly were their options? They could send in troops with flame-throwers, but that might take days. In fact Alex couldn't be certain that the Indian secret service would even pass the message on in time. After all, they had their own agenda. They simply wanted McCain dead.

He didn't like it but he knew what he had to do. He took the map out of Rahim's backpack and studied it. Simba River Camp was clearly marked – and there was the track that he had seen from the air. It led all the way to the dam, rising up the side of the valley. He could follow the river for the first half-mile and then cut across the countryside. It wouldn't be too difficult to pick up the track. There was electricity up there. He had seen one of the pylons. If he could find it again, it would lead him to the dam.

Finally Alex examined the bomb. It wasn't very complicated. All he would have to do was set the timer, which operated like an ordinary alarm clock, then activate it by throwing a single switch. What was it that Rahim had told him? He had to locate one of the two main valves. That was where he would place the bomb.

Alex left Rahim the medicine and supplies, then put on the backpack and tightened the straps. He felt bad walking out on the agent, particularly after he had just saved his life. But at least he could make sure that he wasn't found by the guards. He would follow the path back to the bank where he had first been taken. He would do his best to cover his tracks, and then he would set off in another direction, making sure that he disturbed the vegetation as much as possible. If McCain did realize that Bennett was missing and sent his men after him, they would follow the new path. Rahim would be left alone and Alex had no doubt that, once he woke up, he would be able to look after himself.

The decision was made. Alex glanced up at the sky. The sun was beating down on him. It was clearly now well into the afternoon. Before long it would begin its journey down.

Alex took a swig out of the water bottle and set off. Three miles in this unfamiliar countryside might take him as many hours. He just hoped he wasn't already too late.

MARGIN OF ERROR

Two o'clock in the afternoon, London time.

The navy blue Jaguar XJ6 drove round Trafalgar Square and then headed down Whitehall in the direction of Big Ben and the Houses of Parliament. The weather forecasters had been predicting snow but so far it had held off. Even so, it was a hard, cold day with the wind skittering along the pavements. Inside the car, the heating had been turned up and the windows were tinted. Both of these helped keep the winter at bay.

The Jaguar passed the famous Banqueting House, where the first King Charles had lost his head, and turned into Downing Street. The black steel gates opened automatically to admit it. It stopped outside Number 10 and two people, a man and a woman, got out. As always, there was a handful of news reporters in the street, making their broadcasts against the backdrop of the most famous door in the world, but none of them noticed the two new arrivals and if they had it would have been extremely unlikely that they would have recognized them. Alan Blunt and Mrs Jones had never been photographed. Their names didn't appear on any government or civil service lists.

They didn't need to knock. The door swung open as they approached and they passed into the brightly coloured entrance hall. A surprisingly long corridor stretched out in front of them. They made no sound at all as they walked along the plush carpet, beneath the chandeliers, towards the far staircase. As usual, the walls were lined with paintings that had been borrowed from a central government collection. They were by British artists, most of them modern and rather bland.

Blunt examined them as he walked past, not because he was interested in art – he wasn't – but because they might give him some insight into the mind of the man who had chosen them. There was a new prime minister in Downing Street. He had been voted in just a month before. And what did the paintings say about him? He liked the countryside, fox-hunting and windmills. His favourite colour was blue.

Of course, Blunt already knew everything about the new man – from the state of his marriage (happy) to the last payment he had made on his credit card (£97.60 for a meal at the Ivy). There wasn't a single MP in England who hadn't been thoroughly checked by MI6: their families, their friends and associates, what websites they liked to visit, where they took their holidays, how much they spent every week. There was always a chance that the information might reveal a security risk or something that the MP didn't want anyone to know.

The two of them reached the staircase and began to climb up to the first floor, passing portraits and photographs of past prime ministers, spaced out at regular intervals. There was a man in a suit waiting at the top, gesturing towards an office. The building was full of young men in suits, some of them working for Blunt although they probably didn't know it. Blunt and Mrs Jones went into the office and there was the prime minister, sitting behind a desk.

"Mr Blunt, Mrs Jones ... please take a seat."

The prime minister wasn't happy, and it showed. Like all politicians, he didn't entirely trust his spymasters and he certainly didn't want them sitting opposite him now. It wasn't fair. He hadn't been in power very long. It was too soon for his first international crisis. There were two men sitting with him, one on each side. They were trying to look relaxed, as if they had just happened to be passing and had decided to pop in for the meeting.

"I don't think you've met Simon Ellis," the prime minister said, nodding at the fair-haired, rather plump man on his left. "And this is Charles Blackmore." The other man was also young, though with prematurely grey hair. "I thought it might be helpful if they joined us."

Blunt hadn't met either of them but of course he knew everything about them. They had both been at Winchester College with the prime minister. Ellis was now a junior civil servant in the Treasury. Blackmore had left a career in television to become director of strategy and communications. The two men loathed each other. The prime minister didn't know this. They were also loathed by almost everyone else.

"Well..." the prime minister began. He licked his lips. "I've read your report on the situation in Kenya and it does seem to be very alarming. But the first question I really do have to ask you is why did your agent feel it necessary to send his information via the Indian secret service? And secondly, why did it take them so long to send it on?"

"I'm afraid I can't answer that," Blunt replied. "We only know what you know, Prime Minister. It's all in the file. Our agent was kidnapped and smuggled out of the country against his will. Somehow he must have managed to break free and fall in with an agent from RAW."

"Research and Analysis Wing," Blackmore muttered helpfully.

"We have no idea what RAW were doing in Kenya and so far they've refused to tell us. I'm afraid foreign intelligence agencies are always overcautious when it comes to protecting their own. But if I may say so, Prime Minister, it's completely irrelevant.

What matters is the report itself and the very serious threat it contains."

The prime minister picked up a sheet of paper that had been lying in front of him. "This was sent by email," he said.

"Yes."

"And it suggests that this man, Desmond McCain, is engaged in a plot to poison the wheat crop in Kenya for his own financial gain."

Blunt blinked heavily. "I'm glad you've had time to read it," he said.

The prime minister ignored the rudeness. He put the paper down. "What makes you believe this information is reliable?" he asked.

"We have absolutely no reason to doubt it."

"And yet I understand that this agent of yours, the one who sent the report – which, incidentally, has no fewer than three spelling mistakes – is only fourteen years old."

There was a long pause. The two advisers glanced at the prime minister, urging him on.

"Alex Rider. Is that his name?" the prime minister asked.

"He's never let us down in the past," Mrs Jones cut in. She was carrying a slim leather case which she opened. She took out a thin file marked TOP SECRET in red letters and handed it across. "These are the details of just four of the assignments he's undertaken on our behalf," she continued. "The most recent of them was in Australia."

"Shouldn't he be in school?"

"He called in sick."

"Let me have a look." The prime minister opened the file and read it in silence. "You certainly seem to have a very high opinion of him," he remarked. "And let's say for the sake of argument that it's justified. Let's assume that everything he has told you is true..."

"Then by half past four London time, the wheat will have been activated," Blunt said. "It will have been turned into a million doses of ricin. And as soon as the wind rises, the spores which McCain sprayed over the field will take off and begin to spread across the rest of Kenya. They will settle on the next field and then the one after that. It's impossible to say how many millions of seeds Greenfields has supplied over the past five years. All we know for sure is that within three months, the entire country will be poisoned."

"We can let McCain know we're on to him," Ellis said. "There won't be any charity appeal. Once he knows that, there'll be no point in going ahead."

"I agree." Blackmore nodded, secretly annoyed that he hadn't spoken first.

"We don't have any way to contact McCain, short of parachuting into Simba River Camp," Blunt replied. "And anyway, we're too late. There's a biological clock that's already ticking. The damage has been done."

"So what do you suggest?"

"We need to speak to the Kenyan government and send in troops. The field has to be neutralized, probably with flame-throwers. And we also have to find Alex Rider. We've heard nothing more from him. I want to know he's safe."

Although she didn't show it, Mrs Jones was surprised. It was the first time she had ever heard Blunt express any concern for Alex. Even when he had been shot, Blunt's first priority had been keeping the story out of the newspapers.

"I'm not sure that's possible, Mr Blunt." The prime minister shifted uncomfortably in his seat. "It might be a bit awkward explaining to the Kenyan authorities that a British citizen has just launched a biochemical attack on their country – and let's not forget that Greenfields actually receives government funding! Of course, it wasn't *my* government that agreed to it, but even so the political fallout could be appalling. Frankly, the less said the better. And I definitely think we ought to handle the situation ourselves."

"We can put an SAS task force on standby," Blackmore suggested.

"It would still take too long to fly them to Africa," Ellis said. He glanced at the prime minister, waiting for permission to continue. The prime minister nodded. "But in my view, we can do better than that," he said. "We have an RAF Phantom squadron in Akrotiri, Cyprus. They're already fuelling. They can be in the air in half an hour."

"And what do you intend to do with them?" Blunt asked.

"It's very simple, Mr Blunt. We're going to bomb the entire wheat field. After all, thanks to your agent, we know exactly where it is."

"But won't the bombs do McCain's work for him? You'll blow the spores into the air. You'll spread them all over Africa."

"We don't believe so. The Phantoms will be carrying AGM-65 Maverick air-to-ground tactical missiles with infrared tracking. They'll be able to pinpoint the target exactly. Each plane has six missiles. Each missile contains thirty-nine kilograms of high explosive. The advice we've been given is that there's a 99.5 per cent probability that every single one of the spores will be destroyed in the firestorm."

"That still leaves room for error," Blunt said.

"And what about Alex?" Mrs Jones added. "For all we know, he could still be in the area. Are we going to launch a missile strike against him too?"

"I don't think we have any choice," Ellis said. He reached down and picked a speck of dust off his tie. "There's no reason to believe he's anywhere near the target area."

"And if he is?"

"I'm sure you'll agree that we can't allow one life to get in the way. Not when we're trying to save thousands."

There was a brief silence. The prime minister was

looking more uncomfortable than ever. But then he spoke again. "I think we've come to a unanimous decision, Mr Blunt."

"You certainly have," Blunt muttered.

"And before you leave, there is one thing I have to ask you. Exactly how many agents do you have who are under the age of sixteen?"

"We have only one," Blunt replied. "There is only Alex."

"I'm very glad to hear it." The prime minister looked apologetic. "To be honest, I was rather horrified to discover that the British secret service would even consider employing a minor. I can see from his file that he's been tremendously useful to you and he certainly deserves our gratitude. But putting children into danger, no matter how compelling the reason ... well, I'm not sure the public would stand for it. In my view, recruiting him in the first place was a serious error of judgement."

"Well, if your Phantom jets manage to kill him, that won't be a problem any more, will it?" Blunt said. He was speaking evenly and without emotion but it was the nearest Mrs Jones had ever seen him come to losing his temper.

"I hope it won't come to that, Mr Blunt. But whatever happens, I want to make it clear that my government will not tolerate this sort of thing again. This is Alex's last assignment, do you understand me? I want him back at school."

The meeting was over. Blunt and Mrs Jones

stood up and walked out of the room, back down the stairs and out into the street, where their car was waiting for them.

"The man is an idiot," Blunt snapped as they swept through the gates at the end of Downing Street. "He talks about a 0.5 per cent margin of error. But I spoke to Redwing and she thinks it's much higher. These missiles of his won't kill the disease. They'll spread it – further and faster than anyone could imagine."

"What about Alex?" Mrs Jones asked.

"I'll talk to RAW the moment we get back. But their man has gone silent. Nobody knows what's happening in Kenya." He glanced briefly out of the window as they turned into Whitehall. "It looks as if, once again, Alex Rider is on his own."

"Where did you find this?"

Desmond McCain was sitting behind the folding table that he used as a desk in his own private tent at Simba River Camp. It was similar to the one in which Alex had been kept except that there was no bed and the walls were decorated with photographs of the office buildings which McCain had once developed in the East End of London. Although the fan had been turned to full speed, the air was still hot and sluggish. There was sweat on his head and face. It was seeping through the shoulders of his jacket.

He was looking at a leather shoe which he

recognized. The last time he had seen it, it had been on Myra Bennett's foot. In fact, it still was. The foot, bitten off just above the ankle, was inside.

"It was beside the river, sir."

Njenga was also in the room, standing with legs apart and hands behind his back. He was the leader of the dozen men working for McCain. Unlike the others, he had been to school in Nairobi and spoke fluent English.

McCain took one last look at all that remained of his fiancée. A single tear stole out of his eye and crept down his cheek. He wiped it away with the back of his hand.

Also on the table was a scrap of material, part of Alex's shirt. McCain examined it. "What about this?" he asked.

"It was in the same place."

"By the river."

"Yes, sir."

McCain held the strip of shirt in his huge hands, tugging at it with his fingers. More than two hours had passed since he had noticed that Myra was missing and had sent his men out to find her. They had come back with this. What could possibly have happened? He had left her standing on the observation platform, waiting for the boy to come to the end of his strength and fall as, inevitably, he must. There was no way that Alex Rider would have been able to reach her. Nor could he have escaped. It had all been too carefully arranged. And yet there was something...

"There is no blood on this shirt," he said. "We've been tricked. Somehow the boy got away."

Njenga said nothing. The rule here was to speak only when it was essential.

"He can't have gone far, even with a head start. He has nowhere to go. He won't have crossed the river, not knowing what's in it. So it should be a simple matter to track him down." McCain had come to a decision. "I want you to take the men – all of them – and set off after him. I'm not asking anything clever. I want you to bring him back to me alive if you possibly can. I would like to have the pleasure of finishing this once and for all. But if you think he's going to get away, then kill him and bring me back his head. Do you understand? This time, I want to be sure."

"Yes, sir." Njenga showed no concern about killing and decapitating a child. All that mattered to him was the money that would come to him at the end of the month.

"Go now. Don't come back until the job is done."

A few minutes later they all left, twelve men carrying a variety of weapons including spears, knives and machetes. Half of them had guns. Njenga himself carried a German-manufactured Sauer 202 bolt-action hunting rifle equipped with a Zeiss Conquest scope. He knew he could shoot the eye of an antelope out at two hundred yards. He had done so many times.

They found two tracks at the river. The first one went into the bush and came back again. The second, which was much clearer, headed off towards the north. This was the path they chose. Alex Rider had a head start but they were Kikuyu tribesmen. They were taller, faster and stronger than him. They knew the land.

They set off at a well-disciplined run, dodging through the undergrowth. They were confident that they'd catch up with him in no time at all.

SIMBA DAM

The birds perched high up in the camphor tree were definitely vultures. The shape was unmistakable: the long necks and the bald heads, and the way they sat, hunched up and still. There were about ten of them ranged across the branches, black against the afternoon sky. But the question Alex had to ask himself was – were they waiting for him? It seemed very likely.

He had no idea how long he had been moving but he knew he couldn't go on much longer. He was dehydrated and close to exhaustion, his arms covered in scratches, his face burnt by the African sun. The bits of his school uniform that he was still wearing couldn't have been less well suited to this sort of terrain. The grey polyester trousers trapped the heat and his school shoes had caused him to slip twice. Each time he had come crashing down to the ground, he had wearily reminded himself that there was a bomb strapped to his back. Not that he could have forgotten it. The weight of Rahim's backpack was dragging him down, the straps cutting into his shoulders. Well, if the bomb went off, the vultures would have their feast. It would just come in snack-sized pieces.

The journey should have been simple. After all, he had seen where he had to go from the air. Unfortunately the landscape looked very different at ground level when he was stuck in the middle of it. The sudden rising hills, the thick vegetation, the spiky shrubs that forced him to turn another way ... all these had been flattened out when he was in the Piper Cub. The bush had swallowed him up. The dam, the pylons and the track had all disappeared.

He had to rely on the map and his own sense of direction. To start with he had kept the river on his right – near enough to glimpse the water through the trees but not too close to attract the attention of whatever might be lurking in it. That was his greatest fear. He was in the middle of a killing field – and he wasn't being escorted round like a tourist in a four-by-four. He was unarmed, out in the open. It had been early afternoon when he set out, and most of the animals had been asleep; but the sun was already beginning to cool, and very soon they would awaken and renew their ceaseless search for food. Was he prey? He could imagine his scent creeping out. All around him invisible eyes could be watching his progress, already measuring the distance. He had seen elephants, monkeys and – of course – crocodiles. What other horrors might be waiting for him round the next corner if he was unlucky? There could be lions or cheetahs. He had thought of taking the Dragunov sniper rifle or searching Rahim's pockets for other weapons but in the end he had decided against it. Rahim might need them when he recovered consciousness. Now he wished he hadn't been so generous.

After about half a mile he had turned away from the river, heading in what he hoped was the direction of the dam – and it was then that his progress became harder. This time it was the map that was deceiving him. It hadn't shown that the ground sloped so steeply uphill, although he should have worked it out for himself. Rahim had told him that the water held back by the Simba Dam flowed through two hydroelectric turbines. Since water only flows downhill, it was fairly obvious that he would have to climb.

It was hard work, weighed down, in the hot sun. And the African landscape was huge. He knew he only had three miles to cover but somehow the distances seemed to have been magnified so that even a shrub or a tree right in front of him always took too long to reach. Worse still, after leaving the river behind him, Alex had lost all sense of direction. He wished now he had taken Rahim's compass. The colours were too muted: the pale greens and browns, the faint streaks of yellow and orange. You could hide a herd of elephants here and not see them. There was nowhere for the eye to focus. There were no people, no houses, nothing that looked like a pathway or a road. This was the world as it must have been long ago, before man began to shape it to his needs. Alex felt like an intruder. And he was utterly lost.

But as long as he was climbing uphill, he had to be going the right way. He stopped and took out Rahim's water bottle. He had already drunk from it three times and he had tried to ration himself, but even so he was surprised to find it was almost empty. He finished the last drops and slung the container into the bush. Let the guards pick it up. Alex had no doubt that they were already closing in behind him.

The bush ahead suddenly parted. Alex froze. It was an animal of some sort, small and dark, hidden by the long grass. And it was heading towards him. For a moment, he felt the same uncontrollable terror that McCain had inflicted on him with the crocodiles. If this was a lion, it was all over. But then he relaxed. The animal was a warthog. It stared at him with its small, brutish eyes. Its upturned nose sniffed the air and Alex could imagine it asking itself the same question it must ask every day. Food? Then it made its decision. This creature was too big and probably wouldn't taste very nice. It turned round and fled the way it had come.

Alex looked back. What time was it? There was

a mountain ridge over to the west, lost in the heat haze like a strip of grey silk. The sun was sinking slowly behind it and there was already a faint moon, visible against the clear blue sky. A meeting place of night and day. Alex wiped a grimy hand over his face. A mosquito whined in his ear. He wondered if Rahim had woken up yet. What would the Indian agent do when he discovered he was alone?

A movement caught his eye. At first Alex thought he had imagined it – but there it was again. An animal? No. About a dozen men were making their way towards him. They were still at least half a mile away, far down at the bottom of the slope that Alex had been climbing. They were spread out in a line and Alex could just make out their faces, the combat clothes they were wearing and the weapons they carried or had strapped to their backs. He knew exactly who they were. He also knew that if he had seen them, they had seen him. If he stayed where he was, they would be with him in less than fifteen minutes.

Forcing himself on, he broke into a run. There was a thicket of trees to one side and he made for it, wondering if he might be able to lose himself among the trunks and branches. But it was a foolish hope. Alex knew that McCain's men must have been tracking him from the start and that a single broken blade of grass or fallen leaf would be like a flashing neon sign for them. Now it was just a question of speed. Could he reach the dam before they caught up with him? Could he detonate the bomb? Alex had no doubt that he was going to be captured and killed. But at least he would die in the knowledge that he had beaten McCain.

The wood ended as suddenly as it had begun. On the other side, there was a field, and the first man-made object that he had seen since he set out: the remains of a low wooden fence. He leapt over it and continued running, aware that he was surrounded by a very different sort of vegetation. It was wheat! Incredibly he had reached McCain's wheat field. So the dam had to be directly ahead of him. He still couldn't see it but he knew it was there. If he just continued forward he would have to come upon it.

He was racing through the wheat. He could feel it scratching at his ankles and his hands. It was all around him. And with a sudden jolt of horror he wondered if it had switched yet, if the spores had done their work. If so, he was running through a vast field of poison. Each one of these bright yellow blades could be the death of him. The very air he was breathing could be full of ricin. Grimly Alex kept his lips tightly shut and held his arms high. It seemed incredible to him that McCain could have done this: taken something as natural and as beautiful as a wheat field and turned it into something deadly.

He glanced back. There was no sign of his followers. Seeing them had given him new speed and determination. Over to one side he saw the electricity pylon that he had spotted before, or one identical to it – not steel, but wood, and only four or five metres high. It was still a quarter of a mile away but he made for it. The wires would lead to the turbines and the turbines had to be somewhere beneath the dam. He tried to remember on which side he had seen the track. That would be the fastest way forward. Was it possible that Njenga had come after him in the Land Rover? No. Alex would have heard the engine by now.

The wheat, waves and waves of it, crunched beneath his feet as he drove his way through it. He liked the sound that it made. He wanted to crush as much of it as he could but the field seemed to go on for ever, trapped between the two rock faces that rose up on each side.

Where was the dam? He should have been able to see it by now. The wheat suddenly ended – so abruptly that it was as if Alex had fallen from one world to another. He was on the track! There it was, right underneath him. So how far did he have to go? How much further *could* he go? He glanced back. There was still no sign of the guards but the wheat would cause them no problems. In fact, the trackers would have a field day. Alex had left a motorway for them to follow. He had to keep up his pace. They would surely have doubled theirs.

The track had once been covered with asphalt but it was full of potholes now, with weeds and wild grass sprouting through. Alex guessed it was used both by the farmers coming up to harvest the wheat and by technicians working on the hydro-electrics. He could make out tyre tracks and hoof prints. It was an easier surface for running but he was still going uphill and his mouth was dry. He resisted the temptation to look back. He had no time to waste. But his muscles were taut and his whole body was tingling with the anticipation of a knife or a bullet in his back.

And then the track turned a corner and there, ahead of him, was the Simba Dam.

It was completely bizarre and out of place. That was Alex's first thought. This huge grey wall had been constructed in the middle of all this unspoilt nature and it had no right to be there. It wasn't exactly ugly. Indeed, the great curve, stretching from one side of the valley to the other, had a certain gracefulness. Beaten by the sun, the cement had faded so that it blended in with the rocks that surrounded it. But it was still a scar. In a strange way, it reminded him of what had happened to McCain's face. The dam cut the landscape in two and the two halves didn't quite meet.

Alex stumbled to a halt and stood there panting, his entire body covered in sweat. He desperately needed a drink. He wished now he had taken more care with his supply.

There was no sign of the lake from where he was standing at the very foot of the dam, surrounded by discarded pieces of cement and broken rocks that must have been blasted during the construction. The surface of the water had to be about thirty metres above him and, of course, on the other side. He could see enormous slots in the wall, oversized letter boxes with what looked like metal gates cutting them in half. Presumably these could be raised or lowered to allow the water to spill through. Alex tried to imagine the amount of pressure that must be pushing against the wall itself: the tonnes and tonnes of water being held back. Somewhere – perhaps in Nairobi – someone would press a button and a sluice would open. And then some of the water – just a few million gallons – would rush down a series of hidden pipes to the turbines, where energy would be siphoned off to provide electricity before the water was finally released to feed the crops.

Suddenly the bomb he was carrying felt very small.

As Alex followed the track to its end, the Simba Dam loomed over him, much bigger and more complicated than anything he had imagined. It curved in two directions, forming a letter C around him but also slanting out over his head, away from the water. What had Rahim called it? A double curvature arch dam. Now that he was here, it was easier to understand what that meant.

Two drainage slipways ran up on each side. These were basically curving roads, running up the side of the hill, though so steeply that no car would be able to make the journey. Alex guessed that they had something to do with the water, which could be directed down them and into the valley if there happened to be heavy rainfall and the threat of a flood. Two concrete staircases had been built next to them, one for each slipway, with about a hundred steps up to the top. There was one other way up, a single ladder clinging to the face of the dam, leading to two inspection platforms, one above the other, and finally to the lip of the dam itself. The ladder was dangerous because it wasn't quite vertical. Following the curve of the wall, it slanted outwards. It was also narrow, steep and covered in rust.

Alex took this all in, then turned his attention to a construction directly in front of him. It looked like something out of the Second World War: a pillbox, perhaps. It was a solid concrete bunker with three barred windows. Two fat steel pipes jutted out, pointing at him like the cannon of a tank that might have been parked inside. Both of them were capped, making them look like oversized industrial oilcans. They were connected to the dam by hydraulic steel claws with a network of smaller pipes, wires and taps around them. The concrete underneath them was stained. It had recently been wet.

Alex knew that these were the two valves which Rahim had described. His targets. He took one quick glance back over his shoulder then hurried forward. He had perhaps five minutes to position the explosive before McCain's men arrived. Even as he ran, he wriggled out of the backpack and opened it. The concrete building had a sort of entrance, a narrow slit that led into an inner chamber with more pipes and machinery. While he was in here, Alex would be out of sight. Surely he couldn't have left a trail on the broken rocks and other debris in front of the dam. With a bit of luck the trackers wouldn't be able to find him until it was too late.

He had the bomb in his hands. It couldn't have been easier to activate. That was what made terrorism all the more frightening – the fact that it relied on such simple devices. The glass window in front of the clock face opened and Alex was able to take the single hand and move it as many minutes as he wanted, up to sixty. He made a quick calculation. It would take him about two minutes to climb up to the top of the dam, using one of the staircases beside the slipways. Once he was there, he would be safe from the torrent of water. But what about the Kikuyu?

Suddenly Alex had an idea. He could use the water! The guards were coming up the valley. If he blew up the valve before they arrived at the dam, there was a chance they might all be swept away. Of course, it would give him less time to get away himself if something went wrong – but if it was a choice between death beneath a million gallons of water or at the end of a spear, he knew which one he would prefer.

He turned the hand of the clock to the figure 4, then pressed the two switches. A green light came on and the clock began to tick. So it was done. Alex looked around him. It didn't matter which valve he chose. With a bit of luck the explosion – contained within the concrete walls – would be strong enough to rupture them both. He placed the bomb on top of one of the pipes, wedging it against the ceiling. Now to get away.

He slithered out of the opening and stopped in dismay. There were three Kikuyu in front of him. They had almost reached the end of the track and were gazing at the dam as if it had deliberately chosen to block their path. There were no more than fifty metres between them. They saw Alex at once. One of them called out. Another threw his spear. It fell short. None of them seemed to have guns.

Alex began to run. He headed for the nearest slipway but he hadn't even begun to climb when another of McCain's men appeared at the top, pointed down and shouted. Alex realized what had happened. The dozen tribesmen had arrived at the dam and, as he had hoped, they had lost his track. So they had separated. They were all around him, coming at him from every side.

And he had made a terrible miscalculation.

There were just three and a half minutes until

the bomb went off. He didn't have time to go back into the bunker and reset the detonator – he'd be trapping himself and it would only draw attention to what he had done. He had to move quickly – and preferably up. If he stayed here, he would be killed by the blast or drowned in the rush of water. The staircase on the right was covered. Alex looked the other way. Yet another tribesman had appeared and was heading down the concrete steps. The three men who had first seen him were getting closer.

That just left the ladder.

Alex grabbed hold of the first rung and began to climb.

THE THIRD DAY

The F-4 Phantom II fighter jets had taken off at exactly 4.45 p.m. local time, their Rolls-Royce Spey engines powering them down the runway and into the air, climbing at forty thousand feet per minute. There were three of them. They had levelled off at sixty thousand feet, moving into a classic arrow formation, before turning south towards Africa. Each one carried six missiles. Between them they were confident that they had enough firepower to turn McCain's wheat field into a blazing hell in which nothing, not so much as a single microbe, would survive.

There was, of course, the faintest possibility that the initial force of the impact would propel some of the mushroom spores into the air, ahead of the flames. These spores would then travel very fast and very far and do their lethal work elsewhere. But as is so often the way with British politics, a decision had been made. If it was later shown to be wrong, all the evidence would be gently massaged to show that no other decision had been possible. Not that the public would ever hear about this. The orders that the three Phantom pilots had received were top secret. Their flight plan had not been recorded. As far as the world was concerned, they hadn't even taken off.

And when the three planes crossed the Kenyan border, heading west from the Indian Ocean, the urgent enquiries from air traffic control in Nairobi were ignored. Later it would be explained that they had accidentally strayed off course during a training mission. Profuse apologies would be offered to the Kenyan government. But for now, they were observing strict radio silence.

The Phantoms were equipped with the Northrop Grumman target identification system, essentially a telescopic camera fitted to the left wing and connected to a radar scope inside the cockpit. As Alex began to climb the ladder at the Simba Dam, the planes began to drop altitude, flying towards the Rift Valley at just under twelve hundred miles per hour. Inside their cockpits, the pilots made their final preparations. There would be no need for a fly-past. The target coordinates were locked in. Once they had visual contact, they would open fire.

Alex was halfway up the ladder with the first maintenance platform stretching out above his head. It was hard work, climbing up. Because of the curve of the dam, he was leaning outwards and the force of gravity was against him. Every time he pulled himself up another rung, he felt himself being dragged backwards. The sun was also beating down on him, burning his arms and neck. He forced himself to keep going. He was painfully aware of the bomb that he had activated and that was ticking away even now. If only he had given himself more time! If it went off before he reached the top of the dam, there was a good chance the ladder would be blown off the wall – and him with it.

He grabbed hold of the next rung and looked back, only to see two of the guards who had raised the alarm – at this height they were no more than toy figures – running to the foot of the dam. The third was holding back. None of them seemed anxious to climb the ladder after him. Why? He looked up and saw the reason. They had no need to follow him. Another Kikuyu had reached the centre of the dam and was already climbing down.

There was no way out. Alex consoled himself with the knowledge that nobody knew about the bomb apart from him and that in about two and a half minutes it would explode, releasing millions of gallons of water that would flood the valley, drowning the wheat. It would be mission accomplished ... except that he wouldn't be around to see it. He wondered if anyone would ever discover what had happened. Perhaps Rahim would make a report if he managed to get away. *He died fighting for what he believed in.* Alex could already see the words inscribed on the medal. Jack could wear it at his funeral.

But he wasn't ready to give up yet. He couldn't go back down. He realized that the third Kikuyu was aiming another spear at him. That was why he had positioned himself further back. Well, he was in for a surprise when the valve was smashed. A spider down the plughole! He was about to find out what it felt like. Alex seized hold of the next rung and pulled. Once again the curving wall pushed him backwards, as if it were desperate to make him let go.

The man above him was getting closer. It was Njenga. McCain's second in command had already reached the upper platform and was dragging the rifle off his shoulder, bringing it round to pick off Alex. But Njenga knew that he too had made mistakes. First, as he approached the dam, he had instructed his men to separate. He had been confused by all the different concrete ramps and stairways, the various outbuildings with their tanks and pipework. He had assumed Alex would try to hide, and had given the order to spread out and search for him.

And he had spotted the boy too late. From where Njenga was standing, the slant of the dam put him at a disadvantage. So long as Alex remained underneath him, he was slightly tucked away, out of sight, and he couldn't get a clear shot. Why then was the boy still climbing? He had just reached the lower platform and was continuing up the next stretch of the ladder that would bring the two of them face to face.

Njenga made a decision. There was no need for shooting. He laid down the rifle and took out his machete. He smiled to himself. How far did the boy think he would be able to climb without hands?

He waited. Alex was getting closer.

Alex knew he couldn't risk going any further. He could see Njenga's machete blade dangling in the air directly above him. If he climbed another few rungs, he would be in range. He was going to have to wait for the explosion. Perhaps the shock of it might change things, rearrange them in his favour. It was all he could hope for.

At the bottom of the dam the Kikuyu tribesman threw his spear. The black needle with its vicious silver point flashed towards Alex. He saw it out of the corner of his eye. The man who had thrown it must have been fantastically strong, as there had to be at least twenty metres between them. But the spear was off target. It was going to hit the wall just to his left.

At the very last second, Alex let go of the ladder with one hand, his whole body swinging round as if on a hinge. He stretched out with his free hand and caught the spear in mid-air, then, using all the strength in his shoulder, swung himself back again. At the same time, he lunged upwards.

He had grabbed hold of the spear at the very bottom end. The beaten metal tip sliced into Njenga's leg, just above the ankle. Njenga screamed and toppled sideways.

Then the bomb went off.

Alex was over halfway up the face of the dam. He felt the entire ladder jerk violently. He was almost thrown off – and would have been if he hadn't been expecting the shock wave and had prepared for it by wrapping himself around the metalwork, clinging on with his arms and his legs. He felt himself being slammed away from the wall of the dam and cried out as a ball of flame rushed past his back and shoulders, shooting into the air. But he was still there. The ladder had held. He hadn't been thrown off.

Njenga was less fortunate. Shocked and in pain, with blood pouring out of the wound in his leg, he was caught off balance and plummeted down, twisting in the air before he was dashed onto the rocks below.

And instantly he was gone. Alex had positioned the bomb perfectly. It had completely smashed the bottom outlet valve and ruptured the other valve too. It was as if the two biggest taps in the world had been turned on simultaneously. The water didn't just rush out. It erupted with such force that it seemed to obliterate the entire landscape – the rocks, the vegetation and, of course, the three Kikuyu who had been standing in its path. They were simply blasted away, smashed out of existence by a thundering white locomotive that roared over them, taking them with it.

How many thousands of gallons of water were being released by the second? It was impossible to say. The water didn't even look like water. It was more like smoke or steam – only more solid. Alex saw a huge tree uprooted as if it were no more than a weed, a boulder pushed effortlessly aside. And then the flood reached up for him. He felt the spray whipping into the back of his legs and, looking down, he realized that almost all the ladder below him had been ripped away. The twisted metal ended just a few rungs beneath his feet. If he stayed here for a minute more he would be sucked into the vortex and obliterated.

Once again he began to climb. The sound of the water was pounding in his ears, deafening him, and he remembered the huge lake that the Simba Dam had been containing and wondered how much longer the curving wall could hold it. The lake was a monster that had been given its first taste of freedom. This one torrent might not be enough. It would demand more.

Alex was soaked. He was blistered by the sun. He was close to exhaustion. Somehow he dragged himself up to the platform where Njenga had been standing and then onto the last stretch of ladder that led to the top. He didn't dare look back. He could still hear an incredible, explosive pounding and knew just how McCain would have described it. It was the sound of the third day when God created the oceans. And he knew that very soon the river he had let loose would reach the wheat field. Every last stalk would be drowned. Maybe the water would even reach Simba River Camp and destroy that too. He liked the idea of McCain disappearing in a swirl of mud and stones and broken trees. It was nothing less than he deserved.

Alex reached the top of the ladder and rolled over a low wall with a road on the other side. Dripping wet, gasping for breath, he knelt for a moment, taking stock of his surroundings.

The track that he had followed from the wheat field rose up past one of the slipways and continued over the lip of the dam where it became a bridge, a sweeping curve that crossed from one side to the other. That was where he was now. He had climbed about forty metres. The ground, with the churning water, was a long, long way down. On the other side of the dam, in front of him, the lake stretched towards the horizon, completely calm and undisturbed by what was taking place below. Alex could see distant mountains, the clouds and the emerald sky, all reflected in the mirror of the surface.

He turned back. From here he could make out the sweep of the land, a great plain with the silhouettes of trees and, in the far distance, a herd of gazelles, lost in their surroundings. And there was the wheat field with the first finger of water trickling through it, widening with every second that passed. In another minute it would begin to drown. In five, it would no longer exist.

But he was trapped. The remaining guards were on top of the dam, in two groups, left and right. They had already seen him and were shouting among themselves, excitedly raising their rifles, taking aim. They would have fired at him already, except they had to be careful. If they missed, there was a chance they might hit each other.

They began to move forward. Alex could only stand and wait.

The bridge trembled. Alex felt it, like an earthquake beneath his feet. At first he thought it must be tiredness, that he had imagined it. But then it happened again and this time it was stronger. The entire wall of the dam was shifting. The guards had felt it too. They stopped dead in their tracks, looking at each other for explanation. The answer was obvious.

The dam was breaking up. Perhaps the bomb had damaged some of the joints where the individual blocks of concrete had come together in the construction. Or there could always have been a hairline crack, a weakness just waiting for the moment to bring an end to the whole thing. Well, that moment had come. Alex was thrown sideways as the ground tilted. He saw more water gushing out of a newly formed crack. Part of the wall crumbled, huge pieces of masonry tumbling in slow motion, disappearing into the chaos below. He knew there were just seconds left before the whole thing collapsed. Even if he tried to run, it would be too late.

The guards were retreating in panic. He could see their eyes widening, fear etched into their faces. They had forgotten him. They had to get off the dam and back onto dry land. They were dropping their weapons. One of them lurched into another and then both of them were knocked sideways, thrown off their feet by the cement floor which tilted up beneath them. Alex heard them scream as they were tipped over the edge.

He fought for balance. Something was coming towards him. What was it? A plane – but a strange one, small, like a toy. Alex recognized the Piper Cub. It was flying over the lake, heading towards him, so low that the wheels were almost touching the water. Was it McCain? Had he come for revenge? But then he saw the rope trailing from the back and a dark figure hunched over the controls. Rahim! He must have recovered to find Alex missing and guessed what he planned to do. Rahim had come for him. He had told Alex he could fly. He had also said that he could keep the plane airborne at thirty-five miles an hour. He was steering straight into the headwind, using the air currents to slow himself down. If he went any slower, he would surely stall.

It was impossible. Alex knew what Rahim had in mind. But he couldn't do it.

Another explosion of concrete and water. Part of the dam tumbled like a house of cards, sinking into itself. The ground tilted crazily. Once again Alex had to struggle to stay on his feet.

The plane was so close that Alex could see the concentration on Rahim's face as he fought to keep himself in the air. The end of the rope was skimming the surface of the lake, snaking a line through the water. The plane looked slow but the rope was whipping towards him, almost a blur.

There was no other way. Blindly Alex reached up and felt something lash into his chest and the side of his neck. The plane howled over him, so close that it nearly took off his head. The wheels rushed past. His scrabbling hands caught hold of the rope, tearing the skin off his palms. The end twisted round him. And then he was jerked into the air so hard that he was sure he would be torn in half. Pain jolted through his arms and down his spine. He felt as if he had dislocated his shoulders. He was blacking out.

But his feet were in the air. He was being dragged up and now there was nothing beneath him except white foam, the bellowing water, crashing cement. Higher and higher. He wasn't even sure how he was holding on. Somehow the rope had tied itself around him. The ground was rushing past.

Behind him the Simba Dam disintegrated and the lake surged forward, free at last, hundreds of thousands of gallons pouring down into the valley.

All the remaining guards were swept with it, mercilessly battered to death before they could even drown.

Dangling from the plane, Alex was carried away.

The water, blood red in the setting sun, continued pouring into an ever-widening sea.

In London the prime minister was on the telephone.

"Yes." He listened, a tic of anger beating in his forehead. "Yes, I quite understand. Thank you for keeping me informed."

He put the phone down.

"Who was that?" Charles Blackmore, the director of strategy and communications, was in the office with him. It was seven fifteen but the day's work at Downing Street wouldn't end for a while yet. There were papers to be signed off, a planned phone call with the president of the United States, and at eight o'clock a cocktail party for all the people working on the London Olympics. The prime minister was looking forward to that. He still enjoyed seeing himself in the newspapers, particularly when he was supporting a popular cause.

"It was the RAF in Cyprus," the prime minister said.

"Is there a problem?"

"Not exactly." The prime minister frowned. "It seems that this whole business in Kenya was a complete waste of time."

"Oh yes?"

"We actually deployed three Phantom jets down to this place, the Simba Valley. The pilots had the exact coordinates. Fortunately they decided to take a visual sighting before they fired off their missiles. And just as well..."

Blackmore waited, a look of polite enquiry on his face.

"There was no wheat field – no sign of any crop at all. Just a giant lake. They circled over the entire area, just to be sure that there wasn't any mistake. So either the information given to MI6 was inaccurate or this boy, Alex Rider, made the whole thing up."

"Why would he do that?"

"Well, he's only a child. I suppose he was seeking attention. But it just shows that I was absolutely right. Remind me to call the chiefs of staff. I think I should have a word with them about Alan Blunt. I'm afraid this puts a serious question mark over his judgement."

"I agree, Prime Minister." Blackmore coughed. "So what did the Phantoms do?"

"What else could they do? They turned round and headed home again. The whole thing was a complete waste of time and money. Perhaps we should start looking for someone else to head up Special Operations." The prime minister stood up. "How long until the party, Charles?"

"We have forty-five minutes."

"I think I might change. Put on a new tie. What do you think?"

"Maybe the blue one?"

"Good idea."

The file that Blunt had brought to the office was still on the desk. There was a photograph of Alex Rider clipped to the first page. The prime minister closed it, and slid it into a drawer. Then he went to get changed.

UNHAPPY LANDING

The airport was on the outskirts of a small town made up of brightly-coloured houses and shops and seemed to be a stopping point for tourists on their way to or from safari. There were half a dozen private planes lined up beside the single runway and a smart clubhouse with wooden tables and sunshades where passengers could wait. Everything was very neat. The lawns and hedges could have belonged to an English country house. There was a small playground with swings and a see-saw, and the children who were playing there were well-dressed and quiet. The evening was completely calm with the last rays of sun stretching out towards the great mass of Mount Kenya, and the occasional clatter of a propeller starting up or the buzz of a plane coming in to land seemed strangely inappropriate. Surely they could find somewhere else to go about the business of air travel!

Alex Rider took this all in as the Piper J-3 Cub approached the runway. They flew low over a row of chalets with the word LAIKIPIA painted in large letters across the roofs, and he guessed that this must be the name of the town. They had been flying for about an hour, heading south-east. He knew they couldn't have gone much further. Looking over Rahim's shoulder, he had watched the needle on the fuel indicator begin its downward journey. It had arrived at zero a while ago.

After everything he had been through, climbing into the rear seat of the Piper had been almost too much. Pulling himself up the rope, inch by inch, while being whipped through the air at eighty miles per hour and six thousand feet above the ground, Alex had forced his mind to go blank, to concentrate – totally – on what he had to do. He didn't look down. He wasn't sure he had the stomach for it. But nor did he look up. That would only taunt him with how far he still had to go. All he could do was cling to the rope with his hands and feet, trying to pretend that this was just a PE lesson at Brookland, that there was no wind rush on his face, no engine buzzing in his ears and that when he got to the top he would be given a quick round of applause and then allowed to get changed for French.

The whole thing would have been impossible if the crop duster had been equipped with a closed cockpit. But there were no windows or doors, and when Alex reached the top of the rope, he was able to grab the edge of the plane and pull himself over and into the back seat. He landed awkwardly, his face and shoulder burrowing into the soft leather – but it felt wonderful. He was safe. And he was leaving the Reverend Desmond McCain, the Kikuyu guards and the Simba Dam far behind him.

"Untie the rope!"

Rahim had turned round and shouted at him, the wind snatching the words away even as they were spoken. Alex did as he was told, untying the rope from the wing strut and letting it fall back to earth. He watched it dwindle in the distance until it was no more than a wriggling worm, and reflected that it could all too easily have been him free-falling down to the ground far below. He couldn't believe what he had just been through. He sank back into the seat, belted himself in and let out a deep sigh of relief.

The RAW agent hadn't spoken again and Alex was grateful. He was utterly drained and although sleep was impossible with the wind battering against him, he tried as best he could to relax, somehow to recharge his batteries. He wanted to go home. With his eyes half open, he watched the landscape slide away beneath him, the different patches of green and brown criss-crossed by roads and dirt tracks with tiny buildings scattered here and there, hinting at some sort of life – normal life – carrying on in the vastness of the Kenyan bush. The Piper's engine droned on. Rahim was wearing his camouflage jacket. Alex only had a T-shirt and trousers, and as the evening drew in he began to shiver. Very soon it would be night.

But even though the sun had gone, the sky was still glowing softly when Rahim suddenly shouted into his headset, getting permission from air traffic control at Laikipia to land. The little plane wavered in the air as if finding its balance. The ground, a long strip of tarmac, rushed towards them. Then they bumped down and taxied to a halt. A few airport workers dressed in bright yellow overalls with TROPIC AIR stencilled across their chests glanced curiously in their direction. It wasn't often they saw such an old-fashioned aircraft here. And a crop duster! There weren't any crops for miles. A few tourists, sitting outside the clubhouse, stood up and watched them come in. A couple of them unfastened their cameras and took pictures.

Rahim turned off the engine and the propeller began to slow down. He took off his headphones and twisted round. Alex wasn't sure what he had been expecting but he was taken aback by the anger in the agent's face.

"What did you think you were doing?" Rahim exploded. He still had to shout to make himself heard, but from the look of him he would have shouted anyway. "You could have got yourself killed. You could have got me killed!"

"Rahim..." Alex began. He wanted to climb out of the plane. Couldn't they have this argument over a cold drink and something to eat?

But Rahim was in no mood to go anywhere. "You stole my equipment. I cannot believe what you did. You left me there..."

"I had to do it."

"No! My job was to kill McCain. That was all. We could have dealt with his plan afterwards. You disobeyed my instructions, Alex. Do you have any idea of the damage you've caused? And how do you think my people are going to explain all this to the Kenyan authorities? You took out an entire hydro-electric and irrigation system!"

"Well, maybe you can tell them we saved a lot of lives."

"McCain is still out there. McCain has got away."

"I left you your gun. Why didn't you just go and shoot him?"

"Because I had to come after you." Rahim shook his head in exasperation. "I should have left you to the crocodiles."

There was a brief silence. The propeller was still turning, but more slowly.

"What is this place?" Alex asked. "Why are we here?"

"This is Laikipia. We have to refuel. I'm leaving you here. I've contacted my people and they'll arrange for you to be picked up."

"What about you?"

"I'm going—"

That was as far as he got. To Alex it was as if the

agent had snapped his head right round, and he was aware of a sudden cloud of red vapour filling the air in front of him. At the same time, he registered that there had just been a shot and he looked round to see Desmond McCain, dressed in a brown linen suit, walking towards him, the Mauser pistol in his hand. Alex turned back to Rahim. The agent was dead. There was no doubt about it. He had collapsed forward over the controls, a gaping wound in the side of his head.

Alex felt a wave of anger and disgust. He was also sad. Despite everything, Rahim had come back for him and saved him – for the third time. Alex hadn't even had a chance to thank him.

The propeller stopped.

McCain stood beside the plane, right next to the wing. The gun was now levelled at Alex. How had he got here? Alex was too shocked to think clearly but it occurred to him that if Rahim had chosen this airfield to refuel, then McCain might have landed here for exactly the same reason. All around him he was aware of people – aircrew, tourists, children – running for cover in panic. They had just seen a stumbling giant of a man, with a silver crucifix in his ear, appear from nowhere and commit murder for no obvious reason. They had to think he was mad. And maybe he was. McCain didn't seem to know where he was – or care. He had seen Alex and he had come to settle the score. Nothing else mattered.

"Get out of the plane," McCain said. His voice was steady but his eyes were bloodshot and unfocused, the skin around his face stretched tight. He was trembling slightly. He was doing his best to control it but the muzzle of the gun gave him away.

Alex stayed where he was.

"What do you want, Mr McCain?" he demanded. "I'm not going anywhere. Nor are you. Your wheat field is at the bottom of a lake. There isn't going to be any plague. It's all over."

"Get out of the plane," McCain repeated. His finger tightened on the trigger. He was holding the gun as if he were trying to crush it.

"Why?"

"I want to see you kneeling in front of me. Just for once, I want you to behave like an ordinary child. You're going to cry and beg me not to hurt you. And then I'm going to put this gun between your eyes and shoot you dead."

"You might as well shoot me here. I'm not playing your games."

McCain dropped the gun a few inches so that it was aiming at Alex's legs. Alex knew that the skin of the Piper Cub would offer no protection at all.

"I can make it slow..." McCain said.

Alex nodded. He took one more look around him. It didn't seem as if anyone was going to come to his rescue. The whole airfield had emptied. The other planes – and now he spotted the Skyhawk

that had first brought him to Simba River Camp –
were silent, unmoving. Surely someone would have
called the police by now ... always assuming that
there were any police operating in a remote town
like Laikipia.

"All right," he said.

He unbuckled his seat belt, gripped the sides of
the plane and began to pull himself out. At the
same time, he glanced into the front of the plane,
past the slumped figure of the pilot. He knew that
Rahim had a gun. But there was no sign of it and
no way he could search around without receiving
a bullet himself. What else? His eyes fell on the
metal lever between the two seats. He thought
of the rubber pipes connected to the two plastic
drums either sides of the plane.

The whole system had to work on pressure, with
the drums pumped up in some way by the engine.
They had been flying for an hour so there had to
be enough pressure in the tubes. But was there
any of the mushroom soup left in the drums? Alex
didn't dare turn round and look. McCain was still
under the wing, waiting for him to climb down.

Alex was already standing up. As he swung his
leg over the side, he pretended to stumble. His
hand shot out, slamming the lever down. At once
he heard a hiss – and a second later, a film of
grey, slimy liquid began to squirt out of the pipes
running along the wing tips. McCain was taken by
surprise. For a moment, he was blinded, caught

in the middle of the shower, the mushroom soup splashing over his head and into his eyes.

McCain fired – but missed. The second after he had hit the lever, Alex had thrown himself the other way, tumbling over the side of the plane and down to the grass below. He heard the bullet thwack into the fuselage, millimetres from his head. At the same time, he crashed to the ground and cried out, a flash of pain blazing behind his eyes. He had landed badly, twisting his ankle. Worse still, the drums had only contained a few dregs. Alex had barely got to his feet and begun to limp away before the shower stopped and McCain, cursing and wiping his eyes, was after him.

Alex could barely do more than hobble. His foot wouldn't take his full weight. Every step was an agony that shot up his leg all the way to his neck. He knew he wouldn't be able to get much further; and anyway, there was nowhere to go. Behind him the grass and the landing strip stretched out, flat and empty. The perimeter was fenced off, with an open gate leading to the edge of the town, but it was too far away. He would never reach it. McCain didn't seem to be moving fast but like a figure in a nightmare he was getting closer with every step.

Alex came to a line of drums stacked up on the grass right next to the tarmac, each one marked TOTAL ESSENCE PLOMBÉE. Leaded fuel. Why was it written in French? McCain fired five times. The nearest drum shivered and fuel began to splash out, spouting in five directions. Alex dived for cover behind it. A bolt of pain shot through his ankle. He wondered if he would be able to get up again.

McCain had stopped about ten paces away. Casually, as if he had all the time in the world, he took out a fresh ammunition clip and reloaded the gun. The fuel continued to gush out.

"You can't hide from me, child," McCain shouted. "'Vengeance is mine; I will repay, saith the Lord.' That's Romans, Chapter 12. And now, finally, the time for my vengeance has come. Let me see you..."

Alex tested one of the drums. It was full of fuel and too heavy to move. But the drum that McCain had punctured was emptying rapidly. Lying on his back, he pressed both feet against it and pushed with all his strength. It toppled over. Now Alex was exposed. There was nothing between him and the Mauser. He got to his knees, leant on the drum, then rolled it over the tarmac towards McCain.

McCain smiled. He walked forward and placed a single foot on the drum, stopping its progress. He had a clear view of Alex and at this range he couldn't miss. Alex was still kneeling on the ground. It was just what he wanted.

"Do you know how many years I spent planning this operation?" McCain asked. His voice carried across the short distance. He was leaning forward, one foot still perched on the drum, his elbow resting on his thigh. "Do you have any idea what it meant to me? All I wanted was my rightful place in the world. Money is power, and I was going to have more than you could possibly imagine.

"I'm going to shoot you now. Not once, but several times. And then I'm going to walk away." He lifted the gun. "Goodbye, Alex. You're going on a slow journey to hell."

"Let me know what it's like," Alex said.

The fuel drum exploded. In the seconds before he had sent it rolling, Alex had attached the black gel ink pen that Smithers had given him to the metal surface. He had activated it with a thirty-second fuse. And it had worked. One moment McCain was taking aim, the next he had disappeared in a pillar of flame that roared into the sky. It really was like a judgement from heaven. He didn't even have time to scream.

Alex was already twisting away, trying to put as much space between him and the inferno as he could. He was too close. Blazing droplets of aviation fuel rained down from the sky. He felt them hit his shoulders and back and with horror realized he was on fire.

But the grass had recently been watered. It was cool and damp under his hands. Alex rolled over again and again. His skin was burning. The pain was worse than anything he had ever known. But after spinning half a dozen times, he had put the flames out. He looked back at the tarmac. The charred, unrecognizable figure that had once been the Reverend Desmond McCain was on its knees. One final prayer. The silver earring had gone. There wasn't very much of him left.

He heard shouting. Police and airport workers were running towards him. Alex couldn't see them. He was stretched out on the grass, trying to bury himself in it. Was it really over at last, the journey that had begun in a Scottish castle and had led to an airport in Africa?

He couldn't move. And he was barely aware of the men who lifted him as gently as possible, laid him on a stretcher and carried him away.

SOFT CENTRES

The snow that had been promised in London had finally arrived.

Only a few inches had fallen during the night but as usual it had brought chaos to the streets. Buses had stayed in their depots, the Underground had shut down, schools were closed and half the work-force had decided to take a holiday and had stayed at home. Snowmen had suddenly appeared in all the London parks, standing under trees, leaning against walls, even sitting on benches – like some invading army that had come and seen and decided to take a well-earned rest before it set out to conquer.

It was the end of January and the winter had taken a grip on the city and seemed determined never to let go. The streets were empty, the parked cars huddled beneath their white blankets, but Jack Starbright had managed to persuade a mini-cab to bring her to St Dominic's Hospital in north London. She had been here before. It was one of the places favoured by the Special Operations division of MI6 when their agents were damaged in the field. This was where they sent them to recover. Alex had spent two weeks here when he had been shot by Scorpia.

Mrs Jones was waiting for her in the reception area. She was wearing a black, full-length coat with leather gloves and a scarf. It was hard to say if she had just arrived or if she was on her way out.

"How is he?" Jack asked. She had been phoning every day since Alex had been picked up. She had wanted to see him in Nairobi. But it was only the night before that MI6 had called her and told her that Alex had been flown home and brought here.

"He's much better," Mrs Jones said, and it occurred to Jack that she could have been talking about someone who had just recovered from a bad cold. "The burns are healing and he won't need any skin grafts. He won't be playing sport for a while. He fractured his ankle at Laikipia Airport. But he has amazing powers of recovery. The doctors are very pleased with him." She smiled. "He's looking forward to seeing you."

"Where is he?"

"Room nine on the second floor."

"That's the same room as last time."

"Maybe we should name it after him."

Jack shook her head. "I wouldn't bother. He won't be coming back."

The two women stood facing one another, each one waiting for the other to speak.

Mrs Jones could see the accusation in Jack's eyes. "This really wasn't our fault," she said. "Alex met McCain quite by accident. That business in Scotland had nothing to do with us."

"But that didn't stop you sending him to Greenfields."

"We had no idea that McCain was involved."

"And if you had – would that have stopped you?"

Mrs Jones shrugged. She had no need to answer.

There was a plastic bag resting on a chair. Mrs Jones picked it up and handed it to Jack. "You might like to give this to Alex. It's from Smithers. Some chocolates."

"Oh yes? And what do they do? Explode when he puts them in his mouth?"

"They're soft centres. Smithers thought he might enjoy them."

Jack took the bag. She glanced towards the lift, then back at Mrs Jones. "Promise me that this will be the end of it," she said. "From what you've told me, this time it was worse than ever. It's a miracle he's still alive. Do you have any idea what this must be doing to him – inside his head, I mean?"

"Actually, I have a very good idea," Mrs Jones countered. "I asked our psychiatrists to run a few tests on him."

"That's very thoughtful of you. But I mean it, Mrs Jones. Alex has done enough. I want you out of his life."

Mrs Jones sighed. "I can't promise you that, I'm afraid. First of all, it's not my decision. And anyway, as I said, this didn't begin with us. Alex has a knack of finding trouble without any help."

"I'm not going to let it happen again."

"Believe me, I'll be very happy if you can prevent it." Mrs Jones pulled up her collar and tightened her belt. "Anyway," she said, "I expect Alex is waiting for you. You'd better go up."

"I'm going. Please thank Mr Smithers for the chocolates."

Jack took the lift to the second floor. She didn't need to ask for directions. The layout of the hospital was all too familiar. As she approached the door of Alex's room, a woman came out carrying a breakfast tray and Jack recognized Diana Meacher, the attractive, fair-haired nurse from New Zealand who had looked after Alex before.

"Go right in," the nurse said. "He's waiting for you. He'll be so glad you're here."

Jack hesitated, composing herself. Then she went into the room.

Alex was sitting up in bed, reading a magazine. His pyjama top was open and she could see that, once again, he was heavily wrapped in bandages, this time around his neck and shoulders. His eyes were bright and he was smiling but he looked bad. The pain he had been through was still with him. He was thin. The haircut that Bennett had given him when he was smuggled out of the country didn't help.

"Hello, Jack."

"Hi, Alex."

She went over to him and kissed him very gently, afraid that she would hurt him. Then she sat down beside the bed.

"How are you feeling?" she asked.

"Terrible."

"As terrible as you look?"

"Probably." Alex put down the magazine and Jack saw that even this movement made him wince. "They've taken me off painkillers," he explained. "They say they don't want me to get addicted to them."

"Oh, Alex..." Jack's voice caught in her throat. She had been determined not to cry in front of him but she couldn't keep the tears from her eyes.

"I'm fine," Alex said. "I'm a lot better than I was."

"I wanted to come out and see you."

"I'm glad you didn't."

Jack understood. If he looked this bad now, she could hardly imagine what he must have looked like before. He wouldn't have wanted her to see him like that.

"Are you very cross with me?" Alex asked.

"Of course not. I'm just relieved to see you. After you went missing, I was..." Jack stopped herself. "When can you come home?" she asked.

"I was talking to the nurse just now. She says that if all goes well, it should only be a couple of days. Tuesday. Wednesday at the latest."

"Well, thank goodness for that," Jack said. "You know what Thursday is."

"No." Alex had no idea.

"Alex!" Jack stared at him.

"Tell me."

"It's your birthday, Alex. You're going to be fifteen."

"Am I?" Alex laughed. "I'd completely lost track of the date." He thought for a moment. "So what are you going to buy me?"

"What do you want?"

"I want to go home. I want peace and quiet. And I want that new version of Assassin's Creed ... it's just come out on PlayStation."

"I'm not sure these violent computer games are good for you, Alex."

Jack didn't tell him that she had already bought it and that a few of his closest friends were waiting for her call, hoping to come round.

Fifteen years old. Surely MI6 would leave him alone now. They had stolen almost a whole year of his life. But never again. Jack made herself that promise.

Beside her Alex settled back into the pillows. His eyes closed and even as she watched he smiled and fell asleep.

ACKNOWLEDGEMENTS

It's always amazing how many people are willing to help me, giving up their time and opening doors that might otherwise stay closed – and it seems only right to name them here. I try to make the Alex Rider books as realistic as I can and it simply wouldn't be possible without them.

So to start at the beginning, Martin Pearce and Colin Tucker from British Energy showed me round the Sizewell B nuclear power station in Suffolk. I'm assured that security there is rather tighter than it was at Jowada. I then visited the John Innes Centre, which is part of the Norwich BioScience Institutes (and bears no resemblance at all to the Greenfields Bio Centre in this story). I was given an extensive tour by Dr Wendy Harwood and Dr Penny Sparrow and they very kindly explained the principles of GM technology and demonstrated the gene gun which I describe in Chapter 12. I owe a special debt of thanks to Dr Hugh Martin, a principal lecturer at the Royal Agricultural College, who first suggested to me the method by which Desmond McCain poisons the crop in Kenya.

Jonathan Hinks, who is the chairman of the British Dam Society, introduced me to the concept of the double curvature arch dam and arranged for me to see one. I spent a very pleasant day in Scotland with Kenny Dempster from Scottish and Southern Energy, who gave me an extensive tour of Monar Dam (the only double arch dam in the UK), located in the very beautiful Glen Strathfarrar.

Lea Sherwood, the brilliant stunt arranger who appeared in the film of *Stormbreaker*, assured me that Alex's escape in Chapter 23 would have been possible but perhaps you shouldn't try it at home. The Gaelic translation on page 43 was provided by Dr Robert Dunbar at the University of Aberdeen. And I owe an apology to Professor Robin Smith from London Imperial College, who gave me a lengthy lesson in physics which sadly didn't make it to the final draft.

As always, I have relied on the guidance and advice of my three editors: Jane Winterbotham and Chris Kloet at Walker Books and Michael Green in New York. My agent, Robert Kirby, gave me great support when I needed it. My assistant, Olivia Zampi, organized everything with incredible patience and precision. And my son Cass was once again the first to read the manuscript and as usual gave me excellent advice.

Finally, thanks to my wife, Jill Green, who had to live through the writing of this. It wasn't always fun.

AH

READ OTHER GREAT BOOKS BY
ANTHONY HOROWITZ...

Alex Rider – you're never too young to die…

High in the Alps, death waits for Alex Rider…

Sharks. Assassins. Nuclear bombs. Alex Rider's in deep water.

Alex Rider bites back…

Alex Rider – you're never too young to die…

"Horowitz is pure class, stylish but action-packed … being James Bond in miniature is way cooler than being a wizard."

The Daily Mirror

ALSO AVAILABLE AS GRAPHIC NOVELS...